REDEMPTION ISLAND

By Domingo A. Rocha, M.D.

An Old Line Publishing Book
Hampstead ◊ Maryland ◊ USA

If you have purchased this book without a cover you should be aware that this book may have been stolen property and was reported as "unsold and destroyed" to the publisher. In such case neither the author nor the publisher has received any compensation for this book.

Copyright © 2012 by Domingo A. Rocha

All rights reserved. No part of this book may be reproduced or transmitted in any form or by any means, electronic or mechanical, including photocopying, recording, or by any information storage and retrieval system, without permission in writing from the publisher.

Printed in the United States of America

ISBN-13: 9781937004668
ISBN-10: 193700466X

This book is a work of fiction. Any references to real people, events, establishments, organizations, or locales are intended solely to provide a sense of authenticity and are used fictitiously. All other characters, incidents, and dialogue are drawn from the author's imagination and are not to be construed as real.

Old Line Publishing, LLC
P.O. Box 624
Hampstead, MD 21074
Toll-Free Phone: 1-877-866-8820
Toll-Free Fax: 1-877-778-3756
Email: info@oldlinepublishingllc.com
Website: www.oldlinepublishingllc.com

REDEMPTION ISLAND

To my good friends: Dan Dockery and Opus T. Cat, RIP

REDEMPTION ISLAND

Acknowledgements

This is the book I started to write when I was 15 before I had enough English to do a proper job of it. It is also the book that when shown to my English teacher resulted in a very sad, non-supportive response.

Although it took many more decades than I expected, it is now something of which I am very proud. Nevertheless, I could have not done this alone. The following people deserve special credit:

Ed Lyle for improving the book greatly by making it more readable and the continuity more fluid (or is it the fluid more continuous? At my age it could be either).

To the creators and actors of Gilligan's Island, not only did I enjoy the show but together with Jules Verne's Mysterious Island, I started on the quest to write this adventure, one based on the similar idea of several strangers relying on each other for sustenance, security, support and eventually survival.

To my ever supportive wife of 34 years, who graciously and happily(?) handles my many moods, interests and distractions.

To my many friends, coworkers and patients for providing me with endless material, endless fun, and being a willing audience to test my musings (some of which end up in my books).

To Anne, for showing me what true strength and courage in the face of overwhelming adversity looks like.

To my dear publisher, who made the cover far better than I could have imagined.

REDEMPTION ISLAND

Contents

PART ONE
Chapter One - Out of Options	11
Chapter Two - Second Chances	31
Chapter Three - Introductions	44
Chapter Four - Marooned	51
Chapter Five - Dan	65
Chapter Six - Waiting	75
Chapter Seven - Reversals	100

PART TWO
Chapter Eight - Survival Basics	105
Chapter Nine - Preparations	115
Chapter Ten - Trouble on the Trail	125
Chapter Eleven - Trouble's at Sea	137
Chapter Twelve - Martha's Fate	148
Chapter Thirteen - Reunion	164
Chapter Fourteen - Sunday Service	171
Chapter Fifteen - Marc to the Rescue	183
Chapter Sixteen - Intimacies	203
Chapter Seventeen - The Soap Festival	211
Chapter Eighteen - Escape Plans	226
Chapter Nineteen - Luis	243

PART THREE
Chapter Twenty - Battle Preparations	251
Chapter Twenty-One - Marc in Charge	254
Chapter Twenty-Two - Allie Makes Her Entrance	270
Chapter Twenty-Three - Battle Plans Redux	278
Chapter Twenty-Four - Wicked Witch of the West	285
Chapter Twenty-Five - Arrianna Reaches Her Family	303
Chapter Twenty-Six - Civilization	307
Epilogue	314

REDEMPTION ISLAND

PART ONE

Chapter One

Out of Options

In another era in another part of the world, their unscheduled landing would have been due to mechanical failure. At most it would be considered pilot error. In our profit and time-driven world however, it was a result of the usual mix of greed, laziness, apathy and, most importantly, Life. "Life" in the sense that nothing ever goes the way one thinks it will. Murphy's Law: that there are events beyond our control and even beyond our perception and comprehension.

On this hot, late spring day, this mix of human foibles came together in a form that would eventually transform all of the passengers and crew aboard the *Albatross*.

The pilot of the amphibian, Mike Faraday, was thirty-eight and as lean as the Marine pilot he had been in 'Nam. At this moment he was not reminiscing over those years but concentrating on the problem at hand while trying to maintain his calm, professional demeanor. When it was over, then he would vent the anger that was now building within him. At least that was what he told himself.

REDEMPTION ISLAND

"Still not working?" Mike asked.

The copilot, Dan Dockery, looked up from his dials. Unlike Mike, he did not appear to be upset. He busily and happily went through the procedures that were drilled into all pilots; a procedure for a lost engine, another for loss of pressurization. When the problem finally made itself known, Dan was at a loss because there wasn't a specific procedure for this situation. Eventually he made do with the combined procedures for being lost and being low on fuel. "I couldn't raise a soul. I can't tell if the radio's broken or if that storm is interfering. We are too low to reach anyone else."

"Yeah, that's right. What's our radio range?"

"We're only at two thousand feet and with the VHF requiring line of sight and the storm interfering, figure on thirty to thirty-five miles. The nearest alternate airport is easily twice that distance."

Mike fumed. He could come up with only one acceptable alternative and it wasn't all that acceptable. Patches of sweat started to show on his uniform and on his dark brow. He wiped them away with a sleeve, idly scratched his crew cut head and silently cursed the heat for making it harder to think. If he could transmit his intentions, then he could relax, fly the plane, and let others worry about the consequences. As it was, he was the one on the hot seat. The decision and all its repercussions were his. The responsibility for the safety of all aboard came with the job of pilot and captain of the *Albatross*.

~~~~~~~~

The *Albatross* was an old, but remarkable, flying craft. The company kept it in acceptable working order. Mike was a typical pilot in that he did not care that they did not paint her as often as they should, or that the interior was cracked and faded. Given the choice between a new paint job and a new navigation instrument it was a no-brainer. Unfortunately in his case he was rarely given a choice and he mostly settled for neither. At this specific moment his concern was that Joe, the head mechanic, might have skimped on the VHF antenna.

The *Albatross* could seat up to twelve souls including the crew, but at the expense of a severely decreased range. For each passenger and his typical sixty pounds of luggage, there would be fifty gallons less fuel. With the *Albatross*'s engines using seventy gallons an hour, each additional passenger after the first eight would decrease her range by forty-three minutes. Mike would have given his right testicle (he had an attachment to the left one) for forty-three more minutes of flying time.

On this ill-fated day Dan and Mike had six passengers, but—and it was a big "but"—they had loaded five hundred pounds of cargo that had missed its scheduled flight yesterday. He had cut his fuel reserve accordingly and now was out of gas and out of options.

~~~~~~~~~~

The aforementioned six passengers seemed blissfully unaware of their predicament: all but one of them. They were chatting, continuing making acquaintances for the duration of their journey.

Arrianna was one of the two passengers not involved in these social trappings. She had one of those faces that did not show age and looked young enough to get away with ignoring the adult world. She was fair skinned with nearly black hair that fell several inches below her shoulders. At 5'10" she was tall and her unusually long limbs accentuated the effect. She found vigorous physical activity, especially dance, her escape and this combination of height and leggy dancer's build gave the illusion of her being lanky, uncoordinated and light enough for the wind to blow away. In fact, she tipped the scales at 132 pounds and could bench-press close to that. She wore loose-fitting jeans and a T-shirt obtained at one of the many dance competitions she'd won. The other thing she wore to good effect was a perpetual look of intense, deep thought. It kept the world at bay, which was exactly what she wanted.

Her birthday was only a few weeks away and, if you asked Arrianna she would without compunction say she was "eighteen—almost." If you asked her mother (were she still alive) she would say that she was "seventeen, going on fifty."

At the moment the pilots changed the *Albatross*'s course for the last time, she was playing cards with herself. Not solitaire, but Rook. She played both sides with all of the emotion and surprise that two separate players would have. Her thoughts, however, were not on the game; Arrianna was wondering what to do with her life. The last year had been one of the few good ones and she was no longer tormented by the memories of her mother, but she found school abominably boring and had to force herself to work at it. She had arrived at a compromise with herself and the world. If she consistently made B's her father and her school counselor would leave her alone. They suspected she could do better but would freak if they knew how abysmally little effort it took her to achieve this limited amount of success.

She was now considering a revision in her life. She had one more year of high school left and her future was pressing in. The only thing she knew for certain was that she could not, and would not, stay one extra minute in her father's house. As soon as she graduated she was "outta there." The thought was so delicious that she smiled involuntarily—it was only a year away. It bothered her only slightly that she might need better grades to get a scholarship for college or to go into the military as more than a grunt. She let her thoughts drift to fantasies about the wonderful sense of freedom that was close enough to taste.

~~~~~~~~~~

The other person not socializing, the one who understood that all was not well, was by the window underneath the wing trying to figure out why in the world they were so low and going in a direction away from their destination. He had extensive experience with navigation, albeit on a boat, and at the moment, he was merely confused. He was not yet worried, that would come later. He saw the storm in front of them and thought it must be blocking their approach to the airport. He expected they would gain altitude and circle for the forty to fifty minutes it would take for the storm to move on, but instead they were heading eastward away from the airport, away from any of the populated islands that he knew. And he knew them all.

His name was Seth Martin. He was a short, slightly overweight seventy-two year old with tufts of white hair way too long to be fashionable and enough muscular build to carry his weight well. He thought of himself as a Clydesdale, not a thoroughbred. He wore a clean but well-worn shabby suit without a tie. His white shirt had the top two buttons undone and it looked like he'd slept in it.

The first tendrils of fear began tickling his subconscious and Seth grew restless. He wanted to ask the pilot what was happening. He was only fifteen feet away, but did not want to become conspicuous, yet if nothing changed in the next few minutes he would have to make a polite inquiry, as too much was riding on his successful arrival.

"This is the captain speaking. I have an announcement to make."

REDEMPTION ISLAND

Arrianna thought that adults were always so wordy. It was painfully clear that he was making an announcement.

"All passengers need to prepare for landing. You will need to buckle and make the straps tight. I expect the landing to be a bit rough."

Everyone looked around to see their fellow passenger's reactions. So far no one panicked and all did as instructed. All but one of them felt more uncertain than scared. Seth was scared, petrified actually. Not about his personal safety, since he was not a man easily affected by dangerous circumstances, but about not having a chance to transmit his intelligence. He desperately needed to get this information to his contact, and quickly.

~~~~~~~~~~

Dan had his hands full. He had managed to reach someone at the airport, but between the static and the other planes transmitting on the frequency; he was not getting his message across.

"Dan, call out a mayday," said Mike.

"Right, it's the only way we'll get them to pay attention." He dialed 7700 into their transponder. This would identify them to the nearest Air Traffic Control radar site that they had an emergency. With this done he transmitted what he previously never dreamed he would need to, "Mayday, Mayday, Mayday, November fiver fiver Kilo Lima is critical fuel and heading to..." He turned to Mike, "What is the name of the island?"

"Doesn't have one, but we call it "Mother Island," because of the twin peaks on its central mountain."

"...Kilo Lima going towards Mother Island, with eight souls on board."

"Fiver fiver Kilo Lima, this is Air Traffic Control copy critical fuel, and eight souls on board. Please repeat destination, transmission garbled."

"I need to make a radio call, it is very important," Seth said with a tremendous amount of authority that did not betray his true feelings. He made a grab for the microphone.

Mike screamed, "Who the Hell... get back and buckle up. We have an emergency here."

"I know. That is why I must make this call. I assure you it is vital that I-"

"NO! Get back there NOW! We have to let them know where we are landing."

Seth became quiet but did not leave immediately. He remained, watching the two pilots deal with the problem.

Dan began re-transmitting, but the static was now worse and the controller was obviously unaware of the local name for the island and kept repeating "Brother Island." This was distressing to both pilots because it implied they were on the west side of their destination near the inhabited island called "Little Brother," instead of the small and uninhabited place they were headed. By the time the static cleared, they were too far over the horizon to get a clear signal. They had heard that a rescue effort was on its way, but feared it was heading to the wrong destination.

Mike began readying for a water landing. It would be in an area with which he was vaguely familiar, but had not previously checked out. He prayed there were no shallow obstructions hidden beneath the waves. While going through the pre-landing checklist, he reflected on the series of miss-cues that had brought him and the other seven souls to this previously unimaginable conclusion.

~~~~~~~~

REDEMPTION ISLAND

Sharon, his wife, woke him at the usual time with a mug of hot Colombian Supremo made just the way he liked it, black and hot. He loved this part of the day and resented that it only lasted a couple of dozen minutes at best. They would chat about this and that while he let the Colombian do its thing. He would then get ready for another full day with his first love, flying. He had been in the Air Force back in Vietnam, as far back as he could recall.

On arriving at the *Albatross's* home airport, the passengers were already milling about and the luggage was being loaded. The greatest benefit of being the pilot, he told himself, was that the copilot would perform the pre take-off checks and he would just verify a few things. Unfortunately it meant that the least senior of the crew was the one doing the checking. He reflected that it was probably at that juncture that the trip began to go bad.

Five hundred pounds of cargo had been left behind by the prior night's flight to the main island. The story that the trucks bringing it here had been severely delayed was not in any way unusual or unlikely, but Mike knew it was far more likely that the pilot refused to wait even a few extra minutes for it. The guy was a moron, and would never have been considered for the job, much less hired, except that he was the owner's brother-in-law. Now the boss wanted him to take the cargo and it would eat into his fuel reserve.

He looked at the flight plan Dan prepared and recalculated the weight and balance for the plane. Laypeople did not understand how sensitive flying machines were to not only the total weight but to how it was distributed. Too far forward or too far in the tail created control problems that could be deadly. Today, he could not reasonably object to carrying the cargo. He noted the winds were slightly below normal. He would have a light quartering headwind all the way to Carthage. The passenger load was lighter than usual. He agreed to the cargo and arranged for the fuel truck to remove the surplus Aviation Gas.

REDEMPTION ISLAND

As was the routine of air carriers all over the world, planes were topped off every evening to minimize condensation inside the fuel tank. Water in the tank in any significant amount could have tragic consequences. It usually did not get noticed until the plane tried to take-off and upon the initial rotation of the nose, the condensate, which is much heavier than Avgas, would slosh into the fuel inlet.

He double-checked his fuel consumption figures and verified that despite everything, they still had slightly more than his required hour of reserve. He felt a small misgiving about going with less than his personal preference of two hours' reserve, but the law said one hour and he'd never needed even half of that. He forgot about it and went to help Dan get the plane ready.

His passenger list had six people: three men, two women and one child. The *Albatross* was a relic from a war long ago. It had cost little to purchase and, although it required considerable maintenance, it uniquely suited their needs. Unlike other charter companies, they had the capability to land on water or land, which was why they named the plane *Albatross.* They advertised accordingly and catered to those with a fear of flying. Because they flew from island to island and only used coastal airports, they were able to emphasize the safety of being able to land anywhere anytime. It turned out to have been an inspired idea and they had as much business as they could handle.

The second miscue occurred after an unremarkable take-off. Arrianna had come up and politely asked if they could overfly the island for a few minutes so she could see its beauty from the air. Mike deeply regretted not having kids of his own and she looked so excited that he had been unable to refuse her. Despite this, she had a melancholy aura about her and he had actually let her sit in Dan's chair while Dan checked on the passengers. He circled the island at an altitude of a thousand feet. Arrianna was so polite and so appreciative, and with her enthusiasm growing every minute, the five-minute tour ended up taking sixteen minutes.

When the *Albatross* stabilized at cruising altitude, the turbulence was far greater than anticipated. Mike climbed to nine thousand and then ten thousand feet before he found calm air. It took Dan much too long to discover the third miss-cue.

Winds are faster the higher one goes, sometimes much faster if one is in the jet stream. Down low there is friction with the ground, and trees, as well as the effects of thermals. These were the cause of today's turbulence. When the *Albatross* had reached ten thousand feet they had an extra twenty knots of headwind to fight. Dan should have reacted immediately and made the necessary adjustments to conserve fuel, but he had been in the middle of telling Mike about the new Miata he bought for his wife and neglected to make the appropriate calculations in time.

It was only when it was almost too late that the fourth miscue became apparent. The fuel gauges had not registered any change in fuel. While checking them for malfunction, Dan noticed a small magnet on the right of each gauge. They had been placed there to keep the needle pegged to full. That could only mean one thing. Someone had siphoned some of their fuel out and had counted on normal turbulence to dislodge the magnets so that no one would notice. The new line boy must be the one responsible, and he was probably selling the extra fuel under the table to pilots who did not realize or care where he was obtaining it. They were in trouble, possibly deep trouble.

He ordered Dan to slow the *Albatross* to its most fuel-efficient speed and drop altitude to minimize the headwind. He re-calculated their remaining fuel four times before he trusted it. He had to decide what to do. If he turned back right away, he would have a tail wind and would easily reach the airport, however, if he continued on his current course, he would make it, but it would seem to take forever and they would have turbulence all the way. They would land with slightly less than half an hour of fuel left in the tanks, but hey, that was what the reserve was for. He discussed it with Dan and made a call to their home airport.

The call clinched it for them. Adrian, their boss, was adamant that if the fuel was sufficient, they should go forward. At that time, Mike could not fault him, but he could now. The only positive thought was that he had remembered to mention the magnets and his feelings about their source. In due course Adrian would make a formal police report about the fuel theft and endangerment of the passengers and crew. Besides losing his job, the line boy would spend at least a few days in jail. He knew Adrian well and expected him to make a royal stink about it and insist on the harshest sentence possible.

They should have arrived with at least twenty minutes of fuel left. However, things did not turn out that way. Mike repeatedly failed to calculate the extra fuel used for the climb to ten thousand feet. He could not really be faulted because it usually was so insignificant. Today it turned out to be crucial because the ten minutes of extra flying time it represented put their trip in a precarious position. When they finally approached the Carthage airport and found a stationary thunderstorm raging over the island, their options ran out.

Mike was unsure exactly how much fuel was left because he knew how notoriously unreliable the gauges became when near empty. His first sign that he was low on fuel would be when one of his two engines sputtered and quit. He would then have a few seconds of power left in his last engine. While flying in 'Nam he'd been hit by flack and lost all power. The hopeless, miserable feeling of complete and utter loss of control he had experienced earlier was still there in the reptilian part of his brain waiting for an opportunity to surface. Mike was absolutely determined not to experience that again—ever.

He would, therefore, not risk the half-hour or so of circling it would take to wait for the storm to move away from the airport. If they ran out even a few minutes too early, they would have to ditch in the storm tossed waters without power—not a thrilling or survivable prospect. Their best chance lay with the uninhabited and un-named island forty miles to the west—if they could reach it. The storm generated such a down draft that he would get a very nice tail wind most of the way there. With that, and by trading the little altitude he had for airspeed, he should make it.

The island was too small to support any permanent settlement and was well out of the usual shipping lanes and airways. However, from his years of flying around the islands, Mike was familiar enough with it. It looked so beautiful from the air that Sharon and he had taken a rented powerboat to it once. He therefore knew there was a protected cove on the leeward side where he could make a landing and then even if his power was gone, the waves would push him into the beach.

Here the advantage of the *Albatross* became evident. Being an amphibian it could land on pavement or on water. Once they were down safely, it would be a simple matter of contacting an airplane flying overhead to relay their location. All they would have to do was wait for rescue and fuel—he would be home for a late dinner with Sharon. It was with these thoughts that Mike settled himself on the task of landing in little-known waters with the possibility of the remaining engine running out of fuel at any moment.

REDEMPTION ISLAND

In the cabin, most of the passengers were deeply terrified and on the ragged edge of self-control. Several wanted to vent their fear and anger but no one wanted to be first. Arrianna, despite herself, wanted her father with her. She was struggling not to cry but the tears were at the door, banging to get out. She remembered telling her dad, "I can fly alone, I will be fine." All that bluster and confidence had now evaporated and she would have given anything to have a hand to hold.

"Do you mind if I sit next to you?" said one of the female passengers.

Arrianna looked up startled and a tear escaped in the exchange, but she still would not allow herself to sob. She saw that it was the older, quite attractive if slightly overweight, lady. "Sure, if that is what you want."

"My name is Martha, I know we were introduced earlier, but I know how hard it is to remember those things. I don't like planes much and now that there seems to be a problem I am a dreadful mess. I hope you don't mind if I hold your hand until we land, I think I would feel better."

Arrianna was thrilled. She wouldn't even have to ask. "That would be great...I mean, that would be fine. I am a little scared too." With that confession the two women started a conversation that, with Martha's subtle encouragement, would last all the way to touchdown.

~~~~~~~~~~

Seth was furious. He knew they were moving away from civilization and the radio was worthless. He also knew they were flying away from any major islands. He could just make out the shape of a small island in the distance ahead. Where was that? He did not know of any island in that direction. Why were they going there? The plane appeared to be working well—apart from the radio, of course. No message went out while he had been up front and now no message would get out before they crashed and drowned. All that work and risk, the tremendous success, all for nothing. He was red with rage: at the plane, the pilots, himself and most of all, at God.

When he volunteered to help the *Mossad*, he had not done so because he was Jewish, or because he believed. He had agreed because a debt was owed and he was a man of principle. It did not matter to him that he would die in the crash—he had faced death too many times for it to retain any of its terror. It was that he would die indebted and rankled. To make matters worse, he had just obtained the information that would erase the obligation!

He knew the young men that recruited him so long ago, if still alive, would not feel that any debt remained; even though years later he had left Israel for America. But feel it he still did. If not for them, what would have become of Sophie? Bless her soul. And his children, what life would they have? It had been many years since then, but Seth Martin had not forgotten.

So when in the course of his usual business, he stumbled on a source of information that might be useful, he had approached the Israeli Embassy and started the process of repayment that had weighed so heavily on him all of these years.

~~~~~~~~

Gerald "Jerry" Simmons was talking with two other passengers, Leesa and Marc. All three of them were struggling to make a good show of bravado. For all the world could see, they appeared calm, even when the sphincter tones of any one of them would have crushed a grape. Jerry felt that it was up to him to keep everyone quiet and to be the liaison between the passengers and the pilots when the time came. He hadn't become CEO of his multi-million dollar manufacturing company without having to tough out far worse situations than this.

When interviewed, he was described as tall and portly, with a demeanor of assurance that belied his soft caring smile and kind green eyes. He liked to wear tailored suits but not the latest in fashion. He felt that gave the wrong message—that the money of his investors was being spent in the wrong place. So once every year he went to the best tailor in Dallas and told them to make it look "just a bit better than something he could buy off the shelf." It fit perfectly, and he was always comfortable. His enemies, and he had many, would describe him differently: hard, calculating, without any feelings. Yet even after a particularly vicious competition they would grudgingly admit, if only to themselves, that he did not take as much advantage as most. To insiders, he gave every impression that he enjoyed the contest more than the spoils.

Leesa, on the other hand, was in her twenties, fashionably thin (which meant nearly emaciated) tall and lanky. She spoke, saying "As soon as we land I am going to file a complaint. He did not even mention where we are headed. I hope it won't delay us long."

Jerry nodded, "I completely agree. We need to make sure they know how we feel about it and that they don't soon forget us. Once we land, we will approach the pilot…what's his name? John?"

"Michael," said Marc.

"Right. Mike will give us the details of what happened and then we can proceed."

"They are low on gas—possibly very low." Marc said it in a monotone devoid of feeling, not a question at all, a statement of fact.

REDEMPTION ISLAND

"How do you know that?" asked Leesa, for the first time showing the strain she felt.

"Listen to the engines, they are throttled way back, they also dropped their altitude to decrease the headwind and when we turned with the wind they did not correspondingly gain altitude to get the tail wind. It's just hunch that's all."

"Are you a pilot?" inquired Jerry. Despite his heroic efforts, his voice revealed strain, betraying his feelings of worry, though not fear—that would come later. When the fear came he would not be concerned about ditching. His fear would revolve around his inability to swim and that he was deathly afraid of sharks.

"Nah, but I know a lot about flying them and about engines. I read a lot."

Jerry was re-evaluating his initial opinion of this young man. He did not seem the ignorant and useless youth he had intimated. He realized that it had been the long hair and his generally disheveled appearance that was responsible for that judgment. "What do you do?" he said with unanticipated trepidation over the answer.

Marc's attention was now riveted to the window and, without looking, answered, "I'm a professional student. I enjoy learning how the world works. Right now I'm working on my Master's in Physics. I figure that as long as the parentship holds out, I'll just continue to attend a school of one kind or other."

"Parentship?" asked Leesa, finding renewed interested in this unkempt, polite and seemingly brilliant young man.

Marc laughed, "It's my term. My parents pay all the bills and give me an allowance—not much, mind you, but enough to keep me going—I don't know what else to call it besides 'mooching' and that does not do justice to the hard work I put into my studies."

Jerry asked with clear irritation, "Do your parents know of your intentions?"

REDEMPTION ISLAND

"Oh sure, I've told them many times. But I'm an only son and they're used to spoiling me. The way my father puts it, as long as I do well at whatever I'm studying, he will keep me there. So in a roundabout way I earn my keep. I have a running 4.0 grade point average for the last six years—in what most people would call extremely difficult courses."

He turned away from the window and looked past them to some place long ago. "Let's see, I have degrees in mechanical engineering, chemistry, electronics as well as research papers in biodiversity, history of science and technology…" he let the sentence drift. "I sometimes teach classes, but I suppose someday I'll grow up and get a full-time job, but not right now."

Both Jerry and Leesa revised their judgment of Marc. They were intrigued by his lifestyle and Jerry in particular was impressed with his accomplishments. He knew all too well how hard it would be to maintain such a high GPA in the sciences. He himself had just barely managed to pass the ridiculously few science requirements on his way to a degree in business.

Marc broke the silence "We are getting ready to land. From what I can see it will be on open water. There is a bit of a swell so I would tighten your belts as much as you can stand, it could be rough."

As if on cue the pilot announced, "Ladies and gentlemen, this is your pilot speaking. We will be landing shortly and I request that you tighten your seat belts as much as possible. Please try to stay calm, we will be landing on the water and that is a bit rougher than a regular landing. However, this plane was designed just for that and my copilot and I have hundreds of such landings under our belts. We will let you know when you can unfasten your seat belts. If Mr. Martin and Mr. Simmons could come up to the cockpit, I would like to brief you on the landing procedures." Both Leesa and

Jerry gave Marc a silent look that asked "how-did-you-know?" Marc did not seem to notice.

Mike let go of his emotions so he could concentrate on the landing. It was just like flying a combat mission over 'Nam, or so he told himself, "At least no one is shooting at me." He desperately needed to get it right the first time. There was no extra fuel and besides, the passengers could not be expected to handle an aborted landing. He knew that panic would be disastrous in more ways than he could count.

He briefed the two older men on how to open the doors and help the passengers out, where the flotation devices were as well as the raft. He pleaded with them to help him keep everyone calm and to reassure everyone that, despite the unexpected nature of the landing, there was no cause for alarm.

When they were back in their seats, he reflected that he had picked them simply because they were the two oldest men. He had expected the older man, Seth, to struggle with the news but it was that other guy, Jerry, who'd fallen apart. It was a brief collapse and, within a handful of seconds, he managed to compose himself. However, Mike was paying particular attention and noticed the paleness and the hyperventilation. He hoped that Mr. Simmons, who in the end managed to look calm and self-assured, would not lose his composure.

The old man turned out to be a treasure. Mike could see the courage and fortitude in his eyes. There was no doubt he would be an enormous asset in any crisis. Maybe he would have a chance to talk to him after all this was over and find out what life experience had given him such emotional strength.

Dan interrupted his thoughts, "One thousand feet. The wind is behind us at twelve knots and, from the chop, I can see it is going to be about the same on the surface. We can make our turn to base anytime."

"Right. I have the stick. We'll go out a bit further so that we don't overrun the beach, after all, we don't know how much gas we have left. Have you been able to reach anyone on the radio?" Mike already knew the answer but felt compelled to ask.

"Nah, they know we are making a water landing, but I can't get them to understand our location. They still think we are going down over at Hermanito Island, on the other side of Damascus. And…" Dan paused for effect, "You'll love this. They said that if we can hold out ten more minutes, the runway will reopen."

It was at that moment that the starboard engine quit. "Damn! Right rudder, right rudder! Feather that prop. I am turning on final approach; we have to land this beast now! We don't know how long number two will keep going." With that statement the second and last engine quit. The silence was overwhelming. He braced himself for the inevitable screams from the passengers.

"Switch off all unnecessary electrical equipment."

Dan complied, "Equipment off."

"Ready on the flaps with the manual lever."

"Flaps ready."

"Feather the port prop."

Dan was ahead of him and had already feathered it. Mike had noticed it, but had said so out of training and habit. By feathering the prop, it would not generate as much drag and they would be able to glide at a reasonable angle, otherwise they would have the glide characteristics of a rock.

"Switch off the gas to the engines." Mike knew that this was probably unnecessary, but it was the rule. You never knew if there would be just enough gas in the system to start a fire.

"Switched off."

"We are on final and lined up into the wind, let's just put this baby down gently and then drift into that beach. Any luck with the radio?"

REDEMPTION ISLAND

"Nah, we are too low, probably have been too low since we diverted. It won't reach anymore. Once we land, we can contact an overhead plane to relay a message. We will be out of here by sundown."

Although Mike agreed with Dan's evaluation, part of him remained uneasy as if the final shoe had yet to drop.

The landing went as well as could be expected. The initial contact was hard, by runway standards, and the rapid deceleration once in the water was…unusual, if not downright scary. Nevertheless, the *Albatross* found itself floating in the swells not far from the beach. Dan and Mike congratulated themselves and then Dan unfastened his straps to facilitate the evacuation once they beached the plane. It was when he was stepping out of his seat and still unstable that the other shoe finally dropped.

"Hold on Dan, a wave is going to hit…"

The warning came too late and Dan lost his balance, he reached out and just missed grabbing the bulkhead. He fell in a heap on the console. The lights of the radio, transponder, ELT, and navigation instrumentation blinked once and then died. Dan and Mike looked at each other with the dread of the condemned. One of them would have to tell the passengers that not only were they marooned on an uninhabited island, and that the search would occur many miles from here, but that their only connection with the outside world was now dead.

Chapter Two
Second Chances

Once the landing was over, Arrianna's fear dissipated entirely and she felt an intense feeling of adventure. When she heard they might be stranded on this island for a "couple of hours," instead of groaning and moaning like the others, she was thrilled. She desperately hoped that the rescue would not come too soon and she could not wait to get onto shore. This unexpected predicament was just too good to be true, she wanted to explore and experience the freedom of being a castaway. To her surprise, Martha, who had been so strong through the entire landing episode, was now visibly upset.

In a dramatic role reversal, she was now leaning on Arrianna for emotional support. Had she made up her fear of airplanes to help her out? Arrianna laughed inwardly when she realized that she probably had. She no longer cared. They were down and safe and they were going to have a break from her boringly predictable and utterly miserable life.

The only person who had lost it had been that bitch, Leesa. She acted so superior to everyone and had been so condescending to Arrianna in particular, that Arrianna was now enjoying Leesa's discomfort. Just because she was an up and coming soap star and was about as beautiful as anyone she'd ever seen, it did not give her the right to be so self-engrossed.

Leesa was carrying on about what a disaster it was and how she could not deal with it. Then she started to hyperventilate and it took both the old coot, Mr. Simmons, and that good looking guy, Marc, to calm her down enough to breathe into a vomit bag. Surprisingly that helped almost immediately. Even sick and in distress she looked good. Her banana republic shirt and shorts looked pressed and neat. Her hair was untouched and she did not even sweat. How did she do that?

Arrianna wished she was on the other side of the plane so she could see the island again as they approached it. She had to constantly reassure herself that there would be plenty of time to see it before the rescue plane arrived. She was the first to take her shoes off, tie them together and hang them around her neck, ready to wade into shore when the plane beached. Her thoughts were on how warm and wonderful the water would be and the unimaginable discoveries that awaited her.

~~~~~~~~~~

Mike and Dan were readying for the now inevitable beaching of the *Albatross*. They had to act quickly and decisively as soon as she scraped bottom. They planned to jump off and lighten the plane as much as possible so that the old girl would beach as high as possible. After that, they would have to think up a way to keep her from floating away with the tide. They had postponed telling anyone the true depth of their predicament, hoping that somehow, someway, they would be found soon.

"Dan, you sure you want to go first?"

"Yeah, I like the water and I would rather do that than stay here and face the cargo."

Mike nodded inwardly for he felt the same. He'd also rather brave the waves and hook up the towline to the plane by himself than become the brunt of all of the fear and anger that surrounded them.

"I can help with the towline." Marc said behind them. He was suddenly the scrutiny of both pilots. "That's what you are trying to do, Right? So that you can anchor the plane and it won't drift off?" He looked and responded to the nods. "It will further help to get my weight off the plane…" Both pilots smiled at this, despite his impressive height, he could not weigh more than one hundred and twenty. He was out of proportion. It was as if he'd been at one of those mirrors they have at carnivals that make everyone look tall and skinny. "…as little as it is, but more importantly, while he is hooking the line to the plane I can take the other end to the beach and look for a tree to wrap it around." He then looked at both pilots expectantly.

Mike wanted to laugh, except it wasn't a laughing situation. This skinny, tall kid had read the situation exactly right. They could use the help. If only he could be sure that he would not drown out there. "Thanks, we could sure use the help. My name is Mike and this is Dan. I don't recall your name."

"Marc, Marc Sommers, and don't worry about me, I will be careful. As long as there aren't any cannibals on that island I will be just fine." With that both pilots laughed and felt the most relaxed since the entire ridiculous episode had started.

Mike went up to Seth and Jerry and told them what he wanted them to do. Now that they were down, Jerry looked far more comfortable and had, in fact, been doing an excellent job of keeping everyone, especially Leesa, calm and cooperative. "It is important, that as soon as Dan and Marc jump out, that the two of you get everyone out of the plane as fast as possible. You are to stay clear of the fuselage and the wing float. The surf could throw you onto them. Guide everyone to shore and when everyone is safe help Marc. It would be best if you all went together as a group so that if one of you falls, the others can help."

Seth responded first, "No problem captain, we will take care of it, won't we Jerry?" Although he had said it like a question, it was a statement of fact. Seth was acting like a battlefield commander. Mike wondered what war he had been in. Judging by his age, he wrongly assumed that he had been part of the "big war," W.W.II. Which side of the war he had fought in was up for grabs, lots of people with German accents fought on both sides. "You just go on with what you have to do and let us know of anything else that you need help with."

Jerry was not used to being second in command and only managed to nod and say weakly, "Absolutely. We will take care of it."

With that Mike went back to the cockpit to help steer the Albatross on the beach. Without power the plane would normally not respond to rudder inputs, but today the wind was just strong enough to give him a little control. He saw out the window that Marc was already on shore carrying the end of the towline and could only presume that Dan was hooking the other end. Within minutes he saw the group of passengers struggling against the surf with Leesa doing all she could to make it as difficult as possible. He was having a very hard time not developing a large resentment against her. "There is always one that screws it up for everyone else..."

REDEMPTION ISLAND

~~~~~~~~~

The water was just as warm as Arrianna had expected and she screamed with joy. Martha came next and then Jerry, followed by Leesa and Seth. They had intentionally kept that wimpy, whinny Leesa between the two men so that they would be able to help her the most. She was making every effort at falling apart and being worse than helpless. Arrianna felt irritated that someone like that had to be here but decided she would not allow that spoiled bitch to ruin her adventure. Once they were all out, she led Martha to the beach. The water was translucent cobalt overlying soft, unspoiled white sand. She noticed many differing kinds of colorful fish swimming around them. "If only the rescue would not come until at least tomorrow," she told herself. She wanted a chance to sleep out in the open and look through the jungle that was only a hundred feet or so from the beach.

Getting to that beach took far more effort than she had expected. They were told to walk as a group, which unnecessarily slowed her down. On top of that, Leesa had managed to fall several times. Each time she acted as if she would drown—in three and half feet of water! The only saving grace was that she managed to drench herself and ruin her hair with all her hysterics. When they finally reached the shore, Arrianna took off for the tree line, but at a slow, measured pace, not the run she had intended.

"Arrianna, wait!" Martha shouted. She saw the girl stop, look back and signal to follow her. Martha's only desire was to collapse onto the sand for at least an hour, but her motherly worry won out. Arrianna was young and of the age that would think nothing of doing something rash and dangerous. She therefore ignored the screams from her muscles, joints and heart and trudged up to join her. When Martha reached her, Arrianna said excitedly, "Let's check out the woods before the rescue comes!"

"I think we should stay together. It is not a good idea to wander off by yourself. We don't even know what is out there. Besides it isn't a 'woods' at all. It is a jungle and it is probably filled with all kinds of dangerous and icky creatures."

"Icky? Is that the technical term for it?" asked Arrianna playfully.

"Exactly, there are probably leeches and blood sucking flies the size of cats." Martha was most definitely not getting into the spirit of discovery.

"Don't worry, I won't go far and I have been hiking and camping with my Dad many times." With that she turned and walked into the jungle. In less than a minute, she was lost from sight.

With a shrug, Martha turned around and walked up to Marc, who was working at one of the trees. She noticed that he was looping the rope around the base of a tree and constantly taking up any slack that appeared as the result of the plane bobbing up and down on the surf. "How is it going?"

Marc turned his head and saw Martha, "Great, I think the plane will be fine for the night. We will have to keep the line tight as the tide comes in, but as long as the tree holds out, that won't be hard."

Martha was stunned and tried in vain not to show it. "We will be here that long?"

Marc flushed. He had not meant to say so much. After all, he had only guessed from the pilot's actions that they did not expect an immediate rescue. "I don't know, I was just speculating, that's all. We will have to ask Mike, I mean the pilot, what our situation is."

Changing topics she asked Marc, "Do you think the jungle here is dangerous?"

REDEMPTION ISLAND

"Not really, this island is much too small to support any dangerous wildlife. That is, aside from a few poisonous snakes and mushrooms. Why do you ask?"

Martha looked miserable but did not respond. After an entire minute of silence she blurted out, "Arrianna, that young girl who was with us, ran into it a few minutes ago, I could not get her to wait."

"Oh no! She will get lost. It isn't like a woods, you know. The overstory is probably so thick that she won't be able to navigate and the sound of the surf will seem to come from every direction. There will also be all kinds of dangers, possibly even quicksand. How long ago did you say?"

"Only about five minutes. What should we do?"

It was at that moment of indecision that Arrianna appeared at the edge of the jungle walking towards them. She had been intensely scared within a minute of entering the jungle. It was far harder to traverse than she had anticipated and the sounds had been so strange. She became disoriented and would still be lost except for the occasional screams of anguish from Leesa. She realized that it was exactly her acts of helplessness that saved her and she was struggling to resolve the feelings of thankfulness with those of condescension for the woman.

Dan and Mike joined Marc at the tree and helped him to secure the line. Marc had chosen the largest tree within reach but they all worried that it would not hold. Palm trees were notoriously shallow-rooted and this one was right at the edge of the beach sand. "If we don't let any slack develop, we should be all right." Marc said.

"Yeah, but we'll have to leave one of us watching it until high tide. After that she won't move. Anyone have the faintest idea when high tide is at this time of year?" Dan said this without any real hope of a positive answer.

REDEMPTION ISLAND

Marc surprised all of them by answering definitively, "I would guess about Midnight, maybe ten minutes after. But the peak tide will be rising each night for the next two weeks." He became aware that the two airmen were staring at him in disbelief. He said defensively, "I read a lot, and the tide is connected to the Moon's rotations."

Mike responded, "It's great that you know this stuff, it just seems so incongruous with…"

"…with the image I project." responded Marc.

"Yeah," Dan added, "you don't look the professor type."

The three of them settled on a two-hour rotating watch of the towline and then gathered the rest of the castaways to discuss their predicament.

~~~~~~~~~~

"So you see," Mike concluded, "we ran out of fuel because a long series of events that went against us. The radio communications were intermittent because of the very same storm that would not let us land. Combine that with our inability to gain altitude once we were low on fuel and the accident on landing—"

"You mean this clumsy oaf ruined our chances of using the radio," wailed Leesa. Several of the passengers, just recently upgraded to castaways, glared at her. Only Arrianna spoke up. She faced Dan and Mike and, using an affectation of incredulity, sighed and said, "This from someone who can't stay upright in knee high water with two men supporting her."

"I don't have to take that from you!"

Arrianna was not the least bit perturbed, "Would you like a little cheese with your whine?" Before Leesa could respond, Seth stood between the warring women.

REDEMPTION ISLAND

"Stop, Stop. I will not allow this to continue. I am more upset than any one of you about what happened and I am convinced that the pilots did all they could. In fact they landed us safely. We need to stop this silly quarreling and join together to effect our rescue as soon as possible." This silenced everyone, not only because of the common sense and the implication of childishness in the argument, but because of the speaker. "That's better. Young lady, Ms. Arrianna, if I am not mistaken. I would like you to apologize to this lady for all the things that you said."

Arrianna was too stunned and still too accustomed to following the commands of unfamiliar adults to object. "I am sorry." Leesa looked smug and self satisfied as if she had been vindicated.

"Good, and now you, miss 'high and mighty.' We do not need your constant negative Karma. If you cannot keep it quiet, may I suggest that you go for a walk and come back when your urge to complain passes?"

Leesa was about to complain yet again, when she saw that everyone was looking at her and nodding in agreement with Seth. Well! She would just not give them the satisfaction. She crossed her arms across her ample chest and grimaced from the strain of keeping quiet.

"Excellent. Now Captain, would you be so kind as to tell us what we need to do to get off this godforsaken island as soon as possible?" Seth sat down unceremoniously and focused his already intense, nearly-black, eyes on Mike. Now that they had landed safely and were within sixty miles or so from civilization, his hopes of getting his message out and his debt repaid had surged. After all, sixty miles was nothing; one could walk that in one day if absolutely necessary.

"Thank you Mr. Martin. Dan and I appreciate your confidence in us—"

REDEMPTION ISLAND

"Call me Seth, I certainly think now that we are fellow castaways, we can be less formal." Looking around, Mike noticed that everyone, except Leesa and Arrianna, were nodding.

"Thank you, Seth. Our situation is at least stable. The plane is intact and flyable. No one was hurt in the landing. Dan and I have looked at the console and we found that the two radios appear undamaged, but the control panel that routes the power and signal to them is wrecked. We will of course attempt to by-pass it and contact a passing airplane, but—"

"Why not contact the airport directly?" Arrianna blurted out.

Marc replied before either of the pilots. "The radios they have are VHF and only reach on a line-of-sight basis. Since the earth is round, the radio at sea level will only reach, at most, five miles."

"Marc is right, but if we can get the radio working we will be able to reach a large number of overflying planes who will then relay our message."

Leesa spoke up for the first time since her yelling match with Arrianna. "Why did you not contact a plane before we landed?" She was not being malicious with her question. She was sure there had been a reason and was simply curious to know what it was.

Dan and Mike looked at each other and shifted uncomfortably. Finally Mike took a deep breath, made an obvious and futile attempt to relax his shoulder muscles and answered, "We were busy trying to come up with alternatives and we felt that contact with the ground would clear up at any moment. To contact overflying aircraft we'd have had to switch our radio to a different frequency, and during that time we would not have heard a response from the ground. By the time we were going to do just that, the engines quit and we ran out of time. I admit that we could have done that sooner. Also we felt that we'd have plenty of time once we were safely on the water." He looked up at their faces and in a hushed tone said, "I am sorry."

REDEMPTION ISLAND

A deep unsettling quiet mushroomed over the group. The only thing audible was the lapping sounds made by the waves, the rustling of trees and the myriad animals that called this island home. Mike was clearly defensive and Dan, who had been in charge of communications, felt grateful to him for taking the blame for his very significant lapse.

It was finally Martha who broke the silence. "Recriminations are all well and good and when we get back to civilization we will inevitably have more than we want, but now we need to get ourselves organized and settled, there is a lot to do." Both Mike and Dan winced at the mention of future recriminations. Monday morning quarterbacking was the rule with airplane accidents, usually with people who knew less than nothing about flying making the decisions. Dan shrugged it off, most likely because the greatest blame would be placed on the pilot. Mike had a more difficult time letting go of those thoughts.

~~~~~~~~

The entire group spent the better part of the next hour planning for their immediate needs. Leesa was incapable of accepting that they would need to spend even one night on the island and kept looking for a plane to materialize from the direction that they'd come. At the other extreme, Marc turned out to be a godsend. With his seemingly limitless breadth of knowledge and an equal amount of youthful energy, he helped them establish a latrine area, organize a group to locate and bring back fresh water, and determine the best location for their 'overnight' camp. He then joined Mike and Dan in working on a way to signal their presence.

He suggested fires and Mike agreed, noting that three fires would be the international signal for distress. Mike informed Marc they were well out of any of the shipping or airways, and their chances of them being seen were slim.

"Won't it keep them busy and help them feel involved?" Marc suggested.

"Yes it would do that. Do we have a way of lighting the fire?" asked Dan.

"I noticed that Ms. Vaughn, I mean Leesa, smokes. Supposedly she has a lighter. When night comes it will feel much better having a fire."

They agreed and proceeded to further consider other signaling options. Even though the two older men shook their heads at the hopelessness of the situation, Marc insisted on a look at the console's wiring. The only other idea they had that could be implemented immediately was to bring out whatever reflectors they could find and attempt to signal any plane they could see. Mike knew all too well that the only planes overflying would be in the flight levels of at least 18,000 feet and they would have a better chance of shouting at them than signaling with a mirror.

~~~~~~~~~

By nightfall they had two fires started and were gathering wood for the third fire. To their pleasant surprise, they discovered that there were plenty of snacks in the plane and they all made do with nuts, cheese and crackers. If they did not get tired of the monotony, they estimated that they could eat well for at least two, possibly three days. Even then there was bound to be some sort of sustenance on the island. Food, at least, did not seem to be an immediate problem. Water was also not a problem now that they'd found a fresh water stream within shouting distance of the camp. Shelter would only be needed in case of a storm and the plane would suffice in that circumstance.

REDEMPTION ISLAND

Once the third fire was going, they sat around the middle fire and heard Marc talk optimistically about being able to reroute power directly to one of the radios. As far as they could tell, the radios were intact. It was only the power connections that had been damaged. He planned to start with the fix as soon as he had enough light to see. He would then fire-up the radio and contact the outside world. Marc's tone implied he fully expected to be finished and rescued tomorrow.

Eventually they all fell asleep, even Leesa. Arrianna had the least trouble, while Mike and Dan struggled under the overwhelming burden of responsibility.

Chapter Three
Introductions

It occurred not to a single one of the group to set a watch. These were civilized people used to doors and walls, police and the rule of law. They did not understand, much less appreciate, that a hungry animal obeys a much different, more primitive, and usually much harsher law.

The sun shone two widths above the horizon before Arrianna awoke. She felt great. She idly observed that today there would be no Pop-Tarts for breakfast, but she would make up for it after the rescue plane took them back.

She noticed that the only other person awake was the old man. He was turning out to be a rather peculiar person. She herself did not know if she meant the word with the negative connotations or not. She had no preset role model for someone so powerful yet so kind and attentive at such an old age. He must be at least fifty! Maybe even sixty! He would look at her with such an open and happy expression. Had she experience with such things, the image of a grandparent's concern would have been unmistakable.

Unfortunately, Arrianna had never had grandparents, or even poor substitutes. Her experience with people older than her dad was composed entirely of hard drinking business types; the kind that, if they noticed her, would not waste one moment of their precious time acknowledging that fact.

She decided that she liked Seth but was scared of him. She did not know what to say to him. What would he want to talk about? He had helped them sleep last night with his funny and sad stories of a time so long ago. It had transformed their being marooned into a camping trip. Even that bitch, Leesa, relaxed. "I'm sorry, I'm sorry," she said inwardly to her dad, "but she makes things so difficult and she whines all the time."

"Are you talking to me?" asked Seth.

"Oh no! I was actually talking to my dad."

"You make it sound like talking to me would be a sin," Seth laughed, "and I had not noticed that your dad had come along on the trip."

Arrianna could not help but smile. She scooted over closer to him. Maybe she would try to talk to him after all. "You know he is not here, but I had a bad thought and I heard him correct me, so I apologized to him."

"I don't believe that a beautiful and mature young lady like you could ever have a bad thought."

Arrianna blushed. She rarely received such compliments and she liked it a lot. She instantly decided to hang around Mr. Martin more. Maybe he would say more nice things about her. "I called her," pointing to Leesa, "a bitch that whines all the time." Arrianna braced herself for the onslaught.

Seth smiled and even laughed a little. "That is not a bad thought. That is the truth! Everyone here is thinking that. Probably even Leesa herself. A bad thought would be to wish her dead." He put down the copy of the Torah he had been reading and held one of Arrianna's hands in both of his. "What a sweet thing you are. You remind me of one of my granddaughters. Her name is Allie. She is a year younger perhaps, but you are both so beautiful. You must have many boyfriends."

Arrianna blushed again, this time with the deep red extending into her neck. She felt her face heating up, but she did not mind. She had never had an interaction this strange and it was oddly reassuring. "I don't have any boyfriends. Daddy says I am too young. Anyway we move too frequently for me to find anyone."

Seth sighed, "That is the boys' loss. You would make such a good girlfriend. You must be nineteen, perhaps close to twenty?"

She laughed, "No. I am seventeen. I won't be eighteen for over six more weeks."

Seth pretended to be shocked, "You look so much older, and how are you going to learn about boys and relating to them if you are not allowed to have boyfriends?" Without waiting for an answer he continued, "I think that when we get back I will have a talk with your father. I have much experience raising girls, and raising them well. Maybe I can help your father understand."

Arrianna's eyes went wide. There were so many competing feelings that she could hardly sort them out. A stranger helping dad understand her need to date? Being back with Dad soon? Dad talking to a Jew? He did not say much about them, but she had surmised that he would not be comfortable in such a situation. For the first time in her life she wondered what that was about. "Thank you, Mr. Martin for all of the nice things you said." She stood up gracefully, "I am going to walk and look around."

"Call me Seth, please. When you say Mr. Martin, I look around for my father, and he has been dead for many years," he said chuckling.

REDEMPTION ISLAND

"OK, Seth," she said and walked towards the latrine area. On her way she heard the sounds of the rest of the group waking. She even heard the first whine of the morning but was learning to tune it out, just like everyone else in Leesa's life did.

~~~~~~~~~~~

Marc awoke to the sight of everyone but Arrianna staring at him. It was a disconcerting sight. Their unspoken suggestion was crystal clear. He was to waste no time in fixing the radio so they could all get the hell out of here.

They, of course, did not know that he woke up slowly and in need of tremendous sustenance. He usually ate two huge bowls full of whatever cereal he happened to fancy that day. It was for this reason that several of his friends had called him a 'cereal killer.' Today was no different. He wanted a large and hot cup of coffee, preferably Starbucks, followed by a large number of carbohydrate-laden calories—he would not be able to concentrate until then.

With trepidation, he informed the group of his proclivities and they surprised him by their immediate attention to his needs. They did not laugh and disparage him but instead actually catered to him. They boiled water on the fire and made some instant coffee that, under the circumstances, was more than passable. Leesa came up with three granola bars and gladly offered them to him. The others could not hide their amazement and she just glared back at them.

"If it would get us off this godforsaken island one minute sooner he can have me too."

Marc blushed and had to forcibly close his mouth. He saw that many of the others were having similar trouble with Leesa's forthrightness. Jerry noticed that Leesa looked very proud of herself, but could not understand why. If Marc had been a better judge of people, or even if he simply related with people as well as he did with machines and books, he might have surmised that Leesa was struggling mightily with herself to not complain. That the toughness she was showing was therefore a great accomplishment for her.

Out of deference to the group he consumed his breakfast quickly and walked to the plane

Leesa continued "You contact civilization and get them on the way and you can have me as many times as you want while we wait."

Marc ran for cover. He did not want to think even for one moment what interaction the two of them would have once the radio was working and the rescue was underway. Although Leesa was pretty, drop dead gorgeous actually, the idea of having sex as a reward…and with everyone knowing what they were doing…he decided to leave that line of thought unexplored.

Mike and Dan joined him at the plane. It was time to get to work.

While the three men worked, Arrianna made a discovery. She was so totally lost in her thoughts about it that she jumped when Martha came up to her and said, "What have you found?"

"You scared me! Don't sneak up on me like that." She said it like a petulant child and instantly regretted it. Before Martha could respond, she apologized, "I'm so sorry, it's just that I hate being startled."

Martha beamed, to see someone so young and so aware of themselves was a treat. Why couldn't her grandkids be this way? They were older than Arrianna and still they acted like the spoiled children they had been since they were toddlers. "That's all right dear, what have you found?"

"Tracks! They are fresh and large. I think it may be a cat. Take a look." She said this without concern for her safety. Arrianna wished she had seen whatever it was that had made it. Martha was not feeling the same way.

"They are rather large. You think they are a cat's prints?" Martha was out of her element and knew it. Arrianna could say they were elephant tracks and she would not have been able to dispute it, except that they weren't anywhere near Africa.

"Dad would be able to tell you the animal's weight. He would push on the ground like this to see how soft it is and then he would see how deep the impression is and he would declare, 'forty-five pounds, a cat of the *feline forensis genera*' or some such nonsense. Of course you can never quite check, because the animal doesn't then step up to be weighed." Arrianna smiled and giggled.

"What is so funny?" Martha asked while anxiously looking around their surroundings. She noted the varied vegetation at the edge of the jungle, the uncountable multitude of greens and yellows and the loamy sand underfoot. She wondered how old the tracks were. Had they been made last night? This morning? A few minutes ago? Several days ago? Where was the little monster now? Was he plotting to make one of them his meal?

"Once I made a wooden model of a cat in a way that I could add weight to it. I then measured how deep the imprints were and came up with a weight estimate. Dad was surprised."

"I imagine. Did it turn out that he was right?"

"Probably. It was hard to tell because my model had wooden feet and the animal had furry feet."

"That is a nice memory nevertheless. How old do you think the tracks are?" Martha asked with clear concern in her voice.

"Don't worry, they weren't made this morning. Sometime last night I suppose. The ground had to be soft, but it was before the dew. Look, you can see how the dew formed after the paw print."

REDEMPTION ISLAND

Martha relaxed a little but shuddered at the thought of something wild and undeniably savage walking within sight of their camp. She knew that if the creature came back, she would not be of any use whatsoever. Nevertheless, it was emotionally impossible for her to leave the girl alone. So, she suppressed her need to go back to the group and stayed with Arrianna, while the latter continued surveying the area. She even found herself infected with the girl's enthusiasm for everything. They catalogued a variety of tracks, most of them small and rodent like, a number of fruit trees and, just before going back, they found a stream.

"The water is so clear!" said Arrianna. "I'm going to have a sip."

"Is that a good idea? It might have something bad in it."

Arrianna looked up and saw that Martha, for all of her maturity and sensitivity, was not only ignorant of nature, but also scared of it. "Even if it was, a sip would not hurt. Anyway, almost all dangerous contamination comes from humans. I don't see anyone else here." With that she used her hands in a practiced motion and sipped. "It's cold. It probably comes from that mountain up there. Do you want to try it?"

Martha discovered that she was very thirsty. They had been rationing liquids and she was one of those people that drank for more than mere thirst. Arrianna's confidence overcame her sense of caution and she too tasted the water. "It's wonderful. I did not know that water could taste so good."

"You have never been camping or hiking?" Arrianna said with clear disbelief.

"I have never been much of a nature girl. Maybe it is not too late for this old bird to change her spots." She winked at the mixed metaphor.

It was approximately ten minutes later that the two women heard the screams from the campsite and hurried back.

Chapter Four
Marooned

The news had stunned and terrified the group. No one was spared. Certainly not Leesa, but Seth and Jerry were unexpectedly far more upset. Perhaps it was that she vented her feelings regularly while the other two held them under tight control. Regardless of the cause, what Martha and Arrianna saw when they reached the group was a degenerating, verbally abusive altercation full of more vitriol than either one had ever seen..

"You fucking incompetent moron," screamed Jerry, "you are the one responsible for this and I demand you get us back immediately."

Seth added, "I have to get back soon. I cannot hang about here like some castaway in a movie waiting for a chance rescue."

"I think all three of them should not get any food or water until the rescue comes. That will teach them," said Leesa in a self-satisfied tone.

Mike was trying to regain control, but the abuse of both Dan and himself made his efforts strained at best. "Like I said before,

REDEMPTION ISLAND

Marc here tried everything, he almost pulled it off. It is not his fault."

"Yeah, whose fault is it then?" Jerry demanded.

"I don't think it is anyone's fault, it just happened. A thunderstorm is not anyone's fault." Marc said reasonably.

"Stay out of it you fool, you're on his side. Someone is to blame for this and we are going to make him pay. Just wait and see what my agent does to all of you," Leesa said.

Arrianna interrupted the degenerating discourse, "Would one of you adults," she said the last word with the deep cutting sarcasm of a teenager, "tell us what is going on?"

Martha waded in, "Yeah, why are the three of you acting like ignorant rednecks?"

Marc, who up to now had been quiet, could not resist adding some levity, saying "Miss Martha, that is redundant you know, you can say redneck or ignorant but to say both together is quite improper." Martha and Arrianna laughed with him, but it was clear that no one else felt it merited a response. After a long silence, Marc explained.

"I tried all morning to fix the radio. I even managed to connect it well enough to receive signals. The authorities are still looking for us—"

"In the fucking wrong place!" Leesa screamed.

Jerry stood up in anger, "I can't fucking believe this. And if you think I'm going to sit around so I can listen to your ridiculous excuses one more time, you're sorely mistaken." He offered his hand to Leesa who stood up and walked away with him.

By now, Martha could not get herself to accept the undeniable fact that they were not going to be rescued today. She did not want to spend one more night here. She felt queasy with the impending emotional upset and sat down abruptly. Mike resumed his story.

"We tried to transmit, but each time the circuit would blow—"

Marc interrupted, "The radio requires a lot more power to transmit than to receive. It is not surprising that the jerry-rigged wire connections I could manage weren't up to the electrical load. So I tried again. That time, I was not simply experimenting; I knew what I needed to do. I hooked it up and was about to transmit when…" Marc looked down at his feet.

"When what?" shouted both Martha and Arrianna.

Mike finished, "When we noticed that the circuit switch had been left on."

Martha and Arrianna looked at each other not understanding the statement. It was as if he had started speaking Russian. "What does this mean?" asked Martha in a quavering tone.

"It means that the battery has been draining slowly since we landed and does not have enough power to transmit a message. Since we have no other way of powering the radio or recharging the battery we have no way off the island." With that statement Mike's resolve and command evaporated and he slumped onto the sand with his head in his hands.

On that note, they heard a moan from Seth. He was muttering things to himself that were unintelligible to the others. Arrianna went over to him and sat next to him. On seeing her, his lips made a brief involuntary smile before resorting to their pathetic hopelessness. Arrianna put her hand on his and said, "I know we will figure a way out of this place. Marc is so smart and Mike is so knowledgeable that we won't be here forever. It will be just like an extended outdoor vacation."

Seth looked up with tears in his eyes, "You are such a sweet thing. I know that you are right, but I need to get back right away. I have something urgent to do."

"Yeah, that's right. You wanted to get a message out when we were landing. What is that about?" asked Mike, suddenly animated. "Is there a chance that someone will be making a special effort to find you?"

Seth shook his head, "If they only knew, most definitely, they would scour the very ocean floor, but alas, they do not know that I have the information."

"So what is so important?" asked Martha looking for a distraction.

Seth was startled as if shocked by the question. He looked up at each of their faces, Martha, Arrianna, Mike and Marc. Dan had left and was now rummaging around the plane. Arrianna thought that he looked years older than he had just this morning. He appeared torn as if struggling within himself. "I shouldn't say, but I do not know if it makes any difference anymore." They all remained quietly patient, waiting for him to resolve his inner dilemma. "I have information that could very well avoid a war."

"Are you a spy?" Arrianna asked with disbelief.

Seth smiled, "I don't think of myself as a spy. I did stumble on some information that the State of Israel needs desperately. It could save a lot of lives, and it would get me out of debt."

"They will pay you for the information?" asked Mike with unveiled distaste.

"No, not at all, I owe them my life and the life of my family. We were starving after the war and they gave us a home. It is a debt of honor that I am talking about."

~~~~~~~~~~

"It is the utter mindless incompetence that galls me," snapped Jerry. "First, they run out of gas, then they transmit the wrong coordinates and, to top it off, they do not turn the power off and therefore completely drain the only battery available. If I did not know better, I would say it was a plot by my competitors to keep me away from my office next week."

Leesa perked up at that, "Do you really think so?" Hope sprang from every syllable. "If it is a plot then someone knows where we are and we will eventually be rescued. Maybe it will only be until some business deadline passed."

Jerry shook his head with disinterest, "No, I don't. Despite the deadline next week, no one knows where I am or how I am traveling. I usually use the corporate jet but I have been traveling incognito for the last few days." After a pause, "How about you, anyone waiting for you?"

"No one that would care. The only person that would give a rat's ass is my agent and he won't miss me for a month when my next assignment starts."

"Assignment? What kind of assignment?"

"I'm a model and actress, "she waited a beat and a half. "You don't recognize me? I have a fashion shoot for this winter's clothes starting in five weeks. When I don't show that's when they will miss me and only then figure out that I was on this godforsaken shuttle."

They were quiet for some time. Each was trying to reconcile themselves to the situation in their own way. They understood, at some level, that the situation was far worse than they could grasp at the moment.

~~~~~~~~~~

"We are only sixty or so miles from civilization, couldn't we build something to get us there?" asked Seth.

Sixty miles did not seem that far. Arrianna's dad had run a

marathon and that was almost half that far. Martha was thinking similar thoughts. As a young girl she had been a long-distance swimmer and had swum a quarter of that distance then. The distance did not seem insurmountable.

Marc spoke up, "It is our best hope, yet it will be a difficult undertaking at best. At worst, there are numerous obstacles to overcome." He paused to play with the sand at his feet. "Mike and I have discussed it and with the group's help we could try within a week or so."

"Why so long?" asked Martha, "why couldn't we just get going today. The sooner we leave the sooner we arrive."

Mike responded, "I am sorry Martha, but it isn't that easy. Please consider the prevailing winds at this time of year are easterly. Although the winds may be light, the current also goes east. If not careful, we would be blown out further into the Atlantic. The raft we have, although it would hold all of us, will not hold enough supplies for everyone even if we had them. It was designed to keep us afloat until rescue came, not for a sea voyage. It will require planning and collection of as much food and water as we can find."

The rest of the plan unfolded. The two strongest men would go in the raft with as much water and food as they could safely stow. They would have to wait for the wind to shift a little so there would be a quartering wind instead of fighting it directly all the way. One problem would be deciding who would go. Marc and Dan were the youngest and the fittest, but Mike had more navigation experience. It would be a difficult passage. If they could row three knots faster than the current against them, then they could expect at least four hours of grueling struggle before the current eased and over ten hours before they could catch the main islands' wind pattern. Furthermore, they would not be able to rest during this period. At least one of them would have to row just to stay in place. To make matters worse, they would be at the mercy of the weather. They would need to time the voyage to avoid a storm.

"How can you tell if a storm is coming?" asked Arrianna.

Marc answered. "What we can do, is wait for a storm to pass and take off as soon as it is over. The storm uses up a lot of the atmosphere's potential energy and dissipates it. In fact that is what is thought to be the function of storms. It takes a few days to build that potential energy up again and that is our window of opportunity."

"It could be much longer than a week then." Arrianna said in a matter of fact tone, not as an argument. It seemed like she wanted to plan as if she had a lot to do and needed to know how much time was available. "Do we have enough food and water on the plane for that amount of time?"

"No," Mike answered. "Especially if you consider how much has to go on the raft. Regardless of who goes on the raft, they will be burning calories at a prodigious rate. They will also need a huge water supply if they are to work at full efficiency. What we need to do is work as a team to prepare. That is what we were trying to do when the screaming started." Mike did not try to disguise his contempt for Leesa and Jerry.

Seth came out of his stupor and jumped up. "Then we need to start as soon as possible. If we are not ready by the time the next storm comes up, we could miss that opening and have to wait for the next one."

Marc said, "That is exactly right. The next storm could come this afternoon, I'm not sure we could be ready by tomorrow, but if we didn't fight each other and if we all did our part, we could be ready by the day after."

Everyone looked out to sea. Would the storm hold off twenty-four hours? Could they be ready in that time? Every single one of them set their minds on one thought. They would do everything within their power to be ready as soon as possible. Even if it meant beating sense into some people's heads.

"Then I will inform Jerry and Leesa of the plan." Seth said. "I am sure once they hear of it they will be just as anxious as we are to get going with it. They are both used to being in control, to having someone around to take care of any problem that arose for them. This situation plays on their worst fears." Everyone just looked at him as if he had grown another head. "It's just a guess, that's all." He then added. "A very good guess, but a guess nevertheless."

With that Seth took off walking briskly in the direction Jerry and Leesa had gone.

Marc said, "I will draw up a list of supplies that we will need, Dan has already started cataloguing everything in the plane that could be of use. Could the two of you look for a source of food and water?"

Arrianna beamed, "I have already found them. This morning while I was exploring, I found a cold mountain stream and many fruit trees."

"That's great," Marc said, "what kind of fruit?"

Arrianna blushed, "I don't know what they are called. They are yellow and the size of a softball. I have seen them in the markets of the other islands, so I know they are edible."

Martha joined the discussion, "I saw mangoes, papayas, guavas and a few others I could not identify.

Marc smiled, "It could not have been a mango. They are native only to Asia. It must have been something that looks a lot like one."

Martha appeared insulted, "Sir, I know fruit and when I say I saw mangoes, then I do not mean something else."

"All right, all right. I didn't mean anything by it. Let's go see what we have available and make plans to gather as much of it as possible." Marc stood up and amiably followed the two women to the fruit patch. On arrival ten minutes later, he stared in disbelief. "It isn't possible. It just does not make any sense."

"Are they mangoes after all?" Arrianna asked.

"Of course they are," snapped Martha.

"She is quite right. They are mangoes, but as to how they came to be here, that is a big question." They could see that mangoes were green on the outside and, after he picked one and peeled it, that they were yellow on the inside. Arrianna tasted one and loved it. Whether their judgment was affected by hunger for something different than crackers and nuts she couldn't be entirely sure.

Marc explained "Mangoes are a fruit of Asiatic origin. Although they are now cultivated throughout the tropical world, they have never been found in nature in this hemisphere. A find such as this had huge implications as to the origin of the fruit and the travels of ancient peoples."

Martha refused to be impressed. "A bird could have carried a seed from some fruit that was thrown away and then deposited on this island."

Marc realized "You might be right. My biggest problem in life had always been his tendency to focus on the most esoteric or theoretical solution and miss something that was staring me right in the face. A group of boaters could have had a beach party here and thrown seeds of all of these fruits into the bush. Perhaps this had been a clearing where they had built a fire and left their trash. The seeds would have found fertile ground, particularly if the partygoers had buried their trash. The grove appears to be twenty or thirty years old, with several generations of plants. Maybe I will dig around and see if I can find any remains that had not decomposed." His reverie was cut short by Martha pointing out that they had filled their arms with fruit and that the least he could do was the same.

They arrived back at camp. Their joy of discovery and of filled stomachs evaporated when they realized that there was a heated argument going on between Mike and Jerry.

"I should become the leader and run the rescue operation." Jerry said. "I feel it is a management job anyway and I am better suited for the job than you are, Mike."

Mike insisted "It is my responsibility and that I will not relinquish it because some blue nose company CEO feels like giving orders to everyone."

Seth and Leesa, to their credit, were trying to diffuse the situation instead of fanning the flames. It was a strange sight to see them working closely together. An unlikelier pair would have been hard to find. Despite all their efforts, the two men continued with verbal jabs at each other.

"Don't you think you have caused enough damage for one day?" Jerry spat.

"Not as much as someone unused to real work is likely to cause. I am not afraid of getting my hands dirty."

It was Arrianna that finally stopped the exchange. She screamed. Not an ordinary scream like one hears in horror movies, but a shrill piercing shriek she had worked on and perfected over the years. It did not seem human somehow. It sounded like some huge metal monster was tearing itself apart.

She had first realized her gift when she was four and could get the glass alarms to go off with her shrieks. Instead of tantrums she would start setting the alarms off which would cause her mother to capitulate more times than not. Her dad remained immune and in the past few years she had retained the ability solely out of amusement.

The shriek did its work. "Now that I have your attention, I will tell you I am reassured that it is not only my generation that can act like adolescents. I cannot speak for the others, but if the two of you peacocks want to show off your feathers to each other, do us the courtesy to do so out of sight and earshot. As for the leader of the group, I was happy with Mr. Faraday, but if there is contention and, since all of our futures depend on it, I think we should vote on it."

There was a murmur of approval from everyone, except Jerry and Mike. They did not appreciate a teenager making them look like fools, but there was nothing to do now but to follow her lead. They decided to have an emergency meeting with each of the candidates proposing their position in five minutes or less.

Mike started, "You have all heard of our plan to launch the raft after the next storm. Besides that we need to find food, and water. That's all."

Jerry looked smug. He was a very good speaker and knew it. He was able to wax poetically and convincingly. He was about to start when Arrianna spoke up.

"I vote for Marc. He is the least pretentious and seems to be the smartest one here."

Jerry countered, "I don't think you are old enough to vote young lady."

Martha spoke up, "I don't see why not. She is just as trapped here as we are. She has also shown more common sense and maturity than some older people I could mention. I vote for Marc also."

Marc spoke up timidly, "I wasn't even running. I don't know how to be a leader."

"That's good enough for me, "said Seth, "you have my vote also. We need more leaders like you."

"I haven't had a chance to speak," complained Jerry.

"No need," said Mike, "I withdraw and vote for Marc. I have been working with him and he has a good head on his shoulders."

REDEMPTION ISLAND

Seth jumped up and said, "That is four votes. Not counting the candidates, the majority ruled, now let's start working on the plan to get off this island." There was a chorus of agreement, even Leesa and Dan, who had been quiet all day, agreed..

Jerry stood up and, in a show of disgust, brushed himself off and walked away without saying a word. Had he known how little anyone cared about his show of disdain, he would have acted differently. He was used to being fawned over by the sycophants in his company. His biggest failing was that he did not recognize this but assumed they were responding to his brilliance.

The other castaways cooperated without the least bit of friction. They all had one thing in common. They wanted off that island as soon as possible. Even Arrianna had enough of the adventure and wanted to get back. The scenes of conflict she had witnessed on the island, as well as the simmering resentments, had reminded her of her mother. The endless fights between her and dad, the violence and the insecurity. Most of all the insecurity. She had not known from one moment to the next what would happen and whether she could count on being comforted.

She remembered the drinking and the craziness. It had been six years now, but it felt like yesterday. She could see her mother nursing the bottle of vodka and she would know by the amount left how long she had before she would blow. Her father had been hopeless. He'd tried to cajole her into moderating her drinking and always appeared surprised when she failed. That was the part that could still gall her. Fortunately she was now free forever from her mother. Her only regret was how long it had taken and how much she'd had to endure along the way.

~~~~~~~~

REDEMPTION ISLAND

With six of them working together, they were able to quickly develop a list that included what the two men would need for the trip as well as what the group needed to await the rescue. They had cut the food rations twice when it became clear how much they would have to gather.

All of the high calorie food would have to go with the rescue team. They would not have a lot of time to eat. They would also not profit from large meals. The local fauna would be for those remaining on the island. They would only eat what they could clearly recognize as edible. Fortunately, Martha and Marc were able to identify most of the most commonly found fruits. Martha even helped them identify an edible root plant that was plentiful. They would not have much variety, but they would not go hungry.

Everyone was busy and the day passed very quickly. The women scrounged containers from the plane and gathered enormous amounts of fruit. They placed them in the plane to keep animals and insects away from them. They also separated them by ripeness—most were green since the ripe fruit had been at least partly eaten by the native animals of the island. When the group was done, they had gathered enough for six or more days.

The men inflated and checked the raft. It was old, but in good shape. They then gathered everything that might be of use on the trip, but had to trim the list five times before the two men could get into the craft with enough room to row comfortably. They knew they would have to sacrifice something important. They would either lose some amount of food and water, the life preservers, rain gear, or some other necessity. The raft had been made to hold more than two people, but only to hold them, not as a vessel of propulsion. Although it had paddles, these were intended for close maneuvering, not a long distance row. Also, the heavier the craft was, the deeper it would sink into the water and the slower it would move. This was critical since they would be fighting the current. The difference in half a knot of speed could be the difference in drifting backwards or making slight headway.

By nighttime, all the castaways were exhausted, but optimistic. All they needed was a good healthy storm to pass by and stabilize the atmosphere long enough for them to reach civilization. Jerry had returned early and acting as if nothing had happened, he gathered firewood and water and by the end of the day had made as big a contribution as any of them. All the others put the prior issues behind them.

Chapter Five

Dan

They all rose with the sun, hoping to see cloudy skies. Disappointed, they started to eat a breakfast composed of tropical fruits: papaya, mango, and guava. They talked in spirited tones. They were taking an active role in their own rescue and that energized them.

"Where is Dan?" Mike asked. The rest looked around noticing for the first time that he was not present.

"I was up early, just after dawn actually, and he was already gone," said Martha.

"Maybe he needed a walk to relax him. After all, he is our best rower and a lot is riding on him." Seth thought further how he wished he were younger so that he could go on the raft. He did a lot better being active than waiting.

Arrianna was the first to notice, "The raft is gone!"

"What!" screamed Mike and Jerry simultaneously. The group ran to the edge of the woods where they had sheltered their rescue hopes. They could see the drag lines and the deep footprints from when Dan had pushed the raft down the beach and into the water.

Mike was shaken speechless, but was able to work it out in his mind. With the surf coming in, if he pushed the raft only when a wave broke near the shore, no one would have heard him. "Damn him! Why couldn't he wait?" They all looked at each other and at the tracks. It was Seth who finally spoke up, "I suppose the only thing we can do now is pray that he makes it." There was a chorus of nods before Jerry said, "I for one will not forget this irresponsible behavior, when we get back…" His words were lost in the surf as the entire group walked away. No one wanted to listen to his vindictiveness. Jerry was embarrassed and humiliated. He was unused to these emotions and discovered he loathed himself for having them. The group could not have done anything to infuriate him more. He stormed away.

As the group ambled back to camp, Mike explained what he knew about Dan. "It had been Dan's responsibility to contact overflying planes during their emergency and also his job to turn all the power off in the plane. Dan must have felt deeply responsible for our current predicament, particularly our inability to contact help.

"You mean you took the blame even though it was his job?" Leesa exclaimed. The confusion on her face was evident. It was as if she had just seen Mike grow a second head.

"Of course he did," offered Seth, "he was the captain of the plane. It was his responsibility. What kind of leader blames others?"

Arrianna could see from Leesa's face that she saw it as the leader's job to avoid blame. Maybe in her line of work it was. She wondered what it was that she did, besides look beautiful, of course. "What is it you do, Miss Vaughn?"

Leesa looked surprised to be addressed by the youngest in the group. "What are you? Nineteen, perhaps twenty?"

"Seventeen, until next month."

"Right, a very mature and confident seventeen then, but call me Leesa. I divorced the creep who gave me that last name."

"Why do you keep it, then?" Arrianna asked reflexively and immediately back-stepped, "I'm sorry, I don't mean to pry."

Leesa laughed, "Don't worry about it, it's not prying. Anyway, if it isn't in some tabloid somewhere I would be surprised. I am a model and sometimes actress. Professionally I am known as 'Vaughn,' so I did not see any advantage in changing it."

"That's where I saw your face," commented Martha, "I knew that it looked familiar, but you look different in the ads."

"There are a lot of adjustments done. First, on my face with make-up and then with the computer, they can change any body part they don't like. I am surprised they need me anymore. Pretty soon they will be able to manufacture the entire face with their computers. Can you imagine a computer nerd will be creating the most famous face in the world?"

There was a short silence which she broke. "I married this director, you know, Hollywood and all that. He was oh so nice to me, as long as I drooled over him. Once I started giving him honest feedback, he became quite nasty. The entire industry is ruled by ego with a capital E."

With the ice broken, the group began talking about themselves. Seth told them a little about his trip running the British blockade of Palestine.

Mike told them "My dark skin had been such a barrier to getting a pilot's job that I changed my name so the hiring agents would not make up their mind before they met me. I chose a name as lily white as possible, "Faraday". I still had to prove myself, but after the name change, I have been given many more chances to do so.

When it was her turn, Martha confessed, "I have been a

housewife most of my life and I am now trying to find something to do with my life now that my kids are all gone. This trip was supposed to be an adventure." This merited a small laugh from the rest of the group.

After about an hour, they began questioning Marc and Mike "Do you think he has a chance? How long do you think it will take him? When will we know one way or the other? What do we do now? What else can we do?"

Mike and Marc agreed that if a storm did not come up and if the current wasn't too strong, Dan had a good chance of breaking out of the current that pushed past the island and reached the Atlantic. After that it depended on his endurance and the wind direction but, most of all, it depended on luck.

Marc wanted to start planning in case Dan did not make it, but Mike wanted to wait a few days and give Dan a chance.

Arrianna suggested the eventual solution. "If we have some time on our hands and we already have enough food and water to last us several days, then…" She let her voice trail off.

"Then what Arrianna?" asked Martha.

"Then why don't we survey our island a little better and see what else we may have at our disposal? It will give us something to do without having to focus on Dan possibly failing to reach anyone."

Seth laughed, "Brilliant! You sure act much older than my kids did at your age."

Martha agreed, "Much more mature than any of my kids even five years your senior. Are you sure you are seventeen? Where you there at the time?" she kidded her.

~~~~~~~

Jerry was livid. He could not stand it one more minute. Two

days ago, he had been in charge. No, even better, in control over his life, his work, his environment, over every single aspect of his existence. He had spent his youth working to that end. Now it was all gone. What had happened? How did he miss this outcome? How could he have foreseen it? He knew well enough that it was no use going over the same ground yet again. He had reviewed it a dozen times already. He was here now and reexamining the past would not help him. Wasn't that the way he functioned? Set a goal and let nothing get between it and him? So what was he doing now? This situation had further showed him, to his own chagrin, that he could not help but lose his temper. This deficiency made him even more furious—at himself.

Twice he'd acted like a spoiled child and stormed off, unable to tolerate losing an election or being ignored. The fact was that being discounted like that had not happened to him for so long. He was unprepared and did not have the skills to deal with them. *That isn't completely true* he told himself, *there was Rosetta*. It had been years since he had thought of her. Her lovely auburn hair and her sense of irreverence. She ignored him frequently and certainly had no compulsion about putting him in his place. Is that why he left her? Could he have been that shallow? Was he still that shallow?

"Mr. Simmons? We are planning a survey party, would you like to join us?"

Jerry noted that it was the teenager talking, the one who had started the vote going for Marc, that young hippie who did not seem to know anything about human nature. Jerry suddenly stood up, shook himself and forcibly stopped his thoughts. He did not like where they were leading him. She had invited him politely despite his obnoxiousness and he would make the best effort to be his best self, not the jerk he had turned into since landing on this godforsaken island. "Thank you, miss, I would like that very much.

REDEMPTION ISLAND

Do you think the group will accept me after my pouting?" For the answer he searched her face as much as he listened to her words.

Arrianna had no interest in protecting this guy's feelings. Her life with her alcoholic mother and her co-dependent father taught her early to take care of her own feelings and let others do the same. "Oh, I wouldn't worry about them. We are all on edge and, although a few of them did not want me to ask you, the others did." She then started back. After a few steps she looked back and verified that he was coming and let him catch up. "I am glad that you will join us, if we are to get off this island we will need everyone working together."

"What do you mean? Won't Dan reach the main island?" Jerry said, concerned that something wasn't right. It was more than the content of the off-hand comment. It was the tone she had used. There was a pessimistic, even fatalistic tone that was out of place for Arrianna. Even before she responded, he realized the worst. "The wind has picked up, hasn't it?"

Arrianna looked at him on the verge of tears, "Yes. Marc hasn't said as much but the wind direction is wrong and they think there will be a large storm within a few hours. They think that Dan will drown, or worse."

"Worse? Did you say worse?" He caught up to her, turned her face with a light touch on her cheek and said, "I don't mean to be ignorant or indelicate, but what do you mean by 'worse?'"

Arrianna's eyes focused and locked on his. She was no longer holding back tears. Instead she had a conspiratorial look. "I overheard Mike and Marc whispering. Adults are so funny. They think that if they whisper that others can't hear. Usually they don't even lower their voices much. It is like if they pretend that no one can hear them then no one will." She looked at his face and was surprised by the knowing smile.

"You are much too wise. What you have observed is doubly true in business. People tell you far more than they intend to if you just listen. It took me thirty years to figure that out. You are thirteen years ahead of me."

Arrianna could not hold back the smile. She enjoyed hearing compliments about her maturity. "They are worried that he may survive the storm and be swept out to sea and die of thirst." She then resumed her walk.

Jerry was shaken. He was so far out of his element. When was the last time he had to consider not having enough water? Never, that's when. He could give chapter and verse of financial hell, the severe consequences of financial extravagance or misjudgment. Here, however, life was back to its roots: water, food, and shelter. There was a man out there whose best outcome would be to drown all alone while realizing his failure to atone for the mistake he had made. This was turning out to be a very sobering experience indeed.

When the two of them arrived back, the activity was frenetic. Up to now they had been sheltered from the full force of the wind but now that it had changed direction it was making a mess of their rudimentary campsite. They hurried over and Jerry went right up to Marc and asked him "What do you want me to do?"

Marc was taken aback for a second, "Uh, OK. Pick up anything that might blow away and take it to that sheltered spot in the tree line, see it?"

Jerry looked in the direction that he was pointing and saw an ant line of people coming and going from there, "Right…but… shouldn't we be putting it into the plane?" He said this in an amiable tone that was diametrically different than his confrontational style they had become accustomed to.

"We thought of that, but we are afraid that the storm could

REDEMPTION ISLAND

either wreck the plane or break its moorings. Our next step is to get the plane as high on the beach as possible. We will need it as light as we can get it. Actually, if you really want to help, you could join Mike in getting anything heavy out of it."

"Good thinking. I'll go over and help him." Jerry felt energized. He always felt better when there was a crisis. Sometimes he had even orchestrated a crisis out of sheer boredom and exasperation. He was now in his element. So what if he wasn't technically in charge? No one else was either. It was more of a collaboration. Ever since kindergarten he had never "played well with others." Maybe this would be a time to start learning how.

When he reached the plane, Mike was climbing out. He was dragging a big wooden crate and Jerry grabbed the other side without any discussion. They wrestled it off the plane and carried it up the hill and at the top of the beach, Mike said, "There is no need to get this all the way into the woods. It's way too heavy to blow away." He reconsidered and asked Jerry, "Do you know much about the sea? I am much more of an air person. How high do you think the swell will go?"

Jerry looked at him blankly for a few seconds and then understood, "You're right, the storm is going to push the water level up isn't it? I am like you. It could be one inch or ten feet for all I know. Let's go and ask our fearless leader. He seems to know trivia like this."

Mike looked into Jerry's face but did not find any of the sarcasm or the put-down he was looking for. "Yeah, he sure seems to know a lot. I wonder if it has ever done him any good." Mike paused for effect, "Before now that is." Jerry smiled and nodded.

Marc was directing the women and Seth on the placement of their meager possessions in the jungle clearing. The wind there was markedly lower, but not absent. He had them put the heavy things on the windward side as a barrier, followed by the lightest things, with the remainder of the stuff on top to keep things in place. The plan was well conceived and almost as well executed.

"Marc."

"Yes, Jerry." Jerry noted that Marc looked like he was having the time of his life. There was no sign whatsoever that any danger or risk existed, as if this was just a game. Maybe for him that is just what it was. His entire life could have been one game after another.

"Mike is concerned about the swell from the storm and whether—"

Marc excitedly interrupted, "Good, good, I wondered if it would occur to anyone. That is next on our agenda." He was like a new quarterback, trying on the mantle of power and authority and finding he liked it very much. "I figure that with a moderate sized storm the swell could go as high as two or three feet. With a hurricane it can go as high as ten to twenty feet, but it isn't hurricane season, so we can count on a maximum of four feet."

The rest of the group was clearly awed by the depth of his knowledge. They could not resolve the disparity between his current persona and his prior irrelevant "student" persona. They all trooped over to the waterline and measured the high water mark. The crate needed to be moved another ten feet up the beach to be out of danger.

Once the camp was secured, Marc split them into two groups. The men continued to take the heavy cargo out of the plane while the women dug a trench in front of it. They would all have to help in bringing the plane as high onto the beach as possible. Hopefully, high enough to save it from damage. It may not fly without gas but it was, by far, their best shelter.

It took them several hours of heavy effort to unload the cargo, including the seats and every loose item of weight. By the time they were finished, the women had made a semi-respectable trench six feet long. The problem, of course, was that the further up the beach they went, the deeper they had to dig and the less the water supported the plane. The leading edge of the trench was three feet deep already. With their combined efforts, they extended the trench another three feet before they were all exhausted. They looked at Marc expectantly.

"I don't know. I guess that will be good enough. Realistically we can't dig anymore without proper tools. If we can secure the plane with the towline to those trees, it should hold. Also, we can check it every hour and, as the swell lifts the plane higher, we can pull the plane closer." The group wasn't happy with all his qualifications but they were too tired to protest. Mike and Jerry struggled to their feet against the wind.

"The wind is still building," commented Jerry.

"Yeah, it's going to be a bitch." They were all wondering what it would be like out there in the open ocean in a raft with no help in sight. With those thoughts, they all climbed into the plane and secured it the best they could. Even though their added weight would help keep the plane from floating away, their primary reason to get in was simply to avoid the rain that had finally begun in earnest.

Chapter Six
Waiting

Everyone had expected to have a long and sleepless fear-drenched night. Instead the storm was brief and did not live up to its promise. All of them, at one time or another, drifted off to sleep and the night passed uneventfully.

The next morning, when Arrianna climbed out of the plane, she was greeted by the bright sun that illuminated the starkly clear day. For a few seconds Arrianna forgot about their predicament and felt happy and alive. She walked the beach and looked at the restraining wire. She noted that, although it was slack at the moment, it had eaten deeply into one of the trees—which would probably not survive. The thought saddened her and brought her thoughts back to the present.

When Seth maneuvered his fireplug of a body out of the plane, he did not immediately notice the dramatic change in the weather. Instead, he was mesmerized by Arrianna. She was dancing on the beach. *Well,* he thought, *not exactly dancing, but close.* It had a strange silent rhythm that was simultaneously powerful and oddly gentle. Arrianna appeared to be completely unaware of anything outside her. He unconsciously brushed back the little hair he had, walked up behind her, and watched for several minutes, completely captivated by her performance. Then with a start, Arrianna froze and stifled a scream.

"Oh, I didn't hear you come so close."

Seth blushed and apologized, "It is my fault. I came up quietly so as not to disturb you. Your dancing is very beautiful. I have never seen anything quite like it."

"It's Tai-Chi, a Chinese form of exercise. It works the body as well as the mind. I do it every day. Yesterday was the first time in ages that I missed."

"Is it hard to learn?" Seth inquired.

"No, I can teach you the first few steps if you want." Arrianna sounded so hopeful and happy when she offered this that Seth, although uncertain of the advisability, could not refuse her. They spent the next twenty minutes going over the beginning of the "Form." To his amazement, Seth found it soothing and relaxing. He was surprised how long they had been at it when the rest of the group climbed out of the plane.

They gathered together and, over a breakfast of the local flora, they discussed what was uppermost on everyone's mind. Mike was of the opinion that Dan could have weathered the storm. "I also think that he could have been blown to the main island, right at the end the wind shifted quickly back into a westerly direction. It could very well have pushed him there."

"I agree," said Marc, "the storm was very short and did not build up much, the wind shift came much sooner than I expected. If he managed to stay on the raft, he could easily be at or close to the main island."

Jerry spoke, "I hope so, for Dan's sake. I cannot imagine what it was like in the middle of all that wind and water." He noted that most everyone was looking at him with surprise.

"I suppose we will know soon. If he made it, and I'll bet he did, we should get rescued soon," commented Leesa. Everyone remained quiet while they inwardly agreed with her. However, they knew the longer it was before they heard the rescue planes, the harder it would be to maintain that point of view. In time they were unable to hold on to the hope that Dan had made it. Now, in addition to the anticipated tragedy in case of his loss, they all began thinking of what they would do next—how they would ever get off this island.

It did not take long for them to realize that sitting around and waiting for a miracle would not work. They would go crazy and start picking on each other. It was Seth who eventually suggested going ahead with the survey as planned. Martha and Leesa offered to stay behind. Leesa did not care for the survey whatsoever while Martha knew that her arthritis would make it unpleasant for her, as well as slow everyone down. No one had a problem with this since they needed someone to remain at the camp. The two ladies agreed to gather more food and wood while they waited.

Marc asked, "Could the two of you also take an inventory of what we have? It will be helpful if we need to stay here any length of time."

Martha answered, "Of course, while I gather fruit, Leesa can do that. Is that OK, Leesa?"

"Perfect, making shopping lists is one of my joys. This could not be that much different and I'd rather do that than gather fruit."

Marc and Mike settled into planning the exploration. Rather than an extensive, thorough trip, they decided it should only be an extended half-day reconnaissance. This would not require carrying supplies or necessitate being gone from camp too long. Their goals where to discover how hard it was to move about, something about the terrain, and how long a more thorough survey would take.

They all decided to risk it and not take anything with them, even water. They would count on finding some along the way. At worst it would only be three or four hours before they returned. They had no machete, so would need to rely on animal trails and streambeds.

When it was time to set off, Mike took the point while Marc brought up the rear. He liked this because it gave him a chance to study the jungle without worrying about the path they were taking. Seth and Arrianna kept close together in the middle, helping each other through the ever present obstacles of undergrowth and fallen trees. Jerry stayed close to Mike and, to Mike's surprise, was decidedly helpful in picking which way to go.

They made an early decision to avoid going directly into the interior of the island where the terrain took a nasty uphill turn. Instead they focused on staying at the base and circumnavigating the elevation.

They had difficulty following this plan since their best progress was made along stream beds and those invariably went uphill. Their hike developed a pattern of following a streambed until a promising path or opening appeared and then following that until another stream materialized. This involved continuous backtracking and changes of direction. On several occasions Arrianna mentioned to Seth her fear of getting lost.

Once, Marc overheard her concern and reassured her, "Don't worry, we have the best landmark we could ever need. The overstory isn't as thick as I thought. The mountain up there will tell us which way the sea is and, if you combine that with the location of the Sun, I can tell which way camp is. It may take us a while to get back, but getting lost is not a large concern."

"Thanks, I needed that reassurance. I'll start worrying about other things then." Arrianna gave a big smile with that, and Marc managed a muffled laugh that came out like a snort.

Unlike the other members of their party, Arrianna and Seth focused more on the beauty and diversity of the jungle than the utility or practicality of the environment. They noticed that the jungle brush was not as dense as they had feared and the passage, although slow, was not difficult. Early on, they learned to recognize which bushes had thorns and to step cautiously since the jungle floor was not always visible. To Marc's delight, they found several streams with water so clear and cold that they all cooled themselves and enjoyed a drink.

"If water tasted that good back home I would drink a lot more of it," commented Mike.

"I just hope it doesn't make us sick," said Jerry.

Marc heard his cue, "It should be all right. There is clearly no human habitation on this island to contaminate it. I suppose that the worst we could get is a bit of the runs, but as we agreed earlier, we have no real choice. Aside from any rain that we are able to catch, we have no other source of water." They all nodded and continued with their tour.

The wild diversity of the vegetation was staggering. There hardly seemed to be two of anything. Each tree, bush, vine, ground cover, and shrub had variations that made them difficult to categorize. When they mentioned this to Marc, he told them about the necessary adaptations that jungle species require and how they can change dramatically depending on their microenvironment. "These plants had developed sophisticated defenses against other plants that would crowd them out or the animals or bugs that would eat them. In fact, some of the most promising drug research is conducted in jungles and rain forests. Why invent a new anti-fungal or anti-viral agent when the trees have already done it for you?"

There were far fewer bugs than they had expected, and Marc suggested "It might be because the island probably has a rather small population of mammals to support them. Or it could be the shock of seeing five large meals on wheels voluntarily walking into their home."

"But I saw a paw print the other day that looked like it belonged to a cat." Arrianna argued.

Marc mused, "A cat? On this island? Hardly seems possible, what would it eat? How would it get here in the first place? It is a very small island, you know."

Seth jumped into the conversation, "It's plenty large enough for me." Arrianna concurred nonverbally.

"I know what you mean, all this walking and meandering without any apparent progress does give that illusion. However, for an island to provide a sustainable habitat for the top of the food chain—"

"You mean people?" Arrianna asked.

"People sure, but carnivores in general…Anyway, to provide a long term sustainable ecology, the island would have to be two or three times this size, at the very least."

"How do you know how big it is?" asked Seth.

"I saw it while we were landing. There is just this one twin-peaked mountain, which is undoubtedly of volcanic origin. The island is the shape of a comma. We landed on the fat end, the leeward side. The other side, the windward one, fades into a point."

Arrianna became interested, "Why would it have to be larger? It seems to support a large enough variety of life."

Marc was now in his element. "Good question, Arrianna. The threshold is determined by several factors, one of which you have mentioned, diversity. Another is sustainability–for every carnivore there has to be so many prey in order for them to replace the ones that are eaten. There are also a minimum number of carnivores that will sustain a population, to account for the natural deaths, accidents and disease. But also there is the need to survive environmental shocks."

"Like hurricanes?"

"Exactly! You are very intuitive. Droughts, floods, disease, all of these come in a random fashion and a sustainable habitat has to be big enough so that, despite all of these, some part of it will survive and serve as the nidus for repopulating."

Seth was enjoying the discussion, partly because of intellectual curiosity, but also because it took his mind off the muscles that were beginning to complain. "And you think this island is too small to support small carnivores?" There may have been a slight edge of worry in his voice, or it could have been the exertions he was making in his attempts to keep up with the leaders.

Marc resumed his musings, "Much too small for the animals to have developed here. They could have been transplanted, of course, but even then I think they would have eaten themselves out of prey within a short time."

Arrianna spoke up, "What I think that Seth is worried about is that if it is too small to support small carnivores, then it is completely inadequate to support large carnivores like us. Is that correct?" Seth grunted agreement, and Marc agreed with her conclusion. After a several minutes of significant worry for two of them, Marc added some afterthoughts.

"Remember that humans are omnivores and that would make a huge difference, if we knew which plants were edible. Also, when we talk about sustainability, we are talking about generations, not years. A transplanted cat could have a great life here for a long time. It would be her grand kittens that would suffer."

REDEMPTION ISLAND

"So how long do you think we could survive here if we didn't have a raft and if civilization was not so close?" asked Seth.

Marc did not respond immediately, instead he went into some sort of trance. At first Arrianna and Seth thought that he had not heard them or was no longer interested in the conversation.

They proceeded to resume their casual inventory of the fauna around them. They saw a large and varied collection of fruits, many of which were unidentifiable. Could they eat them? Who would go first? They also heard a huge variety of birds. Could they come up with a way to catch them and have some meat? Did any one of them know how to clean and cook a bird? With Marc's previous comments, the number and variety of the birds appeared to be far larger than the island could support. Then they remembered that the birds could fly to another island. They were not trapped by the sixty miles of ocean. Arrianna thought, *What an idea, we catch the birds and place a message on their legs, if we get enough of them, then one of them is bound to be found on the main island.* She smiled inwardly.

They heard more often than saw a large number of rodent-like creatures that no one could identify, not even Marc. They were half squirrel and half rat. They were not all that shy, probably because they were unused to humans or predators in general. They saw no tracks of anything larger. No sign of predators of any sort. It was a relief to most of them, but Arrianna felt bad. She had seen the footprint and wanted vindication.

Marc started talking as if he had never stopped. "I think that for the seven of us, the island would provide sufficient water and an indefinite supply of calories. Primarily from the fruits we have seen, plus roots and even some of the leafy plants may be edible. The problem would be the protein and some of the vitamins that are usually found in grains. Mostly vitamins in the B complex, and some of the trace elements. It would take a long time for those problems to show up though, perhaps six months, maybe more, maybe less. We can delay the process significantly by finding a way to catch birds and some of those rodent creatures. I think the bigger problem for our long-term survival here would be the lack of access to modern medical care. There might be diseases that have been dormant without the proper host. There are a variety of them such as—"

"Thank you very much Marc, but I think that Arrianna and I have heard as much as we want for the moment," said Seth. Arrianna concurred with the sentiment. The last thing she needed was a cornucopia of diseases to worry about. "Anyway, the far bigger obstacle would be the social issues that had nothing to do with how big or small the island is, but of how few people there are on it. It has only been two days and we have already had several fights."

They spent the next hour traversing rough and steep terrain and were unable to continue their casual conversations. The jungle understory had thickened considerably and their only passage through the matted tangled mess was to walk in the middle of one of the larger streams. They all appreciated the coolness of the water on their legs and did not mind the slippery, mossy terrain that required the use of all four limbs from time to time.

Seth, however, was starting to drag behind. It had been years since he had exerted himself to this degree. He noted that he was, by far, the oldest of the group and regretted his decision to come. He had not wanted to miss the adventure, but now he was holding everyone up and, most of all, he hated not pulling his weight. These thoughts brought him back to his concerns prior to the water landing. He forced himself not to think about that, he had enough worries for the moment.

REDEMPTION ISLAND

The volcanic jungle terrain became less congested and impenetrable as they gained altitude. This allowed for a significantly increased choice of directions. They were no longer bound by the streambeds or the barely passable animal paths, if that was what the gaps in vegetation were. For all they knew, the paths they were taking were simply spots were plant life had not yet taken hold. They further noticed a substantial decrease in both the temperature and the humidity at the higher altitude. At about the time that Seth was giving up, Jerry shouted from up front, "Time for a break." They gathered around him and saw the ocean through a break in the trees below them. In other circumstances, it would have been called a scenic overview. Today it was a reminder of their watery jailer.

"How far do you think we have come?" asked Seth. He was looking at Marc, and Jerry visibly held himself in check. He was making an effort to cooperate, which did not go unnoticed by his fellow travelers.

"Impossible to say. I can tell you that we have traveled about ten degrees around the mountain, but we have come a long way up it and we have gained many hundreds of feet in altitude. If we want to get back to camp this afternoon, we can't go too much further."

Mike spoke for the first time, "Agreed, why don't we find and eat what food we can and, after that, we will try to get high enough on the mountain to have a look see?"

Everyone nodded and started to gather some of the plentiful fruit that grew everywhere. They limited themselves to fruits they recognized and, even so, there were more available than they could eat. While they ate, they asked Marc how he knew so much about everything.

"I don't know that much really, I just read a little."

"Bullshit! I know people. All of them smart, educated,

whatever. And I have never met anyone who has the depth of knowledge that you do." Jerry said this with more intensity than he had intended. Marc looked embarrassed and did not look like he was going to reply.

Mike added, "I agree. It is an unusual gift to have so much useful knowledge; how did you manage it?" It was this last comment that revived Marc's attention.

"Useful? That's a joke. None of what I know is useful. If you must know, I haven't been able to get a job doing anything of any interest for years. I have degrees in Physics, Botany, Animal husbandry, and have read extensively in many other fields. But none of it has ever been useful in the real world—outside the ivory towers of academia, that is." He hung his head down in a clearly embarrassed posture. Had this been anywhere in the real world, he would have walked away at this time. Here there was nowhere to go.

"Until now," said Arrianna, moving next to him, "I think we can all agree that without you we would be in worse trouble than we are." The rest of the group raucously agreed with her. Then Jerry surprised them all.

"When we get out of this I'll give you a job. I promise it will be interesting."

Marc looked up and was suspicious he was being pandered to. He saw no duplicity in Jerry's face and, even though he knew he was poor at judging such things, he relaxed. "What would I do?"

"I don't know yet, but you are far too intelligent and well-educated not to have you. Also, heaven forbid that you fell into the hands of the opposition. It has not escaped my notice that in the 'real world,' as you call it, I have skills that are impressive, if I say so myself. Yet in this setting, those same skills just manage to cause trouble. On the other hand, your so-called useless information has been invaluable. It is that ability to apply knowledge in new and unusual situations that my company desperately needs. Our problem is identifying people like you." Seth stood up and started clapping. Arrianna joined him immediately and the other two stood soon after. They gave Marc a well-deserved standing ovation.

Marc wanted to hide. All his life he had been unable to stand the spotlight and here it was, blinding with intensity. Although feeling desperate to leave and get away from the emotional force, he did not want to run away and perhaps get separated, so he resorted to his other well-honed defense mechanism: humor.

"I guess you are all wondering why I called this meeting…"

~~~~~~~~~

They resumed their trek in much better spirits. Marc felt especially good. He felt better about his general usefulness. Maybe after this he would give getting a real job another try, and then he could afford the therapy he needed to better fit in with people. Perhaps he would even be able to date someone more than once. He cringed at the thought of his last two dates. He was so completely inept that they had both wanted it to end within minutes of it starting. With a tremendous effort of will, he let go of those memories and focused on the present situation. Of the seven remaining castaways, he was the only one that did not want it to end immediately.

Arrianna was similarly introspective. She had little use for school or learning and, up to now, had seen no relevance in either. She was having second thoughts, however. The usefulness of Marc's knowledge had not gone unnoticed and appeared extremely attractive. The sheer extent and depth of knowledge available was new to her. Up to now, she had presumed it was all math, literature, languages and other similarly irrelevant and useless topics. Now she knew that you could study things that actually had real life application, like working with plants or animals. She had one more year of high school left. "I wonder if that is enough time to improve my grades and get into a good college." Although she said it to herself Seth overheard her.

"You have more time than you could imagine in your wildest fantasies, my young child. If only I had one quarter of the time you have I would start an entire new life."

Arrianna blushed at being overheard. She did not want the conversation to stay focused on her so she asked, "What do you mean, 'a new life?'"

"My wife died several years ago and my children have grown up. Although I have a strong heart and my lungs have been spared the smoking I did in my youth, some of my other parts are not working so well. I think I would marry again, maybe even a younger woman, and have children again. Those were the best of times for me." Arrianna shrugged at this, trying to look indifferent. "When I was a young man, I had to work so that my family could eat. I did not have much choice in the matter, or cared about having a choice. Now, I would choose something more interesting than accounting. Perhaps become a veterinarian or tree surgeon—at any rate something to do with life rather than numbers."

"Why don't you do it anyway?"

"Youth, it is so wonderful. Nothing is impossible. Alas, I am tired and don't have the fire in the belly I used to have. Who would want an old worn out veterinarian?"

"I would. Anyway Ray Croc did it."

"Ray Croc? Who might he be?"

Arrianna looked closely at him, "You don't know? He is the one who started McDonald's. He was fifty-two and had just retired from his regular work when he opened his first place." Seth smiled at her and started to think about that. Could he really indulge himself like that? If so, what would he do? "Getting back to your dilemma, don't worry so much about having time for something, pick a direction you want to go and take that first step, beyond that, it is in God's hands."

"You believe in God?" Arrianna asked dubiously.

"Depends when you ask. On the way down to our landing I had my doubts, but when we all landed safe, those doubts eased up a lot. Getting to know you and the others makes me think that maybe it all isn't a huge game of chance. Maybe there is something larger than us in the universe. It is the ultimate level of chutzpah to think we are the top tier of natural development. Don't you think?"

Arrianna had not envisioned the question in this particular way. Her life had been filled with an alcoholic mother, a self-obsessed codependent father, and relatively uncaring grandparents. In many ways, she had raised herself. She had seen no evidence of a higher power, or a higher consciousness or a God—well, at least of one that gave the slightest damn about her. "It may just be that we just aren't all that important in the scheme of things, like ants or worms to us and that we are trying to make ourselves feel better and important by creating a supernatural being that considers us important enough to need our worship."

Seth was stunned to his core. He was speechless at the deep deadly cynicism that flowed so easily and casually from this dear young child. It took him several minutes to regain his composure and his voice. "Why don't we have a nice discussion about this some night; there is a lot more to you than meets the eye."

"Sure, anytime." Arrianna smiled inwardly and outwardly. She was happiest when she had placed an adult off balance, and she was good at it, and she knew it.

REDEMPTION ISLAND

Jerry was feeling perplexingly comfortable. He had publicly acknowledged his fears and, instead of feeling down and shamed by it, he felt great. In the world of boardrooms and vicious company politics, any weakness or vulnerability was not only fair game, but impossible to resist. Had he not used this very useful rule to set traps for his unfortunate opponents? Here all those rules were garbage. He was just beginning to realize how much out of his element he was. In telling everyone his vulnerable feelings, he had let go of the need to prove himself. It was that vulnerability that freed up his joy of being. The drive that had powered him all the way to the top of his profession was interfering with his current existence. He knew that this current anomalous situation was only a short respite before he was back swimming with the sharks again, but for now it felt good. The reality that he was the biggest and baddest of the sharks in his particular pond completely escaped him.

He climbed with renewed energy and purpose. He would enjoy not being responsible for everything and keep on struggling to get along and not boss people around. It continued to amaze him how much this group resented it. It was something he had not experienced in how long? It did not take him long to remember and he had to force himself to bring his thoughts back to the present. He did not want to go back there. It had been since his last close relationship, when Marge left him seven years ago.

Instead, he reflected on his offer to Marc. It had been sincere. He would make him an offer that he would not be able to refuse, treat him well and even overpay him. If he could tap into that well-educated and freely associating mind, he would be worth every penny. But more importantly, it would restore the natural order of things, with Marc being subordinate to him. It would help make up for the current situation where Marc was the top dog. If he handled it right, Marc might not even realize that he would lose the freedom he now took for granted.

~~~~~~~~~

Mike's thoughts remained completely with Dan. Had he survived the storm? If so, was he near land or blown out to sea? Was he, at this very minute, exhausted, disoriented and hopeless—just waiting to die? Or had he already drowned alone in raging angry waters? He hoped that, against all probability, he was, at this very moment, with the authorities telling them of their successful water landing and helping organize the necessary rescue operations. What a joy that would be for him, to see his thick dark hair and that serious Mestizo face break into a grin—yet he did not want to set himself up for the expected disappointment. They would not, at this moment, be making this reconnaissance if any of them felt there was even a small chance of his having survived. They were fooling themselves and they would go on for days until it was clear there was no possibility whatsoever he was alive.

How would his body end up? Eaten by sharks and other predators? On the shore of some unknown beach to be eaten by the crabs and other such scavengers? Or found, but not identified, and buried with a "John Doe" on his headstone? What were his wife and children doing now? He could not quite remember her name. He thought it was "Linda," but it could have been "Louise." Dan had always referred to her as "the wife." He knew the names of his kids, though. He had incessantly talked of them. The oldest, Antonio, was in school now and the youngest, Lupe, was…what?—

not quite a year now? *They think we are all dead.* For all Mike knew, the families of the other six castaways were planning memorial services already. All except for his family.

Besides Sharon, there was no one else out there to mourn him. Well, perhaps his employer would be upset at having to replace his most dependable and hard working pilot, but that would pass in a couple of nanoseconds. The fact was he worked so hard and dependably because he had nothing else going on in his life. No family to care or fight with. The thought no longer sent him into the throes of depression—it had been too long. Sharon, an orphan who had been shuffled around a long list of foster homes, similarly had no one. She wanted to have kids, but he had not been ready. Not ready for kids? Or, not ready to give up the hope of finding who he was? To this day he still did not actually know.

The first thing he could remember was that bed in San Francisco. He "woke up" and was so disoriented that he did not know he was disoriented. The room was dark and he could see the moon and the stars out the window. He did not know where he was supposed to be, but he instinctively knew that this was not it. When the nurse walked in and he asked her a question, she flew out of the room and called in a group of strange people who intensely questioned him and gave him a headache. It took a long time to get the story out.

He had been shot down and had hit his head on landing. He managed to find his way to a nearby jungle outpost and, while awaiting transport, a mortar round had gone off next to him. They had subsequently transported him to the main field hospital at China Beach and fixed everything that they could find wrong, but he had not woken up and they did not know why.

By the time of his waking, he'd been in a coma for fifty days and they had been making arrangements for his permanent placement in a long-term care facility. Everyone was so excited until he asked The Question: "who am I?" They had been hoping he would be able to tell them.

He never recovered his memory, beyond some of his time in the force, and these many years later it was unlikely that he ever would. To add insult to injury, "They" did not know who he was. He had no dog tags when he was found, the insignia on his flight suit had not been catalogued prior to their removal and, most damning of all, the records of his fingerprints had been in the repository that had been partially destroyed in a fire set by anti-war activists. Despite a long and apparently thorough investigation, all they managed to tell him was that he had no prior criminal record and that, in all likelihood, he came from Southern Indiana or Northern California. He had wandered for weeks in those areas hoping that someone would recognize him, but it was all in vain. He visited the families of all the soldiers missing in action around the time of his crash, but the records had not been all that reliable. Mostly this was because it had happened during the Tet offensive and chaos had reigned supreme at that time. Eventually he tired of the continual disappointment and started his life over. He even found someone with as little history as him to marry. It had been three years and they were still happy together. He nevertheless still felt that someday someone might very well recognize him and give him back his life, or at the very least tell his parents that he was alive.

He did not want to think of how bad the current situation was for Sharon. She would feel that she was all alone in the world—abandoned once more. At least he knew that she was still around, even if he could not talk to her.

With these depressing thoughts still lingering inside him, he brought his attention to the present. Today his major concern, aside from Dan, was how to get rescued and how to survive until then. He felt good that the island could easily support them for a long time, certainly longer than the few weeks it would take. They might get tired of tropical fruit, but they would not starve.

They readily made it to a nearby promontory and were able to take in the view. It was overwhelming. They had climbed several hundred feet and could see a long vista in every direction, except up the mountain. Arrianna thought she could see the nearest island. However, none of her companions could convince themselves of it. The carpet splayed before them was composed of thousands of greens and green-yellows with just the occasional accent of blue-green here and there. It was one continuous undulating form all the way to the ocean. In some places, the merest slip of beach was visible, but their specific location kept the plane and camp out of view.

Above them the mountain became rockier and less accessible. The temperature was noticeably cooler and, as the altitude increased, the soil became significantly sparser. Marc commented "This is a thin layer barely able to cover the volcanic rock. I'm surprised that it supported as much as it has. Perhaps bird droppings added enough nutrients to the soil to make the difference."

"Look! Up there, is that a hawk?" asked Arrianna. All of them looked up.

"Some bird of prey," mused Mike.

"I don't know," said Marc. They all looked at him as if he had blasphemed. He was startled and blushed, "I never cared much about birds. I haven't studied them much." He said this in a defensive tone, and turned to walk away.

Arrianna quickly added, "Don't go Marc. We were surprised that's all. You know so much more than all of us combined that we...I mean, I sort of expected you to know everything, I am sorry."

REDEMPTION ISLAND

The rest of the group murmured agreement and Seth went right up to him and grasped his arm, "Come on Marc, we did not mean anything by it, tell us all you know about what we see." Marc recovered immediately and started on a dissertation about the island. He mentioned the lack of even medium sized animal tracks on the climb up here, and that the large birds could just as easily be looking for fish rather than small rodents.

"Exploring the rest of the island is going to be a bear, you can see we are more on the leeward side and the other side gets a ton more rain. I imagine that the jungle over there is impenetrable, even with a machete."

"Couldn't we simply walk around the beach?" asked Seth.

Mike spoke up for the first time, "Not really, there are many rocky crags in the way— regardless of which direction we go. The only way would be by boat or raft."

"More fruit," offered Jerry, "although hopefully we won't run out on this side; if we do, then we will have to consider it."

They started walking back to camp with Marc in the lead. He believed there was a more direct way back and he wanted to try it. They all felt better on the way down. There would be no surprises and going downhill was much easier. They were also hopeful that there would be good news waiting for them when they reached camp. Martha and Leesa planned to listen to the radio in hopes of hearing something about Dan.

The variety of plant life was enormous and every few yards there would be something new to note. Marc started pointing out the various fungi that thrived in this semi-dark, wet and partially decaying microcosm they now called home. He knew a lot of the mushrooms' names but not whether they were poisonous or edible. They found his strange fascination with fungi amusing. In a similar way, he was as removed from living things as the mushrooms were.

REDEMPTION ISLAND

He described the very common Oyster Mushroom that grew on dead trees everywhere, but also pointed out the more unusual saprophytes. The Carmine Coral was beautiful and indeed looked like its namesake. The most noxious they saw was the Dog Stinkhorn—if disturbed, its smell was reported to be foul beyond description.

He pointed to the different types of palm trees and detailed which ones colonize first and how the seeds spread from island to island. He continued his travelogue with the endless variety of ferns around them and he ended with the orchids. His love for them showed through his discourse. It was the plant's reliance on bird droppings for fertilizer that captivated Arrianna's imagination. To become so dependent on a creature so removed from one's own existence filled her with apprehension. It reminded her all too well of her commitment a few years past to depend on no one, ever again.

Before they knew it they were back on level ground and near camp. Marc's intuition about direction had been excellent. Instead of heading directly back however, he veered right to the other side of camp than they had seen on their way out. He wanted to survey the flora and estimate how much food and water was locally available.

It was during this part of the trip that they saw the tracks. "I told you that I saw cat tracks!" shouted Arrianna, now feeling vindicated. The group looked around and saw that the tracks crossed the makeshift trail they had been following and were quickly lost in the underbrush. Marc studied them for a long time. He then looked around to see if he could pick up the tracks again.

A few yards away he shouted, "There are more here." They all rushed ahead to see. While they peered around him he pointed to one of the impressions, "It's the same animal though."

REDEMPTION ISLAND

"How can you tell?" asked Seth.

"Look at the outside of the right rear paw. There is a widening of the print. It is identical to the one before." They all studied it and indeed noticed it. This paw was wider and irregular in shape, as if he had an extra toe. "I still don't understand it, they could not have evolved here and the island could not hope to support more than a handful of feline carnivores. They are such efficient hunters that they would eat themselves out of a food supply.

"Oh, you mean they are like humans!" Arrianna said laughingly. "But I was right wasn't I? There is at least one cat on this island."

"Yes you were, and it brings up the question of how long he has been here and how he got here. Maybe there is some regular visitation by boats of one kind or other and it was left stranded here." They all picked up the optimism in his voice.

Mike spoke, "It is only a few hours away by motor boat. I am sure that boats come over from time to time to get away, especially young people. However..." They all waited for him to finish his thought. Instead it was Marc that finished it for him.

"However they would land on the other side of the island, where there is a natural harbor with a wide beach. Isn't that right?" Mike just nodded. They could tell that he felt miserable.

"So how come we landed on this side? Is that more incompetence?" Jerry demanded, reverting to his old self.

"I don't think that is called for," Seth stated sharply, and he physically intervened between Jerry and Mike.

"I just want to know why we are on the opposite side of the island from the nearest source of rescue and the most likely site of boat traffic." Jerry persisted.

"Wind." Marc said as if that sufficed.

Mike spoke up, "We did not expect to be here long or to need a random boater to rescue us. Our main concern was to land safely, that is why we chose the leeward side. There was a significantly decreased chance of gusty treacherous winds or of choppy surf induced by them."

They all glared at Jerry as if saying "is that sufficient, asshole?"

Jerry backed off and, with an obvious struggle, apologized, "I am sorry Mike, I jumped the gun once again. I am just frustrated by the situation."

They resumed their journey and, within minutes, Marc became excited when he saw the ocean and the beach. It was as if he had not been completely sure he would find his way until that moment. By the time they saw the plane again, five hours had elapsed, the sun was straight up and the heat was overwhelming now that there was no overstory to shade them. All but Jerry went immediately to the water and waded to cool off. Jerry persisted in lagging behind, clearly in his own world.

Before the last incident about the landing, Mike and Jerry had established a working relationship that had surprised everyone. Now that was in jeopardy and everyone, especially Jerry, felt the loss. He did not know what he should do about it and it infuriated him that he was the one continually screwing up the works. His entire life had been composed of eliminating people like that and promoting people who made things smoother. By his own standards, he would be out of a job and that unemployable bookworm would be heading upwards. He shook his head in utter disbelief. He was beginning to realize that people might need to work through their issues instead of getting the boot at the first sign of trouble. He certainly wanted another chance.

After a few minutes of cooling off in the surf, they trudged to camp and immediately became aware that something was horribly wrong. Martha and Leesa were holding each other, crying and rocking. They appeared unhurt and there was no visible disturbance at camp. There was even a large amount of gathered fruit. Whatever it was must have happened recently.

Arrianna was the first there, "What's wrong! Why are you crying?" She had tried to keep the fear out of her voice without success. Martha was unable to speak, but managed to point in the direction of the beach. About thirty yards away, by a rock there was a bright orange stain, too bright to be a natural phenomenon, it could only be one thing—the life raft. Arrianna, Marc and Jerry ran to it.

It was deflated and torn at several points. The rope that had tied the supplies on board was loose and frayed at the end. It clearly had suffered far worse out at sea than they had estimated. Their hope for Dan and their rescue died reluctantly, but died nevertheless. They slowly dragged their flagging spirits back to camp and collapsed onto the sand.

They each tried, in their own way, to comfort the women, but they were inconsolable. "You don't know the worst of it," cried Leesa. That stopped all of them and their attention became fixed on her. They expected to hear that they had found Dan—dead. Instead Martha told them their discovery.

"We thought we would listen to the radio while we worked. Leesa had a Walkman that tunes AM stations. They reported our disappearance and how we are well within the Bermuda triangle. Then they had a breaking story that debris identified with our plane had been found by fishermen. They found part of the raft and have concluded that we crashed into the sea 'with all souls lost'. They are abandoning the search."

This stunned all of them into silence until Arrianna said, "Daddy thinks that I am dead!" With that she jumped up and ran down the beach past the raft and out of sight. No one felt like going after her. After all, it wasn't like she had anywhere to go. They were totally alone. The world thought them dead..

Twenty minutes later, Arrianna returned. She looked different. She did not act normally. There was a deep coldness about her. "Come, you have to help," she said and started walking the way she had come.

They followed her more out of curiosity than concern. Around the bend they saw what she brought them for. The bloated, hardly recognizable body of Dan was lying on the beach, with fresh drag marks leading from the water.

"How did he get up here?" Asked Marc.

"I dragged him up here so he would not drift further out." That was when they noticed that she was wet up to her waist.

"Is he dead?" asked Leesa. No one expected that it would be Arrianna who would answer the question.

"Yes, he is. Probably for some time, he is stiff." She related it without emotion and in a deathly monotone that caused shivers in most of them.

Seth went up to her, held her hands in his and asked gently, "My dear child, how on earth do you seem so familiar about such things?"

Arrianna looked right at Seth before answering. Her eyes were dark pinpoints of black with no tears. There was no trace of emotion either on her face or in her heart. "Because he looks a lot like my mother did when I found her dead."

Chapter Seven

Reversals

They simply could not reach her. On the surface Arrianna was acting "normally," although a bit quiet. If not for the enforced contact of the prior forty-eight hours, no one there would have noticed. However, all of them had seen the real Arrianna and therefore the change was not missed by anyone, even Marc.

Seth and Martha were the most upset by the change. At first they had pushed and insisted that she explain, talk, or simply cry. She refused all of these well-intentioned suggestions, and then created resentment by putting the blame on them. She would say, "I haven't changed one bit, it's the two of you who can't handle a dead body." Eventually she put a stop to their attempts with "Leave me alone, you're getting on my nerves with all this touchy-feely stuff, I'm just fine!"

Regardless of her protestations, it was clear that the lively, energetic, and carefree seventeen-year-old who got on that plane a few days ago was now gone and had been replaced with a polite, but aloof twin. A twin who showed no emotion or energy and could have been one of the nearby palm trees.

~~~~~~~

Mike was beside himself with grief, but more so guilt. He could not force himself to believe that the lifeless, bloated, and partly eaten form in front of him was his co-pilot. They had not been particularly close, but they worked well together for years and shared camaraderie and a love of flying. He kept trying to comprehend the myriad things that had gone wrong and found it very hard to think straight and plan the next move. He heard Marc and Jerry planning what to do next and resented them for doing so. They had not known Dan, why should they decide his disposition? Who were they to take that on? The reality that the world had declared all of them dead and that memorial services for all of them were at that moment being planned completely escaped him.

~~~~~~~

"I don't agree. Why can't we simply bury him here? Yeah it will be hard, but I think he deserves more than being fish food," Jerry said firmly, not yet upset.

Marc hesitated. He thought he had made his point well and did not know what to add. It was these kind of moments that had puzzled him all of his life. His logic was undeniable. It wasn't even a hard decision, but the human emotional component was rearing its despicable head once more. He knew, from bitter experience, that to argue logic and reason with someone arguing emotion would be worse than fruitless. It would generate resentment and cause a further rigidity in opinion. Fortunately, Seth intervened.

"Because it is not about deserving anything. We all feel bad about how he died and the terror that must have been his last few hours on this planet. We are all also furious at him for doing something so stupid, foolish and brave, and by doing so taking our best chance of getting off this island with him. We have to accept that, for the moment, we are little different than pre-Columbian Americans, but with fewer tools and no slaves. Look around you. This is a volcanic island. Scratch the dirt off the surface and you will need a pick and dynamite to bury anyone. We can't spend the amount of energy involved in trying to bury Dan deeper than the animals can dig up."

Jerry knew they were right, but a large part of him could not admit it. This was worse than the screeching of nails on a chalkboard. His very soul felt crushed at the thought of the body sinking into the turquoise waters and all of the slimy creatures taking a turn eating his flesh. "It just isn't right!" he screamed.

Arrianna did not help the situation when she said, "It's only meat and bones, for God's sake, no different than a cow. The person we knew is already dead. He won't care that he's fish food…ashes to ashes and dust to dust and all that rot." Although what she said was not in itself wrong or ugly, her tone was. There was a deep, cruel mocking to her words that cut all of them deeply and involuntarily caused them to step away.

Arrianna seemed pleased with the reaction and proceeded. "I don't see why we can't just drag him into the jungle a ways and leave him there. Within a few weeks, there will only be a few bones to worry about and we can bury those if you want. It will be a lot easier."

The ensuing silence was so intense that no one felt capable of breaking it. The surf continued its endless roar and sizzle, the birds continued with their racket of poorly coordinated shrieks, and every once in a while the wind would cause an audible rustle from the foliage. It was Jerry who finally spoke.

"I can see your point Marc. Let's get to it and send him on his way." He had turned so Arrianna was excluded from the discussion. Mike joined them and the three men started the process of weighing the body so it would sink into the sea.

Arrianna started walking away when she stopped and turned. "Don't forget to vent the belly or the buildup in gasses will cause him to float up again."

Jerry turned white with disgust and whispered to the other two "Did she really say what I thought she said?" The other two men nodded in similar disbelief. Marc had known that they would either have to weight him down well or they would have to cut open his belly to prevent bloating, however not one of them could have been half as callous as she.

Seth and Martha both went after Arrianna and caught up to her. They cautiously placed their hands on her shoulders and turned her to face them. "Are you alright? As a response, they saw a gleam in her eye that quickly went away.

"It got that idiot Jerry moving didn't it? He was being such an ass that I could not stand it. It was obvious that his problem was not Dan, but himself. He did not want to be fish food at some future time. God, how I can't stand silliness in adults." She said the last word as if she had just tasted a particularly unpleasant medicine. "I am just fine, you can use your worry over our fate here, considering how many problems we now have."

Seth and Martha were rooted to their spots in the sand as they watched Arrianna walk toward the plane. "What in the world is happening?" asked Martha.

Seth took a moment to reply. "I have seen it before. I never thought that I would ever see it again in my lifetime. It is an extreme survival tactic, let's leave it at that." With that, the two of them went back to join the others in having a small memorial service before they sent Dan to the depths of the Caribbean Sea. Seth had a difficult time not reliving the nightmare of the German ghetto during the war. The soul-destroying hardness that was required to survive and how high the price of that survival had been.

It did not take the group long to get ready. They gathered a few logs and rolled the body onto them. They then managed to tie a large rock to his foot with one of the multitude of vines around them. They tied him loosely to the logs and the three men pushed the makeshift sarcophagus into the surf and walked it out past the breakers. The tide was going out and they had rushed to catch it. When the water was up to their necks, Mike and Marc swam it out a bit further and pushed it out to sea. The group watched it recede while Seth said a few words that were more consistent with Shiva than any other religious rite the others had ever experienced.

PART TWO
Chapter Eight
Survival Basics

It took several days for everyone to accept their predicament. The practical ones, Arrianna, Mike, Marc and Seth mourned, put it behind them and proceeded immediately with the activities necessary for day to day living. Martha and Jerry went through an initial phase of denial that lasted just over one solar day. Leesa went through anger, blame, depression and, finally, denial before accepting her situation. Even then it was only a temporary, tenuous acceptance.

On the seventh day of their island incarceration, they held what would always later be referred to as THE meeting. All of them had worked hard for the past few days, even Leesa. They had searched, picked, and stockpiled food, collected water in whatever containers were available, inventoried their meager resources, and developed a makeshift, but sturdy, shelter using the *Albatross's* starboard wing as the foundation. They now had to discuss how to reach their ultimate long-range goal. They were not of one mind and it would require all of them working together to accomplish either of the ideas that had been circulating.

REDEMPTION ISLAND

Mike was the *de facto* leader of the "conservative" group, while Jerry was the point man for the "radicals." The former included Martha and Leesa, while the latter had Seth and Marc. Arrianna did not belong to either faction and normally would have been wooed by both, except that ever since she found Dan's body, she had become a very scary person and few of the castaways cared to interact with her in any way.

"Everyone's here, so let's get started," said Jerry. Around him all but Arrianna were paying close attention. The air was cool with the evening breeze chilling them. They had agreed to have a fire during the discussion and used Leesa's lighter to light it. The flame was bright and powerful, giving no clue as to how many more times it would work. They were in a circle in no particular order. With all the heavy work the last few days, there had been precious little time to argue or develop grudges. Even Arrianna was pleasant and friendly as long as she wasn't pushed or forced to do something she considered silly. In that case, the razor sharp sarcasm spewing from her mouth would lash the offender into a bleeding pulp.

The last one to receive this treatment had been Marc. A throwaway comment about how he was finally getting fit and that he should get marooned more often, yielded a devastating attack on how "Everyone else on this godforsaken island has a life. If you knew how to be a real person and interact with others, you would not see the situation as humorous or funny. We are in a life and death struggle and you had better start acting accordingly."

Seth stood up and commanded their attention. "Before we begin the discussion, there is another matter that needs to be resolved. As you all know, there is one among us who has been interfering with the smooth functioning of the group. She undermines authority, creates discord out of thin air and, worst of all, she is singularly responsible for keeping our morale as low as it is." There were nods from everyone. "We all realize that we have been through a highly traumatic experience and that we are not equally capable of dealing with unexpected events, yet…"

Arrianna burst, "Goddamn it Seth, we have been here seven days. Either she gets off the pity pot or we push her off it!" Only Seth was not surprised by the outburst. In fact, he had been intentionally pushing her into it. He smiled inwardly, he liked it when a plan came together—perhaps this would not be as hard as they feared.

"I am so glad you feel that way Arrianna, we know that you are the youngest, and we have given you as much time as we could, but your attitude has become intolerable."

Arrianna was stunned. It hit her hard and deep when she realized that they were talking about her behavior. For nearly a ten count she could hardly get her breath. She'd been sure they were referring to Leesa.

"Me? You're referring to me?" She looked around to see that everyone was in agreement, everyone was against her. She set her mind to take them all on.

Dread and revulsion rose up within to melt her very being into a sea of meaninglessness. She could not live with this one more second. Ever since her mother died, she had sworn never again to be emotionally dependent. To always have somewhere or someone to go—a way out. Yet a mere two years later and she was back in the same helpless situation.

Her feelings of desperation and self-hatred boiled and roiled and began to bring up the desperate feelings, the ones that she had, knowingly and conscientiously, buried deep, never to surface again. She used every trick and willed them to stop, but the more desperate she became, the faster they surfaced. The world collapsed around her at the same instant that she felt the arms of someone enveloping her and murmuring comforting words into her ear. "It will be all right. No one hates you. You are a good person. We want that good person back. We desperately need her to help us."

Arrianna collapsed into Martha's arms and was immediately wracked by heaving, wrenching, and uncontrollable sobs. Seth winked at Martha, who smiled back weakly. He told her it would end like this. How had he known? That disheveled little old man in his torn khaki pants and print shirt. What a strange person he was. In one sense, gentle, typical of a grandfather with a clear indisputable intelligence moderated with high doses of wisdom, but, deeper, there lay the inner strength of a giant.

She recollected the numerous occasions during the past week that would have felled a normal person—in fact, had felled some of them. Throughout every one of these events—the unexpected landing, Dan's disappearance and subsequent death, the fights and squabbles of the rest of them–he had remained his own self, sometimes calm, sometimes intensely animated. In the darkest corner of her mind, she had a vague recollection of his being disconcerted about something, but she could not clarify the feeling and she let it go. He was definitely someone worth getting to know and she resolved to find out more about him. For the first time in the many years of her widowhood, she wondered about a man's marital status.

Seth saw Martha coaxing and encouraging the girl away from the group, meandering toward the plane, and he focused on the next issue. He could not totally deny the feelings of satisfaction for a job well done. He had few doubts that, with Martha's help, Arrianna would come around. Whether that young girl, who had clearly been through too much in her few years of life, would fully open up and completely deal with her grief, he did not know. But he hoped she would. Like his youngest, Katia, had. It would help in reclaiming her life, but this time on her own terms.

REDEMPTION ISLAND

~~~~~~~~

The meeting started for real. They were all ready and excited. No one showed any malice or irritation—yet. Before yielding the podium, Seth reviewed the situation. "You all know where we stand. We have heard on the radio that we are presumed dead and funeral services for most of us have already been held. We have no way of contacting anyone except for burning down the entire island. In short, it will be up to us to get rescued. We have two competing plans, which the respective proponents will expound on. Let me just make one point. No one here, not a single one of us, least of all me, *knows* which way is better or if either one will work. Perhaps both will work. Let us try to remain reasonable and not make a religious issue of this. It will require each of us pulling together to enact just one plan, so when we decide which way to go, let us put our feelings aside, latch onto the harness and pull with all our might, so we can get off this blasted godforsaken island." With this done he sat down amidst signs of agreement.

Mike and Jerry both stood up. Mike motioned to Jerry to start. "As you know we are split down the middle on which way to proceed. I am the proponent for the overland option and it is my job to point out the reasons it is our best shot at getting off the island. Mike will speak on the raft option and then we will field questions and try to poke holes in each of the plans. I know that I have been, and still can be, willful and autocratic but I have endeavored these past few days to accept that what we need here is not leadership, so much as consensus and cooperation."

Leesa spoke up. "That's all fine and good, but really, Jerry, we have been over this many times and we know it is new to you, but can we get on with it? I've broken another finger nail today and I

REDEMPTION ISLAND

have to get back to civilization and get a manicure." Her comment is met with a roar of laughter. Jerry blushed good-humoredly.

Marc spoke, "So you want us to hold questions until both sides have spoken? I am afraid I may forget mine by that time."

"Oh, I forgot," said Leesa, "Martha found paper and pens, so we can write down questions. There is plenty of paper but few pens. You will have to share." She stood up, foraged in Martha's canvas bag, and distributed the materials.

Marc jumped up, "Before you start, let me check on Martha and the girl. It would be good if they could join us. We need everyone involved." In less than a minute, he was back, "They will come closer so that they can listen in, but not disturb us with their comments. They have paper to write down any questions that may come up." He sat down and, as an afterthought, said, "By the way, Arrianna appears to be back to her normal self, but…" He did not know how to finish the sentence.

Fortunately, Seth finished it for him. "She has a lot of hurt and pain to deal with. Today is just a start, and to fully recover may take years. But I have no doubt she'll be fine." He looked around, shook off that topic, and forcefully stated, "Let's get started, we have a lot of ground to cover."

Plan A—This plan had originated with Arrianna (even though she was now ambivalent about it) and been taken on with fervor by Jerry. The group would remain intact and methodically travel inland to reach the other end of the island closer to civilization. Once there, they could expect, within a reasonable time period, that a boat would come to the beach, or at least come close enough to be signaled.

Everyone liked the idea of being at the other end of the island. The issue was how to get there. This plan required abandoning the plane and equipment, for they could not hope to carry much. Jerry liked it because it did not involve the sea, which, after Dan's outcome, had changed his perception of it forever. Marc liked it because he was so much more knowledgeable about the land than the sea. He would be able to contribute more and he liked being looked up to. He wasn't ready to give that up. Seth liked it for much the same reason. He would not be able to row very far and he would be far more uncomfortable in the limited space of the raft.

Plan B—was the idea of building a raft and sending either the entire group, or a small detachment to row into the channel between the islands along the path of ship traffic. Storms were one concern. Winds, current, dehydration, sunburn, and exhaustion where the others. He was sure that, with time, they could rig a sail and the entire group could go. He also knew at least one of them, mostly Martha, would not be physically able to hike to the other side. This way if they all did not go, the rest could remain within the shelter offered by the plane.

Martha knew she would not be able to easily traverse a hilly park, much less a mountainous jungle. She would be left behind or be a tremendous burden on all of them. She did not like the idea of going on a small raft, but she could do it, and that was enough for her to be vehemently in favor of this plan.

Leesa exercised everyday of her adult life. She knew she was fit and could compete with any of the others as long as it was at a gym. She hated the heat, the bugs, and the slimy things she knew would jump out at her at every opportunity. She did not particularly like the sea, but she knew they would send a small group of the men on the raft and she could remain in the relative comfort and safety of the campsite. It also provided a chance for a quick rescue. Plan A was probably safer for all of them as a group, but it would take forever to climb their way to the other side, and then they still would have to wait for rescue.

REDEMPTION ISLAND

They all voiced their concerns and, although no one changed their mind, Jerry, Marc, and Seth were weakening, mostly because of Martha. They could not resolve her inability to make the trip, but certainly could not leave her behind alone. They were quickly adapting their plan to have a small group go ahead to the other side with the hope of a quick rescue. Marc, in particular, argued that it would be no different than sending a small group on a raft, and leaving the rest behind.

It took two hours to hear everyone's opinion and at the end they were more demoralized than when they started. They were still tied at three in favor of each plan. Inevitably the attention focused on Arrianna who was the lone remaining vote. She had shown ambivalence to both plans. How would she vote?

Arrianna was deep inside herself attempting to reconcile her fear of her feelings. Martha had said some very strange things to her: that if she did not face her feelings, they would continue to dominate her life. That it was all right to need and ask for help, as long as the person you asked was competent to provide it. This had thrown her into a tirade of sobs and dry retching, for she remembered her father's inability to help when her mother lashed out in one of her drunken rages. Why did he not defend her? Why would he not lash out at her mother like she wanted him to? For a long time she had assumed it was her fault.

She sat bolt upright as she just then noticed the twelve eyes focused on her. "What? What did I do? I am sorry for being so difficult the past few…"

"Never mind that," said Seth, "We have already forgotten about it. We are deadlocked over which plan to go with. By land or by sea?"

Arrianna laughed. It became very loud and very funny and the rest of them started to giggle and laugh, even though they did not get the joke. She developed the hiccups and that made all of them laugh even harder. She finally managed to say, "Who am I, Paul Revere?" They all got it, and started another round of hilarity. The laughter managed to exorcise much of the emotional poison they all retained and, after it subsided, the mood of the group was as good as it had ever been.

For the first time it could be said that they constituted a cohesive group with each member a vital and necessary part of the whole. Arrianna stood up and made a useless attempt to wipe the sand off her legs. She addressed them, "It seems to me that there really is no choice at all. I don't know how we came to think that we could only do one or the other, but I don't see why we could not do both." There was a confused uproar as the most adamant of each faction wanted his or her say.

Seth quieted them down and asked, "Could you expand on that?"

"Sure. We have Mike and Marc write up a list of what they need for their trip, assuming that only those who want to go will. I expect there will be little or no overlap in tools or equipment, and the main issue will be supplies." She looked at all of them, relishing their rapt attention. When she managed to get off the island, she would have to explore how she could replicate this in the real world.

"So, we gather the provisions the land group needs. It can't be much, because they expect to survive off the land. Then the entire group focuses on making a raft capable of simply sailing to the other side of the island following the coastline. When the raft is ready, the first group can go and the raft group can wait and plan until the weather is right. This doubles our chances at rescue and everyone makes it over to the other side without the need to make a huge sea-worthy raft. Also, if one group gets into trouble there is the possibility of the other one coming to the rescue. Once on the other side, we can decide how to proceed."

She said this very matter-of-factly and could not see why they had not thought of it themselves. The group, however, saw it differently. They saw it as inspired. She had been able to get enough distance from the problem to see it in a new way. They collectively came to a conclusion: it could very well work! Seth added, "And no one is left unhappy or unheard. Brilliant, young lady."

They all felt relief and hope. Spontaneously, Marc, Mike and Jerry all stood up and bowed their respect for her problem solving.

Chapter Nine
Preparations

The castaways' concentration and intensity peaked at a higher level than it had a right to. They were now working as a team. Nothing was done poorly, or even just well. It was all done with as much perfection as they could provide. No one was going to be responsible for any preventable failure. There were no arguments regarding authority or working too hard. For their own private reasons, each and every one of the castaways desperately wanted off that island.

The distribution of labor fell easily into three categories: planning (Marc, Mike, Seth and Jerry), hard labor (Marc, Mike, Seth, Jerry, Arrianna and, to everyone's astonishment, Leesa) and support functions, such as food gathering and preparation, packing and organizing (Martha, Leesa, Arrianna and Seth). They floated from one assignment to another smoothly and efficiently as the need arose. They made lists for each of the two groups and would add to them as need arose.

Needs for the overland trip:

- Water containers, small enough to carry—should need only a few.
- Emergency food supply and some way of carrying it, in case they have to traverse a section of the mountain that cannot support them.
- Weapons—for protection from dangerous animals (it doesn't matter what Marc says. It's better to be safe than sorry)
- Bug repellent (Yeah right, where are we going to get any?)
- Matches
- Machete, walking sticks, gloves
- Compass!!!!
- Rope?

Needs for the rafters
- Water, water, water.
- Sun protection
- Some food—although unlikely to get any during the trip, the trip should be much shorter than the overland route. Might try fishing to see if we can supplement our diet that way.
- Compass!
- Some form of oars to assist with the sail or in landing against the wind.
- Available life preservers for non-swimmers
- Tools and supplies that may be needed in the future (cargo service)

As for the raft itself, they had a sketch of something that, although theoretically buildable, still contained major hurdles. The foremost of these was their desperate lack of rope or some other fastener. The other insurmountable issue was how to cut down trees with no power tools and no manual saws or axes.

REDEMPTION ISLAND

~~~~~~~~~~

Arrianna suspected that they saw through her ruse about finding a walking stick. Yes, she would find something suitable that would serve on the cross-island trek and would be useful to ward off the stray wild pig or whatever. What she was really in search of however, was forgiveness. Her entire body craved it as much as she had craved anything. She could not understand, much less explain how, why, or when she had flipped and become such a hateful being. She decided to call that other her "Hyde," after that famous literary character.

When she was her "normal" self, as she referred to it, she was well aware of the other part of her that would take over her body and will. But when she was in her "Hyde" persona she was unaware there was anyone else residing within. Therefore, she could now remember everything that "Hyde" had done with excruciating, guilt-ridden detail. It drove her to tears when "Hyde" was in charge because she was not aware of her normal life and how self-destructive she was to her normal self.

It was not the first time "Hyde" had come on the scene. *I wouldn't have a name for her if it had only happened a couple of times*, she thought to herself. She had lost count of how many times it happened. In another respect, she was not always unhappy when Hyde showed up. She recalled how much better Hyde could handle her mother's alcoholic induced tantrums and abuse, as well as her father's infuriating weak-kneed defense of her. Arrianna was crystal-clear about liking that other part of her and having her around to help out when needed. She was dying because Hyde had taken over without her bidding or the slightest warning. She had been walking the beach one moment and the next time she was by the campfire falling to pieces in front of everyone.

"Why did I do that?" she wailed. "Now everyone thinks I'm crazy and hates me and I can't blame them." Her heart pounded inside her chest like it wanted out of that bony prison. She felt short of breath all out of proportion to her current exertion and her fingertips were tingly.

"I don't think that is very accurate." Seth said from behind her. The effect on Arrianna was so intense. She yelped and began crying in big, bold, uncontrollable sobs. Seth stepped next to her and put one arm around her and squeezed. "What's torturing you, dear child? I am sure that whatever it is we can put it behind you. Just catch your breath and tell me everything." He did not know if she would run away, start talking or scream at him but he was relieved when he noticed the calming of her breathing.

"I feel so bad, and I don't know why I make such a mess of things," she managed to say.

"What mess? I haven't seen any mess. Last I saw, the preparations were going according to plan.. As for feeling bad, I know you will feel much better if we sit down on that rock and have ourselves a nice chat."

Arrianna looked up at him to see if he was patronizing her. His face was a craggy ancient mask of genuineness. She had not realized before how old he looked, probably because he talked and behaved so much younger. The skin on his face was not smooth like hers, it was composed of patches of rough discolored skin that did not fit well together and resulted in all sorts of folds and wrinkles. His hair was nearly gone with only a small fringe over the ears remaining. She had noticed one last thing. It was the first time he had taken his shirt off.

"You see the number don't you?" he asked, not needing the responding nod. "Do you know what it means?"

"Yes, I saw a film in school on it. In Nazi Germany they tattooed all of the Jews...I forget why it was so important though."

He ignored her last remark and proceeded, "Do you also know of the camps?"

"The concentration camps? Sure, they teach a lot about it at the schools I went to. They killed a lot of Jews. My teacher said that in some ways they were the lucky ones." Seth was startled by the last statement and sat there open-mouthed. Arrianna filled the silence for him. "He never said as much but I always assumed that he was one of the survivors. My classmates made fun of me. They all thought I was crazy and had a crush on him. Which I certainly did not, he was way too old for me, and he was as old as..."

"As old as me?"

Arrianna nodded, her cheeks flushing and her hand automatically coming up to cover her face by playing with two of the long tendrils of her dark brown hair. Seth used his left hand to reach and lift her chin, "Don't be embarrassed, I am comfortable with how old I am and you are perfectly right, I am way too old for you to have even a crush on me." She smiled weakly but felt better. "I have only heard that statement about the dead prisoners being the lucky ones from survivors. If you hadn't been there, you could not possibly understand."

"So you think I was right?" Arrianna said hopefully.

"I don't think it, I know it. When I was in the camp, I felt that way myself. What is amazing, though, is your maturity and intuition. There are adults who will never reach your level of empathy or responsibility."

Arrianna started to cry again, but this time it was the sad cry of a child without hope of being comforted. It broke Seth's heart to hear it again. When the allies had freed them from the camp, he had prayed never to hear that hopelessness again. "Let me tell you a story. It is a bit sad at points, but it has a reasonably happy ending."

~~~~~~

Marc and Mike were working on a makeshift net with which they intended to catch fish. "What do you think?" asked Marc.

"It's hard to tell, it seems so flimsy, but if it holds up to the force of the water and the fish put on it, we may be able to eat meat tonight."

"Are you ready to try it?"

"Yeah, sure but let's—"

"Hello," said Arrianna. Had the two men been paying more attention and had they been unusually sensitive, they would have detected the faint quaver in her voice. As it was, they were barely aware of her as they responded. She took this indifference and concentration to be evidence of their justifiable anger at her. She wanted to turn and run, but Seth's presence nearby and her determination to get it behind her won out.

She looked down at her feet and stirred the sand with her shoe, "I just wanted to apologize." She said the last word as if it would solidify into a hideous beast and eat her alive. She was almost surprised when it didn't.

This caught the two men by surprise and it jerked them out of their focus. Marc, in particular, was so discombobulated by this that he dropped his end of the net, forgetting about fish and meat. He walked up to Arrianna and began a similar toe staring, sand shuffling act. It was Mike who finally spoke. "What are you referring to? We were about to give this net a try. Maybe we could have a change in diet tonight. You do like fish don't you?"

This was not going according to any of the possible scripts that her mind had conjured up. *Why are they pretending to be ignorant?*

REDEMPTION ISLAND

They must be making it harder for me because of how mad they really are.

She could feel the fear rising up inside her about to turn into panic. Worse still she could feel Hyde knocking on the door asking to be set in charge and take care of these two bozos. Yet that was exactly how she had arrived here, by letting "her" take charge. She took a deep breath like Seth had told her and spilled it all out. "I am sorry that I have been so difficult and done such stupid things and hurt you."

To her surprise, she did not suddenly vanish in a puff of smoke and actually felt better for having said it. She allowed herself the slight luxury of a self-satisfied smile and was about to turn and disappear when Marc caught her arm.

"What are you talking about? I don't understand. Please come and join us. We could use the help with the net. He looked at her eyes and saw the depths of sadness that resided there He felt a strange impulse to envelop her in his arms and hold her. He pushed that aside like he did all such feelings. *You couldn't trust feelings. They were not logical. Feelings could get you into trouble.*

Mike added, "You have been difficult and stupid? I must have missed that. Could you give me an example so I won't feel left out?"

Involuntarily, Arrianna let a chuckle pass her lips. Marc broke into a big grin, even though he had no idea what was going on. He pulled on her arm to join them and picked up the net. The three of them began walking to the sea. "Come on guys, you are making this so difficult. I am trying to say I am sorry for being such a shit for that week after we found Dan."

Mike looked up, "Oh that, I wouldn't worry about it. I had forgotten it completely. As far as I'm concerned, you are a great addition to our group and if you had to get some emotional distance for a while...well you came back and that is what matters."

Marc was lost once again, although he had become used to it over the years. *What in the world were Mike and Arrianna talking about? Emotional distance? Came back? Being difficult? Being a shit?* He had not noticed much. He knew the others felt Arrianna had changed a lot, but he only noticed she did not smile as much as before. She was just as smart and logical and willing to work hard. *What was the big deal?* He said, "Yeah, sure, I feel the same way. Anyway, are you going to help us with the net?" He hoped she would say "yes" because he liked being around her.

Arrianna was more confused than ever. This was so weird she would have sworn that Seth had warned them, but he had not been out of her sight since they talked. "You were supposed to say that you appreciated my apology and that I had been awful and you would consider whether you would forgive me and I had better make myself useful before you cast me out of the group."

Seth laughed when he had heard this and told her "You are quite mistaken about the entire situation."

Maybe he is right. She thought.

"I have something to finish, but as soon as I'm done I will join you." She walked away, shaking her head in utter befuddlement. Maybe the other two would act more according to plan. She could not reconcile that she was so out of touch with reality. She approached Jerry and Leesa who were going over what to take on the raft.

Jerry saw her coming and waved to her. Leesa just gave the slightest of nods. She went right into the apology, but this time right away. They both acknowledged it and she felt better for it but then both of them added stuff that made her just as uncomfortable as Mike and Marc had.

REDEMPTION ISLAND

~~~~~~~~~~

The net worked remarkably well—the first two times. Then it began falling apart and it was all they could do to haul it back in while still repairable. The entire group sat around a fire that evening, enjoying their first meat meal since running out of the plane's supplies. Even Martha and Jerry, who normally avoided fish, enjoyed it thoroughly, and they all repeatedly thanked the three fisher-persons for it. They were amazed how hunger combined with a repetitive diet can make the simplest of foods so savory.

They had worked well together the past few days, but the fraying of the edges of cohesion was just beginning to show. Many of them could not abide being unable to bathe properly. They knew that they were filthy and smelly and even though their noses had adjusted, they disgusted themselves. Others felt like the world was leaving them behind and their usefulness, their reason for living, was gone, possibly for good.

Jerry, in particular, could go into a fit of rage when he imagined what the board was probably doing to his company. Marc alone felt redeemed, as this was the first time in his entire thirty-two years that he felt a part of a group , not to mention inordinately useful and essential. For these, and a myriad of individual reasons, the group that was being held together by a desperate need to be rescued had a limited life span.

Seth asked "Mike, Jerry, how's the raft coming along?"

Jerry answered first, "Not bad. We're using vines Marc identified as related to Manila hemp, the stuff that they used to make ropes out of. It's a bit stiff at first, but we started soaking them in seawater before we beat the shit out of them to get the pulp out and leave only the fibers. We then braid them laboriously. They look awful but work better than expected. It takes an enormous effort to tie them but, with three of us doing it, we're managing well enough."

Mike added, "Even then we'd be nowhere if Marc had not thought of a way to get the trees down. It is amazing what you can do with a hand drill and fire. It would never have occurred to me to build a fire at the base of the tree, protect all but the base with mud, and use the drill to accelerate the process by allowing the fire to reach inwards. Once weakened this way, Arrianna climbed the tree and tied the towline to the top. With that leverage, we've been able to bring these bad boys down in a hurry. If we push hard we can have all the materials we need by tomorrow or the next day and then, in one more day, we can have the raft built and ready."

"I don't know," equivocated Marc, "That seems too optimistic a pace. We should test the raft first and maybe we should build it a bit larger than we planned, besides..."

Seth interrupted abruptly, "That's great, Martha and I have the sail ready to go and Arrianna said the rudder will be done tomorrow. As you know, the preparations for the overland expedition were completed days ago. I think it's time to plan our departures."

All but one of them cheered and shouted their agreement. The entire process was moving too fast for Marc, but not nearly fast enough for anyone else.

Chapter Ten
Trouble on the Trail

It was time to leave. The entire group worked doggedly from before dawn to way past dark to finish. The raft only needed the rudder to be inserted in its collar and the sail to be tied onto the mast. Then the supplies would be placed aboard and they could leave. All of the above could be easily accomplished by those going on the raft, so the rest of them, those going by foot, had rested and were aching to go.

The three hikers were rather fit. Marc was a long distance runner and had run the occasional marathon. In addition, he was slender with long legs and a huge wingspan. All of these attributes made hiking an easy adventure for him. Arrianna was used to physical activity and loved sports. She had played most of them— and played them well. Her experience with basketball, field hockey and baseball would not be of much use, but her triathlon experience would help her through the upcoming intensely exhausting days. Jerry, fit by the modest standards of North Americans, was the weakest of the group and he knew it better than any of them.

REDEMPTION ISLAND

However, he was desperately afraid of drowning and he hoped this motivation, plus his daily workouts at the gym, would keep him from being too embarrassed.

Since it would take most of the day and the day afterwards for the rafters to be ready, the hikers had, at least, a two-day head start, not counting upcoming storms. They further estimated that the trip around the island would take the better part of a day. Knowing this, the hikers talked confidentially amongst themselves and made a pact to surprise the rafters by being on location when they drifted by. They counted on a minimum of three days to arrive there and, with a brisk pace and some luck, they should have no trouble doing just that.

Spirits were high, backs straight, and the pace way too fast. They began singing a myriad of hiking songs that they taught each other. They managed a good start and broke for an abbreviated lunch. None of them were emotionally distant enough from the situation to recommend the kind of slow methodical pacing appropriate for a trek of this magnitude. With the slightest of forethought, the reality of the situation would be clear. After all, they were not following a pre-made and well-marked trail. They were blazing the trail as they went along. They should have expected that backtracking would be required. They were further deluded by their accomplishments the first day. As they say, "Those whom the gods choose for failure, they first are given a goodly amount of success."

They had made reasonable plans and, rather than climb all the way up and down each mountain, they were going to try to skirt the shoulders of the peaks at as low an altitude as possible. Unlike last time, they were not trying to get the best view, but to exert the least amount of energy and use the least amount of time.

"Let's break for the day," said Marc, excited by all the fauna and flora about him. Jerry just nodded, for he was too tired to talk.

Arrianna was relieved at not being the one to ask to stop, "Great idea. We can get a good night's rest and an early start in the morning," she fooled no one with her false bravado. They were all exhausted and could not imagine repeating the hike tomorrow.

Jerry voiced this concern. "Maybe we should rest as much as possible rather than aim for an early start? After all, we may have several days of this to go."

"OK," said Arrianna a mite too quickly. "If it's all right with the two of you, we won't set the alarm clocks or have the desk give us a wakeup call. We'll sleep until the sun wakes us." This energized them enough to look around and gather their dinner.

While they were eating their tropical fruit special, Marc began ruminating. "I hate to say this, but I've been thinking..." Both Arrianna and Jerry looked up, the latter with the dread of the condemned and the former with the intense curiosity of the young.

When Marc did not finish his thought, they both said almost in unison. "Yes?" "What?"

Marc looked decidedly uncomfortable and even managed a squirm or two before replying. "We may have been a mite too optimistic regarding our timetable." Marc was ready for the anger to come out but, as was his nature, he had totally misread his companions.

"Duh!" Said Arrianna.

"No shit, Sherlock," croaked Jerry, though both still had optimistic smiles.

Once it was out in the open, the three travelers were able to discuss things honestly. "The beginning was so easy because we had already explored it and we knew where not to go, also the terrain did not start uphill until after lunch."

"I thought I was going to die during that last hour," Jerry admitted.

REDEMPTION ISLAND

"Why didn't you say something?" asked Arrianna.

"I didn't want to be the one to quit. I didn't want to be the weak one." Marc nodded in understanding. He knew what it felt like to be the odd man out, the one who did not fit in. Arrianna had a harder time since she had worn her difference from everyone as a badge of honor.

They were stuck because the only leader amongst them did not feel empowered to move on. Only after an extended silence and the start of the many night sounds of the jungle did they resolve their dilemma. It was Arrianna who spoke, "Before we all pass out from exhaustion, can we agree to be honest with each other about how we are doing? And I think that Jerry should be in charge of the expedition, we need to make thoughtful decisions, not haphazard ones." Jerry was surprised and only managed a cough.

"I agree," said Marc, "I can't do it and I would feel much better if that was taken care of, that way I can concentrate on the route and the local fauna. What do you think, Jerry? Are you up to it?" They both looked intently at the CEO and, even through the fading light, they could see a strange combination of pride and concern.

"I am the slowest of the group and I know next to nothing of hiking and jungles and navigation…"

"That's not what we are asking you to do. Marc can handle that part of it. We want you to be in charge of the group, planning rest stops, being aware of our general situation, such as amount of provisions and exhaustion level. It helps that you are the slowest. That way no one gets worn out by the other two."

Jerry only managed an, "Oh." followed by a "Sure, I can do that. Now that I think of it, I know very little about the nuts and bolts of what my company produces. I just manage."

They could see the pain in his face at the thought of his company, and they left him alone with it. He would have to find a way to deal with it on his own. They were all asleep within minutes.

~~~~~~~~~

After the threesome had left, Mike, Seth and the two ladies ate a leisurely breakfast and began final preparations. Mike and Seth attached the sail and practiced taking it down and putting it back up. Seth could see that Mike was nervous and went along with the practice to help ease his concerns. The women were using the leftover vines to tie the supplies together and then to the raft itself. They did not want to lose something if a rogue wave happened by. Neither one of them would acknowledge to themselves the reality of the sea.

"It's fortunate that Marc knew how to make rope out of vines, isn't it," said Martha. Leesa looked up and nodded. "I hate to say it, but I think the six of us would be bones by now if he was not here with us."

"Do you think any of the others realize that?" Leesa asked. "I didn't know anyone besides me realized our dependence on him. I am so used to massaging weak male egos, like Jerry's. I never know when to say something and when to keep my mouth shut, so usually I say nothing."

"That must be an awful way to live." Martha said.

"Oh, you get used to it, I guess. And then years later, you start wondering why you don't have any close friends. I suppose if one is not willing to reveal themselves, they shouldn't be too surprised if they find themselves all alone." Martha looked up, surprised by Leesa's honesty and intimacy. Leesa caught her look and smiled. "You, surprised?"

"You could say astonished or thunderstruck and it would be

more accurate. You have not been the most...Um...forthright person in the group."

Leesa nodded. She continued with her work while she talked. "This experience," she waved her arm around to include everything around them, "has been ... Well, I don't know what to call it, but I can tell you this. It is the first time that anyone has stood up to me or my tantrums or my attitude. And it is certainly the first time that I could not get what I wanted when I wanted it. I may be delusional, and I probably will revert to form once we make our way back to the "real world," but I feel closer to the people here than to anyone else in my life."

Martha raised her eyebrows and quickly lowered them back. Leesa did not fail to notice it, however. "I know, I am not all that close to anyone here, but by contrast we are intimate friends."

There was a long silence which Martha broke. "I want to thank you for confiding in me, it helps me get through this ordeal. Some of the time if I think too hard on what my family is doing, I feel I will go mad. Some days I can hardly stand it. I have cried myself to sleep more times than not."

"I know. I hear you every night. Don't be so surprised, we all hear you. Seth wants to come and comfort you but is afraid that his intentions will be misread. Mike and Jerry don't know what to do with it, so they pretend it doesn't happen. Marc is so incompetent with all feelings that he doesn't even realize it's not normal. As far as the girl, I'm not sure. She worries me. She sure appears normal, but there are depths to her that I would be happy to leave unexplored."

Martha remained speechless and was unable to continue working. Leesa could see the flush of embarrassment come up her neck into her cheeks. Leesa knew that, at any moment, Martha would walk away and leave her alone. Worse than being alone actually, she would be with her own thoughts and feelings. The panic pushed her to share more of herself.

"Do you know how many people probably came to my funeral?" Martha shook her head. "Probably over a hundred; my agent would see to that. My films and commercials probably went up in value and he wanted to capitalize on it. Now, more importantly, can you guess how many of those people actually cared?" Martha did not know where this was going and wanted to leave as soon as possible, but Leesa did not give her a chance.

"Not a single bloody one of them! I have no one out there who cares one iota for me. That is what I have been thinking about for the last week, ever since we heard on the radio that they had presumed us dead." This honesty and vulnerability touched Martha's heart and she went over and hugged her. The two remained that way until they each felt better.

"What is going on here? What did I miss?" The two women quickly separated and looked at Seth, who then saw the tracks of the tears on both their faces and backpedaled. "I am sorry to interrupt, I'll come back later."

"NO!" shouted Leesa louder than she had intended.

"Please don't go," pleaded Martha. "We were just consoling each other over our losses."

Seth nodded sagely, "I have heard you cry every night, is it related to that?" Martha nodded. "I couldn't tell if you wanted to cry alone or if you preferred company. I took the coward's way out by leaving you alone." The last few words were barely audible and vanished in the sand at their feet.

"It's quite all right. Leesa told me about your concerns. It is nothing earth-shattering. I just can't get over that my children and grandchildren think I am dead. The pain they must be feeling. And..." she sniffled, "they will sell my house and all my stuff."

Seth nodded, and she saw his deep understanding and even that he felt the same way.

"It isn't my apartment that bothers me but my collections. I have collected something ever since we arrived in Israel after the war. At first, all I could afford to collect were used postage stamps, but later I was into coins, books..." He shook himself and came back to the present. "...I am afraid that it will all be gone. That there won't be anything left of me."

~~~~~~~~~~

The four of them finished every last bit of their preparations at the peak of the heat on the second day after the departure of the hikers. The sea was calm, they had many hours of daylight left and they looked at Mike as children might look at a parent when requesting candy. To their disappointment, he would not leave until morning. They were to rest, chat, and drink as much fresh water as possible prior to leaving at dawn. He warned the women that even though there would be no privacy on the raft and the trip would be far longer than their bladders could hold, they were to drink as much as possible. They would be on short rations until he knew that they were able to get back to shore.

Leesa and Martha looked at each other with alarm, the privacy they could deal with. After all, the accommodations up to now had been less than optimal. They had become used to the latrines, the flies, the smell, the lack of adequate paper and, the worst part of all –the abysmal lack of soap. The plane had carried no soap and, when the tiny hotel soap bars ran out, all they could do was use seawater and sand.

What alarmed them was having to deal with the reality of the trip. It wasn't going to be Tom Sawyer's raft ride at Disney World, it was the real thing. They could fall overboard, be blown away from the island, or be unable to control their direction and end up on their own. Fortunately for them, they did not truly appreciate how bad things could actually get, and the two men, who did know, kept their mouths firmly shut.

Seth went quickly and easily into a deep restful sleep. The ladies joined him out of physical and emotional exhaustion, but not before they had solved their privacy problem. They tied together two of the lap blankets from the plane's stores and intended to put it over themselves when needed. The sense of being unable to see would help them feel that the others could not see them. As Leesa put it, it was the "ostrich solution."

That night, Mike had the hardest time of all because he carried the burden of responsibility. Around midnight, exhaustion forced him into a troubled sleep. His last coherent thought was to wonder how the other group had fared on their first two days and how close they were to reaching the other side.

~~~~~~~~~

The second day of their overland trek was an utter and desperate disaster. Their only consolation was that the three of them were still alive, although how long that would last remained unclear. Jerry could not reconcile how, despite his best efforts, events had imposed their will upon them and how disgustingly helpless they had been to intervene.

The day started poorly with all of them sleeping long past sunrise and, even then, no one was anxious to start. That first day they'd pushed harder than their muscles could handle. They forced themselves to start, and it might have gone well if they had not taken the wrong path. They made the common mistake of tired travelers. When a choice presented itself, they took the path that looked least strenuous without taking the time to investigate. Before they knew it they were in the pits of a vine and underbrush infested hollow that, given their lack of equipment, was un-passable. They then had to climb back out.

Their mood worsened with every retraced step and Marc slid down the hill only stopped by a tree. That left him bruised and limping. When they took a break to eat, all the food that was visible was out of reach, either too high on the tree or tantalizingly protected by a tangled web of needle sharp thorns. They rested hungry, frustrated and disillusioned.

They only managed to forge ahead when the sun was noticeably approaching the horizon and fear of the solidly dark jungle night drove then to a better site. That was when all hell broke loose.

Some burrowing animal came out of nowhere and attacked Arrianna. She had a nasty bite on her ankle and a huge egg on her forehead where she ran into a tree limb while chasing after it in a reflexive gesture of spite. She had then gone into what looked like a seizure to Jerry. He could not help her. There was no 911, paramedics, medical personnel or medicines. He had crawled up to her and, unable to rouse her, he had wailed out of a pit of total hopelessness.

Thankfully Marc retained his cool and made a mudpack for her bite and told Jerry to watch over her while he scouted around.

Now that the crisis was over Jerry noted how well Marc handled these events. Marc handled everyday life so poorly, but he was in his element when backed into a corner, much like he himself was when backed into a financial corner.

Marc was gone only ten or fifteen minutes, which felt like hours, when Jerry heard the rustling. He could not distinguish the real rustling from what he kept imagining. When they finally broke cover, he saw fox like creatures, but smaller and far more aggressive. They were also gaunt and clearly desperate for food. He was not able to count them, as they circled him and the girl. They were clearly interested in her. He used the walking stick that Arrianna carried to poke at them. However, whenever he poked at one, the others behind him came nearer, trying to take a nip out of her. He tried to rouse her, but she only mumbled softly and moved her limbs aimlessly. Marc still did not return, despite his shouts.

He knew he could not overpower them or keep them at bay through force, and it occurred to him how many times he had won a negotiation on chutzpah and guile alone.

He grabbed both water bottles, took the tops off, and then stood to his full height and, in a bizarre ritual dance, proceeded to swirl the bottles while dancing, shouting, and jumping in a circle around the girl. He made a point of ignoring the creatures as a show of disdain. When he next looked, they were gone and Marc was gaping at him with a look that would give him fits of laughter until the end of his days.

Marc had found water, food and a flat clearing not too far from there, but had not heard Jerry's shouts. He explained to Jerry "The huge amount of vegetation provides an enormous surface area for the absorption of sound. When we build a sound proof room, what we do is introduce a large amount of surface area of soft material that will absorb sound."

Jerry eventually forgave him and accepted that he would have come running if he'd realized they were in trouble.

With each of them on one side of the girl and with her waking slightly, they just made it to the clearing before the sun went down. He and Marc munched on a few mangoes and guavas. Now he could hear Marc's steady breathing and Arrianna seemed better.

Marc estimated "We netted about one hour's march and

exhausted ourselves doing so." Also, if Arrianna did not get better...well, he decided he would not think about that for now.

His companions might not realize it, but what had happened today was caused by a lack of leadership. He, Jerry Simmons, CEO and tough guy had let them wander about without direction or discipline. *No more*, he said to himself. *If I am in charge, then, so be it. They would have discipline and decisiveness and, if they still got into trouble, at least it would not be out of sheer stupidity or carelessness.*

Chapter Eleven
Troubles at Sea

Back at the beach, the four rafters woke simultaneously, anxious to get going. They looked eastward into the wind to see if there was any trouble brewing. The haze obscured the horizon, but they all relaxed when they saw no sign of a storm. Mike looked at the rest of them, "Shall we go?"

"I am ready," said Seth.

"Let's get it behind us," said Leesa.

"I am with the rest of you," said Martha. The others did not notice, but her statement had far less energy and far more fear than theirs. The wind was mild but was stirring up the water more than she liked. She remembered that she became seasick rather easily.

With that start, they pushed the raft into the surf. They loaded the two women aboard and they guided it past the breakers, swimming the last hundred meters. Mike climbed aboard, and then he and Leesa helped Seth aboard. Seth had not appreciated how difficult it would be to lift his old battered waterlogged self out of the water and into a makeshift moving platform. Nevertheless, despite looking ridiculous in a *Three Stooges* sort of way, they were now all aboard and, as full of trepidation as they were, excited to be on their way.

The wind came out of the south at 170° and since they wanted to go north that worked out just fine. Once Mike and Seth set the sail, there was little to do but rest, look around, and wait. The sun came out of the haze at midday and lashed at them with its fury. They had prepared for this and all of them wore long-sleeved light clothing. Martha reflected that it would have been nice if she had worn cotton, but in this day and age, who had the time to iron? The irony brought her a smile. They had saved the little sun screen lotion they had scrounged and applied it to exposed parts. Mike and Seth were used to the hot Sun, but the ladies were mandated by the group to apply it well. There was no way to treat sunburn or sun allergy and the luxury of tanning was beyond their current means.

They ate their midday meal in comfort even as the wind became erratic in its aspiration to become a storm. All of them were concerned, but adhered strictly to the policy of not being the one to cast the first stone of fear and doubt. Soon enough, the sea rolled more and the raft magnified the effect. Martha regretted eating and picked a corner of the raft to retch over.

They had reached the northeast corner of the island and needed to change direction to a more westerly course. Mike said, "We are finally making some headway back to the island, I think we'll be all right, but it will take us much longer than I anticipated."

"Good. Seth and I were worried we would not get our money's worth out of this Caribbean Sea cruise. You know how much I hate to complain…"

Seth was drinking some of his water and her deadpan humor caused him to snort it out his nose. "OK, OK, make fun if you have to, but the food on this cruise is the pits, I mean fruit, fruit, and fruit. Enough already with the vitamin C...."

Martha joined in "...and don't get me started on the service!" All of them joined in on the charade and their spirits lifted markedly.

After great efforts, they finally had the island between them and the wind, but at a much farther distance than planned. The island did provide a noticeable reduction in the chop and wind and Martha was particularly grateful. They prepared for the last change in direction as the next point of land came up. This time Mike was going to lead the turn and, in fact, timed it rather well.

Mike pointed ahead, "The beach we want is just up ahead a few miles, at the far end of this shoreline. We aren't moving fast though, so it will take the rest of the day to get there."

Seth looked where he was pointing and the shoreline was moving past them. He then took a sight on the sun to estimate how much time they had left. Since being marooned, he had become very good at this.

He was trying to piece together all the data when he noticed Mike's sly and subtle head motion. Since it was just at this time that Leesa went to comfort Martha during another violent retching episode, Mike and Seth used the opportunity to discuss the problem.

Seth stated, "I estimate that we will be in sight of the beach at sundown." Mike nodded his agreement. "Is this as bad as I think it is?" Mike nodded again. "Shit! Shit! Shit!"

"What's wrong?" Leesa asked.

Mike looked at Seth before replying. Receiving a shrug and knowing he could not tell a convincing lie, he told them the truth. "We are going to run out of sunlight a few minutes too early."

Leesa looked at Martha, who was in no condition to worry, much less comment on the dilemma. "How many minutes and why is that a problem? So we set a makeshift camp by night, what's the big deal?"

Mike swallowed and was about to speak when Seth explained, "We aren't sure, but at least half an hour, maybe as much as an hour. The reason it is a problem is that there are absolutely no lights anywhere. Not on the island, not with us and we will have clouds tonight, so no moon. The sun sets fast at these latitudes and it will be pitch black. We won't be able to tell which way to go. We could as well run into a rock outcropping as the beach or the open ocean."

Leesa gave her opinions "So we have to land sooner or find a way to go faster." They all looked at the rugged coastline. There had not been a spot to land for some time. "We have one of the paddles from the raft and a make-shift board, shouldn't we start using them?"

"Yes we should!" Seth said and started looking for them under all the cargo. "We could also lighten the raft if you think it would help."

Mike shook his head, "I don't think that will help much and we need a lot of that stuff. We should set up a rotation on the paddles, so that no one gets too tired. To make a significant difference we will have to row continuously."

It was an hour later when they had to make a difficult decision. They spotted the small cove at the same time. Their rowing had made enough of a difference and they now expected to reach their destination slightly before dusk. Still the cove represented a bird in the hand, and they could proceed in the morning. It would take them no time at all. With the memories of the last hour, they did not take long deciding to land now. Their tired muscles won the day. It was Martha who changed their minds.

"Aiiyee!" Martha screamed. When they reached her she was inconsolable and could not explain why she was so upset. All she could do was point at the corner of the raft. At first, they thought she had seen a large fish or manta ray, but after a few breaths she calmed herself down enough to tell them "The raft is falling apart!"

All of them ran from corner to corner and tried to look at the bottom of the raft. It was true, the makeshift ropes were fraying badly and the joints were already loose. Seth and Mike checked the mast and rudder joints. Everywhere that the rope had been in constant contact with the water it was fraying in the same way

"What's the matter with the rope?" asked Leesa. I braided it exactly the way Marc showed us. Her tone was slightly defensive.

"It's not your fault. It must be the goddamn vines we used. We did not have the time, inclination or the materials to properly cure the fibers. Marc and I tested it in water, but it was in the stream. We should have tested it in ocean. Something in the salt must be dissolving or stretching the plant matter and fibers." Mike paused, looked around him at his fellow travelers, the raft, and the endless ocean, before speaking again, "At least that's the only thing I can figure."

Seth added "I will be frank with you. We knew well enough that we weren't building the Queen Mary here and that we would have to rebuild it if we wanted to try for the main island, but bloody hell! Not one of us felt that it would fall apart in a few hours!"

They calmed down and decided very quickly that if they landed at the small cove, they would be stranded there with little hope of ever being found. They did not know if they would even be able to walk out of it. The surrounding landscape looked formidable. If they rowed hard and used the dry rope from the cargo, they should be able to hold the raft together until they reached the beach. Even Martha joined in the rowing. The adrenaline energy of raw naked fear was fantastic and their progress increased accordingly.

Seth had just finished his stint with the board followed by a stint with the paddle and had collapsed on the privacy blanket, when an idea struck him. "Mike, listen a second, I think I have an idea that will help. "The ladies continued to row while Seth explained. "I read or heard that making a jib sail is the single easiest way of increasing a boat's efficient use of the wind. It could perhaps increase our speed by as much as twenty to thirty percent. It also does not require any boom, just tie-down sites."

It did not take them long to jury-rig the new sail and the increase in speed was noticeable immediately. They estimated another two to three hours to sunset and hope was high: the ropes were holding, the sail was speeding them on and the end was nearly in sight.

Nevertheless, they continued rowing. It was with an hour left to go that Mike shouted," I see it, I see it. Over there! We've made it!" The rest of them did not get a chance to respond, much less celebrate, because nature answered Mike with a lightning flash and a corresponding thunderclap. It was seconds before the soft rain started.

The island had intervened with the wind but it had also hidden the approach of a storm until it was nearly on top of them. "Brace yourselves," shouted Mike, "the wind will start gusting soon and then the rain will get much harder. If we don't panic, we will still make it—" He did not get a chance to finish his thought, for at that moment Martha fell overboard.

~~~~~~~~

The third day of the overland trek started slowly, only some of which was of Jerry's doing. He had insisted that they become a cohesive group with leadership from him, common sense provided from Arrianna, and Marc's education. The two men were amazed and relieved when Arrianna woke up rested and feeling well. The animal bite was obviously not infected and it was already showing signs of mending. She had a tender knot on her head but her mental acuity did not seem affected.. The two men relaxed noticeably and readied for the day.

They filled their bottles with water, sated their thirst, and ate a hearty breakfast. They also packed extra fruit in case they were caught again in an area where the food was inaccessible.

They began their climb slowly and thoughtfully and when the most promising path was uphill, they went without complaint. All of them had their fill of the easy way. An hour into the hike, Jerry mentioned the seizure. He had been ready for almost any response from the girl. Her actual reaction left him disoriented.

"Oh, I had another one? Well that's all right, I don't seem to have hurt myself during it." And that was all she said about it. Jerry was dying to ask more, but forced himself to hold back. Just like in a negotiation, you don't want to show too much interest or it weakens your hand.

The three of them made far better decisions together and, if in doubt, would send someone ahead to scout it out. They avoided many dead ends and much backtracking that way. Their pace picked up considerably. When four hours had gone by, Jerry called for a lunch break. The other two felt great and wanted to continue, but he insisted. "We are not going to repeat yesterday's mistakes. Pacing is important and I could go a bit further, but there is no point. We have many hours of sunlight left in which to exhaust ourselves." They saw the wisdom in that and set about looking for food.

Marc found different fruits and even some nuts. He said "Perhaps the altitude helped them grow here." Regardless of how they came to be, they all enjoyed the variety. No one voiced it but they all had the same thought: maybe it would help make their stools firmer, instead of the loose, runny mess that a continuous fruit and coconut diet produces.

They could see the sea and figured they were just over halfway there. They hoped the second half would be far easier, if only by virtue of going downhill and probably being able to follow a streambed. If it turned out that way, and they pushed hard the rest of this day, they might reach the beach late the next day. Of course these thoughts led them to wonder about the others and how they might be faring. They looked closely, but could see no sign of the raft in the small slice of visible sea.

Arrianna looked around and shouted, "If I climb to the top of this palm tree, I would have a view of the entire coast line, without the trees getting in the way." And before the two men could protest, she was up and climbing.

When she arrived at the top of the tree, fronds kept getting in the way. She pulled at one after another until she had a minimally obstructed view of the sea. The beauty of it overwhelmed her. She could not talk. It was so stunning. She almost forgot to breathe. The nearly white beach blended into the light turquoise blue waters that drifted into the deep aquamarine blue of the horizon. The sky was cloudy and hazy and the horizon was lost to her almost, as if it did not exist. She was in a glass bubble without seams or joints or problems. She did not want to ever come down again.

Her thoughts were broken by Jerry's agitated question. "Do you see them?"

She then remembered why she had climbed the tree. She scanned the shoreline carefully and saw nothing. This worried them because if they had taken off today, they should be somewhere around this part of the island. She looked carefully one more time, from one end to the other. "I see them! I see them!" They have just rounded the bend, but they are a long way out to sea. That's why I missed them the first time."

She came down and drew them a sketch on the ground. "Why in the world would they go that far out? They were supposed to stay near shore. It will take them forever if they go that far out." Jerry was clearly confused. "You don't think they were going to try for the main island, do you?"

Marc was shaking his head morosely, "No, that is not their intention. Their problem is that I screwed up, and they are having a hard time steering the raft."

"What do you mean?" asked Arrianna.

"They don't have a centerboard. It will make it very hard to turn, there is almost nothing to counter the force of the wind and help them tack back and forth."

"For whatever it is worth, they are pointed in our direction, back to the island. As far as I could tell, they appeared to be making headway. I can climb back up in a half hour or so and double check on that." The two men agreed and they waited not-so-patiently for the thirty minutes to pass. When she made it back down, she verified "They are indeed headed back, but at a much slower rate than I would have expected."

"The wind is probably unfavorable," said Jerry.

Marc added, "It will only get worse as they get close to the island and into the wind shadow. They may have to resort to paddling."

"Paddling? Won't that exhaust them?" Arrianna asked no one in particular.

"Yes it will, but they probably have little choice. At the rate they are going, they will be unlikely to make it before dark. Even with paddling, they will probably need to land on a beach or cove somewhere and finish the trip tomorrow."

REDEMPTION ISLAND

"That won't be a problem, will it? asked Arrianna, "Unlike us, they are carrying tons of food and water. If they land they can replenish both and still have a much easier time than us."

"You are exactly right. And despite my fear of the sea and its creatures, I was quite wrong. We should all have gone by raft."

As Marc started hiking he said, "It certainly looks that way, doesn't it?"

They kept checking on the raft's progress as they hiked. Every time they reached a promontory Arrianna would shimmy up a tree and report on them. They were relieved when they had made their way back to the shoreline. This more than anything else relieved Marc's sense of guilt. When the sky darkened on the windward horizon, they knew that the rafters should leave to, but had no way of telling them. Each time that Arrianna did not report their landing added to the anxiety level. They considered that the shoreline might be unfavorable and Arrianna confessed that she had not taken notice of it. It being an hour or so from dusk, they decided to climb to the highest possible site for the night so they could see their progress.

The group reached an unexpectedly beautiful clearing at the same time that the rafters had seen the sheltered cove. There were no trees obstructing the view and they all could see what happened.

"The shoreline is bad, except for that little cove. I think they see it. Yes, Mike is steering to it. They must be exhausted from rowing."

Marc said wistfully, "Too bad that we can't make it down there in time or we could all finish the trip together."

They all saw how fast the raft was moving and would have relaxed their worrying, except for the storm which was now almost on top of them and clearly churning up the sea. They were about to get in out of the rain when they saw someone fall overboard.

"Who was that?" asked Jerry. "I could tell someone fell in but I couldn't make out who it was." Marc also looked at Arrianna, who was concentrating on the raft.

"The rain and spray from the sea is getting in the way, I can't s...wait! I see Mike. He is rowing. Now who is that at the tiller?" she asked herself. "It can't be Seth, he is too wide. It could be either Martha or Leesa, hard to tell...there! Leesa is at the rudder. I saw her long hair fling about. I can't tell who is at the other oar, the sail is in the way, but from the splashing that the oar is making I don't think it is Martha."

It hit them all at once. It did not matter who was in the water. Someone was, and the raft had not stopped or turned about. They were leaving the person behind to drown. Arrianna screamed at them in rage and would have started running downhill towards the shore had Jerry not anticipated it and been there to restrain her. Marc helped him and they all sat down.

They were oblivious to the rain, the wind, or the raft. The events they had just witnessed drained every ounce of energy any of them had. Arrianna alternately screamed and cursed and wailed. She always came back to, "How could they abandon her? Leave her to drown?"

By the time the three hikers regained awareness of their own predicament, they could no longer see the raft, they were soaked as if dunked and it was much too dark to forage.

Chapter Twelve
Martha's Fate

When they shivered, it was not from cold; despite their altitude, it was still balmy. They had not discussed it, but had collapsed into an exhausted pile of aching flesh and broken spirits. They woke quickly, one after the other. Without a single comment, they broke camp, gathered some food and ate breakfast on the way down to the shoreline. They placed Arrianna last in line because they could not trust her to go slowly and carefully. They had seen and experienced how quickly things could go bad, and were resolved to keep from duplicating those mistakes.

They were fortunate that the cove was exactly on their way and they would not have to retrace their steps back up the mountain. Each of them had thoughts of who it could have been and what they would find once they reached the shore. Jerry desperately hoped there would not be another body for the girl to see. He didn't think she could handle it. Dan, after all, had been a stranger to her, but either one of the two possible alternatives, Seth or Martha, were close to her. It would devastate her. He winced at the thought, but it would be far better if some big fish had made a quick meal of the person.

Marc was unusually quiet that morning. When asked about it, he told them he was puzzling out the weird behavior of the rafters. He believed he had sorted some of it out. "I don't know why they did not land at the cove, but I don't think they made the decision lightly. Maybe they could see something we could not. They clearly understood how desperate their situation was and Mike is much too levelheaded to have taken any chances, regardless of what the others said. Besides, I don't think any of them is that kind of risk-taker. They would have all wanted to land. They came up with the jib out of desperation, that's why it wasn't up before. They continued rowing even after it was up. I am convinced they were intensely aware of the danger they were in."

Jerry nodded, "That makes sense. They were stuck in a desperate situation and were doing their best to get out of it. One thing bothers me. The person who fell overboard was near the edge. Wouldn't they have had the sense to stay to the center if not rowing?"

"Martha gets seasick." Arrianna said with no emotion. It was the first words they had heard her utter since the accident. The two men instantly understood what had happened. It hit Marc with a tingly numbness in his fingers. Jerry felt his headache worsen. He always had a headache when he was in charge of an important project and he was used to it. He rubbed his temples as a supplication to his temporal muscles to relax while Marc shook his hands violently. Neither tactic worked.

Jerry stopped and turned around to face her, "They really could not have turned around to look for her, no matter how much they wanted to. The raft did not turn well, the storm was on them, and the light was fading." He expected her to yell and scream, but instead she fell into his arms and cried, managing a garbled, "I know, I know, but it still hurts so much." This was a novel situation for Jerry and he wished that Marc had been closer so she had turned to him.

After a second's reflection, he changed his mind. This poor unfortunate child who kept losing people needed someone who could handle feelings and he was that person. She would never have turned to Marc for comforting. He almost laughed at the thought that she considered him the most sensitive and nurturing person available. Having no option, apart from pushing her away onto the jungle floor, he stayed there and did not run away from the situation. It felt similar to jumping into a cold pool on a hot summer day. Once the initial shock was over, it felt very good.

He held her head and stroked her hair, and whispered reassurances that he himself did not believe—remembering how his mother had comforted him. She accepted his efforts and he struggled mightily to remember how it felt to be comforted. It had been so very long ago…

They felt no rush and, if pushed to the wall, at least two of them would admit to not wanting to go down there at all. They had a quick lunch, which included coconuts. This was such a welcomed change that they implored Marc to get more. He liked being needed and was happy to oblige. When they resumed, their spirits were not altogether happy but were at least past the initial shock and beginning the journey to acceptance of the second death since they were marooned.

They reached the cove at mid-afternoon and were brought to a halt by the sheer beauty of it. The sand was pristine without a mark on it. The water was a translucent teal revealing a diverse and prolific sea life. The trees at the beach's edge formed a sort of secluding shield that made them all feel isolated, safe and comfortable. Flowers were everywhere, large, small but not subtle. Colors upon colors everywhere, so diverse, intense and deeply saturated that they vibrated on the retina. The accompanying smells were just as delicious. One after the other, they slowed their pace, took deep lungs filled of air and absorbed the experience.

It took a small, but significant, part of an hour for them to remember why they were there. They fanned out and cautiously combed the water's edge. Each hoping that one of the others would find whatever there might be to find.

"Over here," shouted Jerry. The others joined him at a reluctant pace.

"What did you find?" asked Marc. Arrianna remained silent but observant.

"A shoe. It was bobbing at the water's edge. Look, the shoelaces are still tied." They waited for him to make clear the significance of the statement but Jerry either felt it was self-evident or there was no significance.

They searched in circles from the discovery site. Without discussion, Jerry and Marc flanked Arrianna and the three of them searched as a group, expecting the worst. "The tide is going out, and the high water mark was close to the trees, we should look there."

Jerry responded without a pause, "That's right, good idea Marc, you go ahead while we continue to check the beach." He received a glance from the girl that he took to say "thank you." They all knew now that they were looking for Martha's body..

It was only a few minutes later that Marc called them to join him. From his manner they were relieved that he had not found the body. On a small bush Martha's scarf lay still and dry.

"Where did you find it? And why on earth did you put it there?" asked Arrianna, her voice close to cracking but still with control.

REDEMPTION ISLAND

"I haven't touched it," said Marc defensively. "That is exactly where I found it."

"I can't imagine that any wind would have picked up a soaking wet scarf, maybe a wave threw it up there." Jerry mused.

"At high tide," Marc added.

"Or a bird played with it," contributed Arrianna. The all sat around the artifacts, but shared no thoughts. Feelings were expressed by an occasional tear, sob, or sniffle. No one was immune to the sadness. Later they would talk about what to do next, right now they all needed to mourn a tough and courageous lady who they had all known too well to ignore, but not nearly well enough.

~~~~~~~~~

Martha did not remember falling into the water. One second she was retching her guts out and pleading to her merciful God to take her and avoid the torture, the next she was underwater and sinking fast.

Two things had colluded to prevent her from drowning. One was that the shoreline did not become deep water for a long way out, and she touched bottom at about fifteen feet. The second was her water instincts. As soon as her feet felt the bottom, her knees reflexively bent and pushed her up as hard as they could. She was used to holding her breath and, as long as she did not need to barf, she would be all right.

She broke the surface to see the dark, lightness clouds, but no raft. She should have then panicked, flailed about until exhausted and drowned, but she heard an inner voice reminding her that her wish to not be nauseated had been granted. Her stomach felt great! The saying, "Be careful what you wish for little girl, for you might get it," flowed through her head.

Her body decided to swim and to not give up. Once she started the familiar strokes, the calm that she felt during her daily swim sessions took hold. Sure it was salty undulating water with no lights, no lifeguard, but the strokes were the same and the comfort of competence took over.

Which way to go? Could she see the shore? She then remembered that the waves were headed more or less towards the cove they had passed, and she swam with them. The warmth of the sea enveloped her, energized her, and empathized with her. She felt thousands upon thousands of shipwrecked sailors urging her on. She was not to join them, at least not yet. At first she had tried the crawl but the unpredictable nature of the open sea caused her to take in water too much of the time. She switched to the breaststroke and found it restful and she could keep a lookout for the island. With every lightning flash she could adjust her course and, within a lifetime of indeterminable duration, the waters calmed dramatically. She was within the shelter of the cove! If she could only avoid being smashed against some rock...

She reached the beach quickly and with no effort. Then she discovered that she could not get herself out of the surf. The waves would drag her out each time. While in the water she felt rested, but when she climbed out and tried to reach the high ground, the fatigue and exertions of the body revealed themselves and she was unable to develop the intense burst of energy to get out of the reach of the waves. She let herself drift with the water, remaining a few feet from the beach while she rested and planned.

That was when providence intervened once again in the form of a floating stick. It was a few feet long, thicker than her thumb and felt strong. She grasped it with desperation and, when the next wave sent her on the beach, she plunged it deep into the sand and held on with all her remaining strength. The next wave sent her a little further. She repeated the process of plunging the stick into the sand at the peak of her travel. Each time holding on was a little easier.

After many waves passed without any further progress she made one final heroic lunge forward. It only netted her a few precious inches, but the tide had peaked. It was just enough to keep from being floated back out again. She was out of the unrepentant reach of the sea.

She woke ignorant of her situation. She cried until the tears ran out and her thirst became overwhelming. Reluctantly, she pushed herself to her knees and then to her feet. She looked at her surroundings and, in the same way that the hikers would be in a short while, was overwhelmed by the beauty of it. If she had not been parched from the salt, sand and exertion, she would have taken more time to appreciate it. One look and she went into the jungle in search of drinkable water.

Before she made three steps, her scarf chafed her. Atop everything else today, it drove her annoyance into fury. She ripped it off her head and threw it away. It drifted and landed on top of a bush. She did not need it. What she needed was water, and fast. She plunged into the brush with one shoe and gave no thought to leaving a message or indication of her direction of travel. She was intending to go to the beach and had no illusions that the raft could come back for her.

~~~~~~~~~~

"We could make camp here and try to get to the other side in one day," said Jerry, although he was not happy at the thought.

"No!" shouted Arrianna too loudly. "I'm sorry. I mean that I don't want to do that. We should leave right away and get this cove as far behind us as possible. Then we will be sure to get there tomorrow.

The rest of them will want to know what happened to her."

Marc nodded in agreement and, after a pause, added, "She is right, we don't know what obstacles we have yet to encounter and I don't want to feel rushed. You know how much we need to get this trip finished before something else happens."

Jerry knew they would want to go. However, he felt he needed to offer to stay. He also knew that the remaining rafters might be in trouble. He had no way of knowing if they made it safely or not. They had to push on and be there tomorrow, regardless of the dangers. The group was not doing well and it was up in the air as to how many would still be around when, *if,* they were ever rescued. "All right then, let's get started. Marc, why don't you scout around for our best possible path? Arrianna, you and I will look around for water and fruit."

The three of them began their assigned task, glad to have something to occupy them. Marc looked for animal paths and streams which could be followed. Arrianna wanted to find the supplies quickly and get going. Jerry was wishing, for the first time in his life, that he was no longer in charge and thereby responsible for the outcome. He was sick of the death around him.

~~~~~~~~~~

Martha struggled in her quest for water due to the lost shoe. She had previously had no idea how important shoes were and was ranking it as one of man's greatest inventions. That's when she heard it. She stopped and concentrated. It was unmistakable. There was water falling on water somewhere near–but where? The sound bounced off the trees and leaves and she could not take a bearing to it. Had she heard it before? No, she was sure of it. She would just keep walking forward slowly, listening intently. She plunged ahead, her thirst overcoming her good sense. In front of her lay a small and rippling pond with a wide, short, and beautiful waterfall at the other end. She did not take even a second to enjoy the view, but jumped into the pond and drank to her parched tongue's content.

She swam and she removed her clothes to better remove the sand and salt from. She felt a fleeting moment of modesty and laughed hysterically at herself. She was lost, alone, with no realistic hope of rescue and her mind was worried that someone would see her unclothed. *What utter silliness,* she told herself. Her life expectancy was abysmal and only in her fantasies was there anyone near enough to see her. *Modesty! Who could afford it at this time?* What she needed was to get the sand and salt off her and her clothes, so that she would not rub herself raw and invite every blood sucking insect on the island over for dinner.

The pond and the waterfall changed her outlook dramatically. She felt it was placed there just for her and that she alone would ever know about it. She swam from one end of it to the other, enjoying the sparse water spray under the falls. There was even a little cavern underneath, which provided shelter. She drank and swam and floated for what seemed hours, and finally dragged herself were her clothes were drying.

"I haven't been skinny dipping in ages! I'd forgotten how much fun it is," she told herself. "Well, like I have always told you, if you weren't so damned proper and stuffy, you would have more fun," she answered herself. "I know, but at least I am having fun now, before it is too late. Although, it was spicier when there was at least a small chance of someone finding me." She went on in this manner, talking and answering herself. The conversation did not bother her much because she felt like it would be the last she ever had. She would try to go overland to the appointed place, but she had no illusions as to her chances of surviving the next few days.

REDEMPTION ISLAND

~~~~~~~~~

Marc scouted the jungle surrounding the cove and found a good and easy path to follow. When he returned, both his companions were ready and they took off at a fast, but measured, pace. He estimated that after an hour of distance from the cove, the pace would slacken. He took some of the fruit and water and again he resumed his point position. If he remembered the topography correctly, there was only one more bluff to climb, and it would be downhill to the shoreline. "What would that bluff be like?" he wondered. The past few days had cured him of his hopeless optimism and flipped him into what he would call "intelligent cynicism," but, in actuality, was desperate pessimism. Would they be able to climb this last hurdle without injury? What other dangers lurked in front of them? He was so busy predicting their demise that he almost missed the sound.

Was that water he heard? Sure, that's what it was, it sounded like a waterfall. They had as much water as they would need for the day and they were in a hurry to get to the new camp. *What the hell?* He told himself, *I am going to check it out*, he made the appropriate marks on the trail to let them know not to go any further, and he went in search of his waterfall. He did not know why he was looking for it, but he felt he had to. Perhaps he needed an emotional lift and a swim under a waterfall would help. Perhaps he just wanted to have his curiosity quenched.

He saw the top of the fall before he saw the pool. He smiled and, indeed, felt better. When he saw the pool, he gasped at its sheltered beauty. "What a discovery. It is beautiful! I have to get the others." He ran back and found them waiting for him. "There is the most unbelievable waterfall with a pool we could swim in. You have to see it! It makes the cove look commonplace."

Jerry was dubious, "Are you sure? It will set us back a while, and we did want to get as far as we could."

"Please, "Arrianna pleaded. "I am so hot and sweat-sticky that I can't bear to be myself. If I could cool off and rest, I am sure that I could climb better and safer."

Marc jumped on the same train, "We don't know what is in store for us, and the more rested and relaxed, we are the better off we will be."

Jerry too was hot, sticky, and tired. They had only put a quarter of an hour behind them, but it was too good to pass up. "Let's go. Too bad we don't have swim suits."

Arrianna retorted, "Sure we do, we were born with them. I don't know about you, but if it as good as he says it is, I am not going to let a little modesty get in the way of a comfortable cooling swim." Both of the men remained quiet and glad that she could not see their faces or elsewhere.

They almost missed each other. Martha had been swimming under the falls when Marc had first spied them. The noise of the falls had prevented either of them hearing the other. This time, Martha had just climbed out of the water and was ready to return to the beach to begin her solo hike. She was letting herself drip dry before putting her clothes back on, when she saw the three of them break past the foliage. They saw her at the very same time. The shock of the encounter on both sides was such that for the longest time, neither side took much notice of her complete exposure. Even then their reactions were muted. Too much had happened to give it the huge importance it possessed on the outside world.

Martha slowly turned around and started dressing without any hurry. She had wanted to just run to them and hold them to make sure she wasn't imagining it, but many decades of training, and the men's embarrassed reactions, slowed her down. Nevertheless she had no intention of putting on her bra again. She had decided that while swimming, and she was sticking to it.

Arrianna had started running once the shock had worn off and she reached and enveloped her in a desperate embrace before she had managed to button her blouse. Nevertheless, neither of them noticed and they held each other for the longest time, each crying out of sheer relief. The men stayed behind, waiting for her to finish dressing. Marc in particular was already extremely uncomfortable having seen her naked and would have gone elsewhere had there been somewhere to go. Jerry, sensing this, grabbed him firmly by the elbow and forced him forward. "If it doesn't seem to bother her, then who are we to make a fuss?" he said with a wink.

Martha felt delivered. Although she had not given up, she knew her limitations and accepted her inability to rescue herself. Arrianna had been struggling not to give in to the other part of her that was desperate to take charge, to once again anesthetize the feelings of loss. The two of them were now closer than either had ever been to anyone else. A new mother-daughter relationship had been born, and only time would tell which one of them would feed and nurture that relationship more.

Jerry was relieved. He felt no personal connection with the lady, but finding her not only alive, but obviously in very good health and spirits was more than he could possibly have wished for. The burden of leadership eased slightly, despite there being one more person in the group. There was a definite sense of security in numbers, but more importantly, there was comfort in Martha's survival. Maybe they were not as fragile or vulnerable as he had thought. *Maybe we would not all die based on one bad decision or one piece of bad luck.*

Marc had never seen an older woman naked before. He had

hardly ever seen any woman naked, and each time he struggled with his embarrassment. His heart was racing, his hands were clammy, he could not swallow, and he was starting to hyperventilate. Besides running away, he could not come up with any plan and he was about to faint from his efforts when Jerry said, "You look like shit, why don't you jump in the water? It will help you feel better. I'll be right behind you." On his way in, he wondered if Jerry suspected what was going on inside him.

It was after Jerry had joined Marc that the two ladies separated and started laughing uncontrollably. "You got me all dirty and sweaty again! I will have to go back in. And my clothes had finally dried."

Arrianna, knowing she was being teased, smiled. "Just take them off again. Marc is too much of a nerd to look and Jerry, despite everything, is very much a gentleman. In fact, watch this." She waited until the two men happened to be looking her way and she quickly pulled her shirt up and off. Predictably the two men could not turn around fast enough and, in trying, Marc lost his footing and went under. He came up spurting water and coughing. Of course the ladies laughed themselves to giggles and Jerry could hardly keep his own laughter in. "See? You could not have more privacy if there was a steel fence between us."

Arrianna finished undressing and walked into the water, carrying her clothes. She allowed herself to be enveloped by the soft comfort of the water. It was absolutely heaven. The water was cool and cleansing. She could just about forget all her problems and concerns. Nothing existed outside herself. Her clothes nearly drifted away before she reeled them back in and started working on them. Once the clothes were rinsed and laid out to dry, she allowed herself the luxury of soft steady swimming to and from the falls. In deference to the others, she remained underwater and did not stand up to feel the spray of the falls on her body. She was feeling much more like Arrianna now and wished no one harm.

She looked around the small world of the pool. The waterfall was a series of cascading streams down a steep sided cliff that resulted in countless numbers of rivulets running back and forth across the rock face, all eventually meeting in the pool they were all swimming in. The vegetation was lush, even by the island's standards, and grew tall, wide and with abundance. This place would be hard to find, if not for the sound it made. After some time, she began to notice more wildlife: little rodent creatures sipping at the opposite shore, many birds, most of them multicolored in the expected fashion of the tropics. None of them made any trouble for the castaways. Nevertheless, she was enough unnerved that she put her underclothes on as a makeshift swimsuit and made the most of the fall's spray.

Martha could not accept the events. *I had made peace with my situation and accepted that I would not survive. I set myself up to give it my all in a final attempt at survival but I knew the outcome. Then without warning they were there. Right in front of me, real and solid and actually looking for me! Who had sent them? Were they the handiwork of God? The God that I turned my back on for so many years? I am no longer a believer, so why would he do something like that? Does he want me back?*

She smiled as she watched Arrianna cavort in the water. *There is a jewel in the rough. God only knows what had been done to her in her few short years of life, and how, despite that, she had managed to become such a wonderful person. If only my daughters were that mature and ...*but she had decided not to dwell on that. They were grown, had made their wishes clear and their lives hardly, if ever, touched hers anymore. She felt as a mother to Arrianna. What did she feel in return? Would she get another chance at mothering, however small?

It was not long when Jerry began to pepper Martha with questions. "What happened on the raft? Why didn't you land at the cove? When did Mike realize he was running out of daylight?"

She patiently recalled all of the events and had to repeat the part about the ropes fraying.

"So that is why you made such an about face. You were afraid of being stuck in the cove, not knowing whether there was a way out," said Jerry with clear understanding and agreement. "I would have done the same thing."

"From our vantage point on the water, the walls of the cove looked steep and unsurpassable. Mike has been to coves in Hawaii where the only access is by boat. We knew that the four of us could not repair or rebuild the raft. We had no other choice but to make a run for it."

Marc was still lost in thought, "Are you sure they were actually fraying? They did not simply look frayed?"

"For crying out loud, Marc! The joints were loose, half the rope was gone, Mike and Seth came over and, although they did not say anything, their faces showed us girls how bad it was."

"OK, OK, I'm sorry, it's just that…well, you know…"

They all looked at him, "No we don't know. What are you getting at?" asked Arrianna.

"That it's all my fault. First I did not think of placing a center board of any kind. Then I pick a vine that disintegrates in sea water."

"It's not your fault!" They all screamed in unison.

Jerry took the lead, "We know you did the best you could. We also know that, without your help, we'd all be still on that beach where we landed without an idea in the world of how to rescue ourselves. Marc blushed, wiped a tear from his face, and accepted the handshake that Jerry gave him. Martha and Arrianna independently had been about to give him a comforting hug, but realized that, under the circumstances, it would not be a good idea.

~~~~~~~~~~

"We need to decide what to do, people." Jerry said with authority. "The day is getting old. We have to find a place to spend the night before we lose our light." He looked around at the others and could see how serene they were, even Marc. They did not want to think of anything, much less their situation. He did not want to either, but he would have to shake them out of their complacency. "Martha is not the only one who was in trouble. We do not know that they made it safely to the beach and, if so, what their situation is. They may very well need our help."

Martha looked up startled. Her own desperation had blocked this line of thought. "Oh my! Jerry is quite right. They may be as desperate as I was…or more, if they are hurt." She immediately lost interest in the pool and made it to the shore where her clothes lay and finished dressing. No one looked away, but no one looked at her either. Everyone was struggling with the weight of real life intruding on them—once again. They all agreed to push on as quickly as possible. Marc would take the point and find the best way. Jerry would follow and the two ladies would make the best possible time after him. This way, if there was any backtracking, then Martha would be spared the effort.

They made good time and fortune smiled on them. Marc reached the top of the ridge at twilight and hurried back to help the others find it. They settled in for a good night's sleep, expecting to be off at dawn. It did not work out that way.

Chapter Thirteen
Reunion

They all saw Martha fall overboard. There was nothing they could do. If they managed to remain afloat for the next thirty minutes, it would be a minor miracle. They did not have the ability to either stop the boat or turn around and try to save her. It had only been that morning that they were safe on the beach. They looked at the spot she had fallen until it was lost in the rain, waves and spray.

Mike yelled, "Leesa could you look at the bindings. Are they fraying more?" The anxiety was clear in his voice. They were making good time and the storm was getting rough, but they weren't yet lost. Still, if the vines gave way suddenly, then all of them would be in the churning water.

Leesa kept her death grip on the rudder and looked about. "They are fraying more, but they still look all right to me. None of them are any looser."

"Then, as long as they don't suddenly snap, we should be all right."

"Over there!' screamed Seth. " Look! The beach. It's right

there. We could swim if we had to." Mike looked, and for the first time since the unscheduled sea landing they saw a smile, however small, settle on his face. He gave Leesa directions with the rudder and he stopped rowing and began adjusting the sail. Within a minute, they were tossing in the surf of the beach and they were at last sure that they would at least survive the trip. They wanted to get the raft ashore however, so as not to lose all their precious supplies.

They did not have much time to worry over it. The wind had shifted and between it and the waves, the raft was going ashore quickly. One second they were in the water, longing for the beach, the next the raft was aground and they had collapsed on the sand out of emotional exhaustion.

"Come on! One more thing before we rest," yelled Seth. "We need to secure the raft." He was trying to do so single-handedly and failing miserably. Leesa joined him and the two of them were fighting to a draw with the surf. However, it was an unfair duel because the surf would not tire.

Mike took over the leadership once more. He attached three short ropes to the raft and implored the other two "Help me pull it even higher!" They did not want to help, they were collapsed on the sand, breathing hard, hardly moving any muscle. "The tide is coming in. In no time the waves will reach it."

"Then at that time we will get up and push it up further until the tide peaks," contributed Seth with only a little irritation. Mike tried in vain to pull it up by himself. He gave up and collapsed next to the other two. "Besides, in our exhausted state, the three of us together could not budge that POS. Here, hand me one of those ropes. I will wind it around my ankle. That way if we drift off to sleep, I will feel the tug."

Mike readily acquiesced and helped him with the rope, but he placed it around one of his few remaining belt loops. Leesa was already asleep. The two men joined her forthwith. It was forty minutes before the raft pulled Seth into the rising surf.

~~~~~~~~~

Despite many hints from Mother Nature, the hikers once again failed to post any kind of night watch. In general they pushed too hard and too long for them to do so, but they were running risks that were clearly under-appreciated. In the pre-dawn twilight, danger surfaced to the forefront.

Martha, on a good day, slept fitfully. This was not a good day. She was lying on the ground with no cushioning of any kind. Bugs were buzzing about her, muscles were protesting and her spirit was unsettled by the severe and sudden changes in fortune she experienced. There was a noise at the edge of the makeshift camp, and she was now incorporating it into her dreams. She startled awake. Not ten feet from her was the largest untamed cat she had ever seen outside a zoo. And the beast was not in the least bit happy.

At first, she could not summon her voice. It must have gone elsewhere and left no forwarding number. Only by a very concerted effort of will did she manage to squeak out an alarm. "Help. Help!"

The sudden movement of so many others kept the mama cat from lashing out as she had intended. Yet she would not give ground. She had gone hunting when the sun went down, and if that was not hard enough, when she arrived at her den, these interlopers were right at the entrance. Her babies needed her and she did not care if they were so much larger than her, she would overcome.

Jerry was the one who took charge. He woke quickly and instinctively settled on a course of action. He focused on the cat and approached her so as to be the one closest. He then barked out commands, "Quickly, gather our stuff and back away. Let me know when you are done." He then focused all of his attention on the feral beast. To the other three hikers, he was absolutely insane. He stayed on all fours facing down the cat, easily within reach of a long leap. He hissed and growled and arched his back, while slowly giving ground. The cat just as slowly advanced such that the gap between them stayed constant.

It took thirty seconds for the three non-combatants to gather everything and retreat. "We're clear," said Arrianna, her voice quivering. Jerry increased the pace of his retreat, but did not ease up on the intensity of his feral behaviors. At fifteen feet, he stood up, resumed his usual persona, turned his back to the cat and slowly and deliberately walked away. He non-verbally impelled the others to do the same. Marc took one last glance behind them and saw the cat staring them down and, at the last second before going out of sight, retrieve something in her mouth and disappear.

~~~~~~~~~~

Dawn came in a glorious banner of colors. The travelers were so awe-inspired that it was another hour before the three confronted their fearless leader and implored him to explain. Jerry was uncomfortable, explaining, "I have this ability, you see. In certain, very intense situations I can detect the emotions of others. It is subcortical…"

Marc turned to the others, "He means that he does not think about it."

"…right. Anyway, this is how I have succeeded in business. I learned to trust these…intuitions… and to put my brain in the penalty box. I can sense fear, rage, and most of the intense emotions. I therefore know when to call a bluff, when to back down, when to stand my ground." He paused to look around at their surroundings. The flora was different on this side of the island. More greens, thicker underbrush, more birdcalls. The overstory was much denser and they could hardly see the sky, much less the sun. He started to wonder how they would direct themselves when the rising irritation of the other three penetrated to his consciousness. "At any rate, when Martha woke us, the overwhelming feeling was fear. My mind was still half asleep so the feeling was clear. There was no rage, or hate, just fear. We appeared to be some sort of threat to that animal and it did not really want to fight, just to scare us off, so that is exactly what I allowed it to do."

Arrianna voiced the question on all their minds. "But weren't you scared?"

"Scared? You mean of the cat?" The others resisted the urge to say "DUH" in unison. Jerry looked pensive. "No, I can't recall any fear on my part." After a short pause he added, "I guess I'm accustomed to shutting down the fear. You see, in my line of work, once they see fear you're dead, more likely worse than dead." He looked around and saw blank faces. He clarified, "In the business world, they do not just kill you. They pick your bones clean and incinerate the remains. By the time they're done, you can be so far in the hole that you will never, in a lifetime, regain your position or financial freedom. This situation wasn't that hard, the worst that could happen is that the cat would have killed me. Believe me, there have been several times these weeks I have wished for just that."

The group resumed their trek in silence. Jerry had inadvertently reminded them of how desperate their situation remained. Perhaps the four of them were all that remained of the original group of eight. Arrianna stayed close to Martha and held her hand whenever possible. Marc, as usual, led the way, sometimes having them pause while he checked the path ahead. Jerry trailed the two ladies to make sure Martha did not push too hard.

The physical demands were significant and Martha required large doses of encouragement and assistance. Nearly every obstacle was insurmountable to her. Their pace slowed significantly and Jerry was worried they would not reach the beach.

Marc came back from one of his forays. "It's there! Just around the bend. We made it!" This charged everyone up. The two men assisted Martha and the four of them broke out on the beach ten minutes later. Seeing it deserted with no sign of a raft or of the others broke their hearts.

~~~~~~~~~

The reunion was as dramatic and wonderful as it was sudden. One second the hikers were at the beach looking for debris, the next Leesa was screaming at them from the top of a small dune, just tall enough to unobtrusively block the view of the camp. Leesa was overcome by seeing the ghost of Martha with them. She was drowned and fish food two days ago and now she was with them and intact. For the hikers to find the other three in good shape was of equal relief.

They sat about comparing notes. Marc examined what was left of the raft. It was in pieces, apparently the disintegration had continued even after it was out of the sea. Only the mast and rudder ropes were in any semblance of good shape. They all reassured him again that no one could foresee how the salt water would dissolve the fibers of that particular plant.

After all of the arguments and struggles over which way would prove the best, it turned out that neither were easier. The hike had been much more strenuous than anticipated and would have been much too tough for the rafters. The larger raft necessary for the trip to civilization would have proved too difficult to steer back to shore and would have disintegrated under them. They all settled on the same thought. In some it was a disturbing thought but in most it was agreeable and confirming. Only by the combined efforts of every single one of them, had they managed to successfully make it on the first leg of their journey back to civilization.

Chapter Fourteen
Sunday Service

Early the next day, Seth and Martha awoke early as prearranged. Silently they rose and walked together out of sight and sound of the others. Both were alert, intense and determined. They began with a silent moment of prayer and proceeded with the preparations. They had discussed it by themselves just before bedtime and decided not to tell the others. They would present them with a *fait accompli*.

Martha slowly and methodically copied the words twice. Seth attended to the seating and the instruments. It took them a full half-hour to prepare, and then they walked back, hand in hand.

Surprise was clearly registered on the faces of their fellow castaways. They had been missed for a short time and their side-by-side footprints had been noted. No one had ventured to look for them. Now they were holding hands.

"We have an announcement to make," boomed Seth with a deep resonating timbre to his voice. He looked at Martha and signaled for her to continue.

REDEMPTION ISLAND

"Seth and I have carefully determined that today is Sunday." No one moved. They were sure that more was to come. "We have prepared a small service and invite any of you who wish to join us in giving thanks for our deliverance to follow us." And without waiting for comment or reaction, they both turned about smartly and started walking back from whence they came. They did not turn around until they reached the "chapel." They saw their congregation straggling over. Jerry led the procession and looked more curious and tickled than thankful. Marc and Leesa were chatting on their way and looked markedly uncomfortable. Arrianna was the last and it wasn't at all clear if she intended to join them or not.

Martha's sadness lifted when she saw Leesa and Marc look back and call to her. When she still made little effort at coming over, the two of them resolutely walked back, hooked each arm in one of theirs and she was very gently frog-marched to her place in the sand.

Both Martha and Seth stood up in front. All but Arrianna had a look of happy expectancy. They had worried that some of the others would be put off by the religious nature of a thanks-giving service. They need not have worried. Although they might not agree with their intent, none but Arrianna were having any trouble with it.

"You are probably wondering why we have gathered you here under these circumstances." Seth said.

"Yeah! And when are you serving the refreshments?" Leesa answered back.

"Could you speak up? The PA system is not working." Marc added.

"I hope that this is not going to take long. I have a lunch appointment and they don't like it when I'm late." Jerry chimed in.

Mike added solemnly, "Preacher man, please forgive these poor misguided gentiles, for they do not know what they say." This could have been taken seriously, which would have put an insurmountable damper on the exchange. His disposition however showed that he was playing along and everyone continued having a good time at it—all but Arrianna, who sat stony faced, barely able to keep her tears at bay, but too stunned by the discourse to make the effort required to leave.

Martha and Seth, of course, relaxed immensely. They had wanted this to be a group effort, but not maudlin. They had no problem at all with the humor and pretended irreverence. They were bonding as a group. Even serious, rational Mike had joined in. Arrianna's reticence had been a surprise, but Seth thought he knew how to help her over it.

Martha spoke, "We do not have a rigid agenda or format that we intend to follow. This is for all of us. It is intended as a forum to give thanks in any way that feels comfortable to you. If you have suggestions or want to contribute, we encourage it. When we run out of things to do, we will wrap up. We do, however, ask you to play the instrument in front of you whenever we are singing. Everyone looked down in front of them. There was what someone might call a musical instrument—well, only if that someone was on drugs. Regardless, they all picked up their assorted sticks, rattles, and containers and tried them on for size.

The resulting clatter was not music, but it would do. A bit heavy on the percussion and without any cohesion, but it was a joyful noise nevertheless. Martha started the process by giving thanks for her deliverance. They could all easily understand her feelings. After all, she had literally been plucked from the sea, been deposited into the wilderness, and then been found and restored to her people. She went further to detail how she had fallen away from God and the church many years ago after the senseless death of her husband. How this had further alienated her children and how alone in the world she was. She finished by telling them she felt closer and more cared for by the members of this "ragtag congregation' than anyone else she could name.

"During that day by myself at the waterfall, I had made my peace and accepted my fate, such as I thought it would be. Now that I had been given more time and another chance, I am determined not to waste it away by fretting over my situation. I do not know how my life would continue when we got back to the 'real world', but I know I could not continue on my prior life path. I was waiting for death to take me. Now I am more determined than ever to live and to make a difference."

Upon finishing, she sat down next to Arrianna and reached out and held her hand. She gently kissed it and placed it on her lap, held between both of hers. Arrianna resisted, more out of instinct than choice, but quickly absorbed the determination in the touch and allowed herself to lean on Martha, who quietly started to stroke her hair. It was so calming and soothing that Arrianna wished she could allow herself the luxury of letting the caring in, of opening her walls and becoming vulnerable.

Seth spoke, "I have been in better circumstances." There was a chuckle in the crowd. "I have been in worse circumstances." He could feel their attention focus. "I have been in much worse circumstances. Perhaps even worse than you could imagine." Now he had them. They were all riveted to his every utterance. "I am not going to bore you with the details of my life. Truthfully it would bore me senseless."

"So that's what happened!" shouted Jerry.

"Have you tried therapy?" added Leesa. The joking kept going and even Arrianna joined in.

She said hesitantly, "We could have a memorial service for

your sense." That was the final touch. Any tiny amount of decorum that previously existed evaporated in the joyful release of the tensions built inside. The service succeeded beyond the hopes that Seth and Martha placed on it.

When the laughter was almost done, Seth added, "Order, order, or I will be forced to detail you with a lecture on parliamentary procedure." They all knew that he was kidding and his facade of mock seriousness stimulated their laughter once more.

Eventually they resumed their thanksgiving. They sang songs, any song that anyone wanted to sing. Marc requested, "You can't always get what you want" by the Rolling Stones, which was remarkably appropriate to their circumstances. They also sang, "Country Road" by John Denver, "Poor Wayfaring Stranger" and "Let it Be" by the Beatles, among others. After the song requests died out, Seth attempted once again to talk.

"As I said before, our current situation is not the worst I have experienced. Truth be told, it doesn't even rate. I tell you this so that you may take heart and not despair. Our situation is far from hopeless and our combined abilities have proven to be remarkable. I will confess that, for many reasons, I have been a religious man for most of my life. At every point that I felt despair and hopelessness, God has provided. I did not always get what I wanted, but I always received what I needed. Even when my baby died in my arms, before most of you were born, He gave me the chance to hold her and care for her and the comfort to persevere. As you may suspect, I am Jewish and for no better reason than habit I have remained so. But I have worshipped with Catholics, Muslims, and others. I do not feel I have the market cornered on God and you need not fear my being either rigid or controlling. I am willing to share my experience with any who wish it. I'm done."

There was a long silence that became uncomfortable. Then the length of the silence prevented anyone from speaking. The tension continued to build when, to everyone's surprise, Arrianna stood, cleared her throat and with a barely audible and trembling voice said, "I don't know about the rest of you, but I want to be bored senseless." The departure from expectation dissolved the tension and they all resumed their laughter and sense of ease.

Seth wagged a finger with deliberate overstatement, "Now young lady, I will ask you to respect your elders, and if you can't, at least talk lower so I can't hear you make fun of me."

When the merriment died down, Arrianna remained standing. She was forcing herself to continue and they all paid close attention. "Like Martha, I left the church. It never helped me and its so-called 'good intentions' disgusted me. I was reluctant to come this morning but I just could not be alone. I want to thank Leesa and Marc for assisting me in my decision." She then formally bowed to each of them. This had the desired effect of decreasing the serious tone of her confession. "This 'service and I use that term loosely, is nothing like I have ever experienced."

Seth jested, "In your long and ecumenical experience, you mean."

Arrianna threw her head back and gave a loud peal of laughter. When she recovered she simply said, "*Touché*! I am trying to say that I did not know you could feel good and happy and laugh at a service. That it did not have to be a somber and miserable experience. I do not have Seth's hundreds of years of experience and I certainly do not have any more to say, but I do want to contribute to these proceedings..." she paused, "to be honest, mostly because I don't want them to end." She walked in front of the others, several feet further away than Seth had been. She moved the makeshift podium they had constructed out of driftwood and rocks, then closed her eyes, took a deep breath, stretched her arms wide, and began dancing.

Everyone except Seth was surprised. He had after all seen her warming up the day after they arrived. How long ago had that been? Three days? Three weeks? It seemed forever. She looked to be in another place far away, but she was nevertheless conscious of her audience. She remained facing them even after turns and flips. The style was athletic and gymnastic. She vaulted, somersaulted, completed handstands and still was able to combine subtle, soft and slow elements. She looked flawless. Every part of her was in concert with the others. There was no hesitation, no double stepping, no restarts. She continued with her nonverbal devotion with all of them holding their collective breath. Her sense of motion and body was so developed that no one could tell when one motion ended and the next began. The entire ten minute performance appeared to be one continuous flow, with no discernible breaks.

When she finally wound up to an ending, she was standing on one foot with the other crossed in front of her, her outstretched arms slowly bringing her palms together at the center of her chest. She then opened her eyes, focused on her surroundings, and, with only a second's hesitation, returned from whatever inward place she had gone to. She smiled and resumed her seat.

They were awestruck. Each one of them was left speechless by the emotion expressed in her dancing. Then one by one, slowly at first, they stood up and started applauding and cheering. She blushed and hid her face with her hands. The chanting, however, did not cease and she was forced to face them, bow and cry in appreciation. Martha was the first to go up to her, but in no time they were all in one big group hug.

REDEMPTION ISLAND

Around the fire at dinner, she explained "I always wanted to dance. I practiced every day, took as many lessons as I could afford, and entered every competition I could find. My father did not support my interest, thinking it useless and possibly even sinful."

Whenever she would talk of her dance she would become a different person—alive, intense and timeless. This made a sharp contrast to her persona when she mentioned her father. "I suppose he is right. There is no future in dancing. In fact, that is what I was doing on the island; I was at a dance camp for the summer trying to figure out what to do with my life."

Seth and Martha just shook their heads and stared straight ahead, Leesa shivered in surprise and Marc did not understand what was going on around him. *Once again*, he thought, *I am completely out of touch with everyone's body language. What did she do that has everyone in a tizzy?*

Jerry stood up and cleared it up for him. "What is going on? Martha? Seth? Aren't you going to say anything? Leesa, you are in the business, aren't you going to help her? Why is no one saying what is obvious, even to someone like me?" Still no one said anything. Arrianna looked at him, but was confused enough not to be scared. She was simply curious to find out what Jerry was making such a big deal about.

Mike stood up. He had been very quiet since they had arrived at this beach and they were not used to him speaking. "I agree with Jerry. I expected one of you to say the obvious. I must be missing something. Why is no one telling Ari that her father is an unmitigated jerk and that she should follow her heart and become a dancer?"

"Damn straight!" exclaimed Jerry. "I could not have put it better myself. "Look young lady, I don't know your father and I suppose that these good people are reluctant to step on his toes, or usurp his place. However, I have no such compunctions. I am not the most sensitive man, but the dancing you did this morning was not just perfect, it was moving, spiritual even. I can recognize it as a gift. I also saw how much at peace you were while dancing. I would give my right arm for a small piece of that serenity. Don't you dare consider giving it up!" With that he sat back down and started eating his mango.

Seth said, "It's not our place to-"

"I'll be damned if it isn't. She is one of us now. Here she does not have a father, but she has a family. In two weeks we can see what she was put here on earth for. I am not a west coast, new age type of person, but I was deeply moved this morning. It touched me in a way I had not thought possible and helped me accept our situation. I could see what Jerry saw. For the first time since she saw Dan, she was at peace. Now her father, in some misguided sense of parenting, is telling her to become a goddamned secretary or something? And you two are going to stand by and say nothing? I don't get it, I simply don't get it."

Arrianna was now sobbing quietly. She had never received any support from anyone she cared about before. Her father ignored her, her mother was drunk all the time, her other relatives stayed away because of her father's "religion." Now these two dear men that she hardly knew were defending her desire to dance. No, that was not right. They were impelling her to dance, to follow her dream, to be herself. She stood up and went over to Mike and Jerry. She gave each a kiss on the cheek and a quiet "thanks" and she walked away to the church to practice her art and her future.

~~~~~~~~~~

REDEMPTION ISLAND

Immediately after the service ended, they had assigned Jerry to serve as leader during meetings and such. They had to plan their escape. Working together, they came up with various choices.

Now that they were on the nearest shore to civilization, they could light the three distress fires and keep them smoking. The chance of someone seeing the smoke and responding to it was slim, but that became the first project. They had to develop a routine of maintaining the fires under all possible circumstances. This involved gathering the wood and leaves for smoke, watching the fires and watching for ships on the horizon.

They also assigned the job of gathering rocks to spell SOS on an unobstructed stretch of beach. It had to be large enough to be seen from a small plane.

The next plan was to build a raft of better design. The choices here were more difficult. Make it large enough to carry everyone? Or smaller so they could be done quicker and go faster? If so, who would go?" If the strongest and brightest went, it would leave the rest with little help and no hope of mounting their own expedition. If they did not send their best team, then they might not manage to overcome what obstacles came in their way.

They left it to Marc, Mike, and Seth to work out a plan. Marc would look at design with Mike, helping out on the practical aspects of construction. Seth would be liaison and could contribute whatever common sense dictated.

Then there was the more immediate problem of survival. They were fortunate that there were no real animal threats on the island. It was only a matter of water, food, and shelter—in that order. The water source had been secured, but the food only partially. With improved nets they could easily capture as many fish as they could eat, even though cooking them remained a challenge. With their limited utensils, the cook ended up burned and the fish overdone.

REDEMPTION ISLAND

Marc had the additional assignment of searching for a suitable shelter. They no longer had the plane to keep them dry during a rainstorm. They hoped that their boy wonder could dream up something that would serve the same function.

The ladies complained loudly and vociferously that they needed soap. They were sticky and disgusting and each promised anything for a bar of soap. They did not want to hear reason. They cornered the four men and demanded soap as if they were hoarding it. Jerry smiled, shook his head and walked away. Mike said "As far as I know, soap comes from soap plants, wrapped in paper and all."

"Isn't there a plant or root that has soap qualities?" pleaded Leesa.

"Or a fish," demanded Arrianna.

"Or couldn't you make some?" insisted Martha.

"Ladies, ladies, please listen to reason. I am not purposely defying you. It just isn't possible, that's all. We would require all sorts of basic elements that are simply not available on this island. As far as a natural source of soap, if it exists I have never read of it." He pushed his way past them made his way toward Mike and Seth. He found them snickering. "If they hear you, your names will be mud for the rest of our stay."

Seth said, "That is very insightful, Marc. I think you are learning a little about people. Women in particular."

"If we aren't careful, Marc might learn a lot about getting along with women." Mike added.

Marc mustered the courage to ask these two worldly men questions that had always plagued him. He started with, "Do either of you understand women?"

The response was immediate, in unison and as adamant as it was sincere, "NO!" Fortunately for Marc, it did not end there, for the two older men understood that Marc was trying to overcome his

REDEMPTION ISLAND

limitations, so they helped him out and began mentoring him on relationships.

Over the next week, they would continue with their tutoring of Marc. His biggest struggle remained with the lesson that might have been titled. "Women don't always mean what they say."

"In particular, Marc," said Seth one day, "if a woman you are in a relationship with is acting different, moody or whatever, and you ask her what the problem is, and she says something like, 'Oh, nothing.' IT MEANS THE EXACT OPPOSITE. Dig deep, become obnoxious. Make her tell you what the problem is. That is what she will want you to do."

Marc felt that Seth was being ridiculous so he'd gone to Mike with the same question and he had confirmed it. "Absolutely correct! Don't take it at face value. If there was nothing, you wouldn't have asked or she would have told you."

By the end of the week, Marc felt like an utter moron and, for the first time in his life, estimated that he deserved a D in his studies. To his surprise, the two men gave him B+/A- for his efforts. Seth said, "Don't worry. All men feel like morons when they try to figure out women." He paused and added, "But I will tell you a secret. Women have the exact same trouble with men. They can't understand that we actually mean what we say. They are constantly adding imaginary meanings to things."

Chapter Fifteen
Marc to the Rescue

Over the next several days the group remained close, but the strain of being castaways wore heavily on them all. Without exception they were more than ready to be off this "frigging island." They had kept the fires burning, but the three ships that they had seen at a distance paid no heed. A few light planes had flown reasonably close, possibly even near enough to see the SOS, but nothing had come of that either. They found precious little evidence of any regular partying or camping on the beach; a beer can with an expiration date two years old, an old cigarette lighter, and a rust-covered, dented, but still intact, pot. Everything pointed to their salvation being completely and utterly contingent on their own efforts. That was not what any of them had wanted to discover.

Initially they held services daily, but over the ensuing weeks they irregularly attended. Their spirits were diving to a deep low point. They were losing their focus and even Marc was beginning to tire of being so heavily relied upon.

Not the least of the reasons for their emotional doldrums was the numbing invariance of their diet. Even with the addition of fish, there was only one way to cook it and salt as the only spice. Even the most salt-loving of them grew tired of it.

They were all suffering from prolonged exposure to sand, Sun and seawater. Those more prone to keep clean became raw from the increased exposure to water.

By the end of the second week, it was harder and harder to motivate them to keep the fires going. Apparently no one but Marc, Mike, and Seth understood the significance of three fires burning together on an isolated island. Marc explained it away, "We are so close to civilization. It probably does not occur to anyone that we could be marooned here. They probably think we are high schoolers having a good time."

Their only alternative to waiting for fortune to smile upon them was to go and get help, and that meant building a sea-faring raft of some kind. This required, at the very least, two able bodied persons, but optimally three. Mike, of course, would go. Seth agreed to go with him, but no one else wanted to join them. Understandably Martha, Leesa, and Jerry adamantly refused to go. There was absolutely no way they would get on a raft. Marc and Arrianna, although not particularly scared, had little motivation to put themselves at such risk. Neither one had anyone to go back to.

Marc was now a leader, an important member of the community, respected, with his opinion frequently sought out. Arrianna had received more loving attention during their stay here than in her previous 17 years. Martha was not going on the raft, so she saw no reason to separate from her, and if she did not go, then Seth would not go either. She knew all too well that rescue would mean separation from those two. She could hardly bear to think about it. She realized, in fact, that if it wasn't for the lack of soap and the limited diet she would have few major complaints.

REDEMPTION ISLAND

Morale picked up a few notches when Marc managed to manufacture an effective slingshot out of the elastic from Martha's bra. She had almost left it behind at the waterfall, but had been unwilling to pollute such a wonderful spot. Even then he was working on a weapon to bring down some of the birds for meat.

Arrianna and he became the most proficient at stunning the birds with it. Then Seth or Mike would finish the bird off and field dress it for Martha or Leesa to cook. The birds were small with little meat but bird meat was always in high demand.

Marc still had not worked out a solution to their lack of an adequate substitute for rope. At any given time he had from three to five materials under study. Not only did he try other plants or plants in combination, but he was also working on coatings for the fibers. He tried fish oil, coconut oil, and various root extracts. He refused to give his blessing to anything until it had survived in salt water for a week without losing any noticeable strength. It was probably too severe a test, but after their harrowing experience the first time around, no one objected.

~~~~~~~~

Jerry, who was no less depressed than the others, was nevertheless in charge and could recognize a morale problem when he saw it. He was struggling mightily to come up with something dramatic and unexpected to reverse the situation, but so far it was in vain. He had approached Marc and Mike for help, but they also could not come up with anything workable.

The three members most affected and, in some sense leading the group into depression were Martha, Leesa, and Seth. The latter had become morose and uncommunicative recently. It seemed to have started a week or so after the first thanksgiving service. It coincided with Marc's announcement of the summer solstice. It is a rather elementary day to establish, given a stick and a sunny exposure, yet it did no good for the group to realize how long they had already been marooned without being any closer to rescue. Seth had missed some event of importance and he was unable to reconcile himself to it.

Concurrently, he and Martha developed a significant relationship and though no one would refer to it even in their absence. They all felt that they had become intimate. The two of them would disappear for extended periods of time and reappear, clearly emotionally lightened. Normally this would have a very positive effect on both their dispositions, but the synergy of both of them being depressed was intense and deep. Whatever joy and comfort they derived from each other, both physically and emotionally, was not enough to overcome it.

The situation might have stabilized at a level that maintained the functionality of the group, had it not been for their colonic distress. The timing could not have been worse. They were already struggling with the day-to-day necessities when the inevitable consequence of their severely limited diet struck.

Their meager diet, combined with the increasing stress, both physical and emotional, caused them to develop the runs. These were accompanied with intestinal cramps, sometimes severe and debilitating. Work came to a standstill. The latrines were in constant use and new ones were required. There was no paper and cleaning up afterwards, which became an increasingly difficult and sensitive issue. Seth, Martha, and Leesa suffered the worst, Seth being the oldest by far, Martha eating little fish and having a history of colitis to start with, and Leesa, who ate hardly anything at all anyway and refused to eat the meat.

When, a few days after the start of the runs, the rest of the group adjusted and put it behind them, these three did not. The gap in energy level and emotional outlook between them and the other four increased with each passing day. The gap itself became an issue. A split formed. One side complained that the others did not do their share of the work and the understandable counter-complaint was that they did not understand their suffering.

When Mike discovered a large, but localized, patch of pineapple plants, there was a temporary truce while they all enjoyed having not only something new to eat, but something recognizable to their taste buds. Leesa, in particular, improved the most—she apparently enjoyed pineapple and it agreed with her gastrointestinal tract. This lasted as long as the pineapples did. They searched locally to find more, but without success. Unfortunately, each pineapple plant produces one or two of the fruits and then dies. Marc deduced that some time back the top of one of the fruits must have taken root and spread locally. Probably from some picnic.

"How long ago? asked Arrianna.

"I don't know. There were many generations of plants there, but I do not know how long it takes a plant to propagate. Several years at least, possibly many years." Marc replied. He did not notice the look that she had for him and would not have known what to do if he had.

"Could there be more patches around the island?" She continued. She loved to hear him talk and explain things.

"If the people left their pineapple droppings somewhere suitable." He looked at her and realized his mistake. "Oh, you mean from these plants. Could they have spread widely?" She nodded her agreement. "No I think that would be clearly out of the question. They are not propagated by wind or by animals. I think we have eaten all there was, until next year."

"Next year?!" cried Arrianna. "What on earth do you mean?"

REDEMPTION ISLAND

Marc was taken aback by her reaction and managed to murmur, "Just that they produce a fruit a year that's all. What did you think I meant?" The last sentence came out as if a child had said it, scared and uncertain.

"I thought you were trying to tell me that we might still be here in a year."

He smiled and shook his head. He did not voice his conviction that they would either be off the island soon or that they would perish way before even the New Year started. Besides the malnutrition, disease, and emotional and social issues, there were the storms. Without much better shelter than they could hope for they would not survive a bad storm.

By the end of the third week on the windward side, Seth and Martha were in deeper despondency and made no effort to associate with anyone, even each other. Leesa's overall mood had improved, but she started having sudden panic attacks which were coming more frequently. Marc appeared unchanged, but could not deal with the changes in everyone else.

Mike and Jerry fared better than most. 'Nam had unexpectedly prepared Mike well for the current situation, while Jerry had survived a vicious father and the sometimes savage business world. He eventually adjusted to adversity well.

Arrianna, on the other hand, was thriving. She was the only one of the group whose status could be called improved by the desolation. For the first time in her life she did not have a parent holding her back. Her mother had been dead for a while, but her father's co-dependency and incompetence had continued unabated. Here, she was on her own as an adult and finding that she loved it, even if it was in such a desolate place. She had plenty of time to dance, practice her Tai Chi, and she had begun making up dances. Since there was no paper, she was forced to memorize these, but she did not mind.

REDEMPTION ISLAND

During her hours of practice, she would leave the island and live in her own world apart from people, pain, and time itself. As the days went by she increased the time she spent on this to the point where her legs would no longer function.

She felt free for the first time in her short, but largely miserable, life. Her attention turned to the person about her who most stimulated her, Marc. She followed him around asking questions, helping him with whatever he was doing, and eagerly accepting whatever crumbs of attention he gave her. Marc was the only one to miss noticing the significance of her behavior and treated it simply as if she were an exceptionally curious and receptive child.

~~~~~~~~~~

Marc had not mentioned his project to anyone, least of all the ladies, lest it fail and leave them even more miserable. He had not intended it to be a morale booster. He was simply and coarsely trying to make points with Leesa. His logical brain was constantly casting about for something to ease Leesa's misery.

The idea had come to him when they discovered the old rusty pot. The pot was useless as a cooking implement, but he might be able to make some soap. He still did not understand their desperate need for it, but he accepted that it was important to them. The men had told him that, although it was not important to understand women, it was important to accept them, to pay attention to them, to let them know clearly and directly that they are important to you—that you are thinking about them. Do not take it for granted that they know this simply because it was clear yesterday. Each day starts with a clean slate.

He argued "I do not question whether two plus two still equaled four. It had before and, unless something changed drastically, I presume it would remain. Why, then, was it necessary to 'repeat' things all the time? Would they think that I am making fun of them? Or putting them down?"

Mike shook his head in melancholy mirth, Seth threw his hands up in the air with clear disgust and it was left to Jerry to explain. "We have repeatedly told you that relationships are not of a logical realm. Take it as an article of faith that as surely as you need to breathe and drink and eat each and every single day, women need emotional sustenance each and every single day.

~~~~~~~~~~

Marc knew vaguely that to make soap, you need fat, fire, lye and a recipe. The relative mixture he could guess, but he was worried about the results. Soap can come out so harsh that it will burn skin—not the statement he wanted to make. Cleaning Leesa's skin was the goal, not destroying it. He also vaguely remembered that it was possible to improve the soap by adding myriad other things such as vegetable oils, scents and fruits, but had no idea how to go about that. "Well," he told himself, "all you have to lose is your time and energy and you have a relatively unlimited amount of both."

He knew that lye was the chemical Potassium Hydroxide and readily available back in the real world. He thought about it for some time, and decided to attempt to leach it out of ashes. And lo and behold, he had ashes up the wazoo. He would volunteer to remove the huge amounts generated by the three fires. Then he would construct a drip leaching set-up. The water would drip into the ashes and slowly distill through them into his container as fairly concentrated KOH. He had no idea how concentrated it would be and he would have to come up with a way to test it.

REDEMPTION ISLAND

The real limiting factor was going to be the fat. Ordinarily, pioneers would use the hard fat, known as tallow, around the cow's internal body organs. "What was it that guide had said?" He thought deeply and used his highly tuned memory skills to go back to the time he toured the pioneer museum in St. Louis. He had been fascinated by how self-sufficient the pioneers had been. They made everything they needed, or did without. Cheese, butter, preserves, smoked meat, clothes and soap.

He could see the guide clearly now and she was talking about soap. "It's the quality of the fat and the ratio of lye to fat that determines how irritating the soap will be. Back then it was an art form and every batch was different. If the batch came out well, they bathed more frequently, if it came out harsh, hardly at all."

What kind of fat could he obtain? Fish fat, in small amounts, and coconut oil in large amounts. He quickly became the fat-eating machine of the castaways. They even made jokes about it. He had made it clear that if anyone did not want fat, he would take it. He pretended to eat it and gathered as much fish fat and bird fat as he could muster before it became horribly rancid.

On the day of his experiment, he disappeared before dawn. He had intimated to the others that he was bored and wanted to explore. He refused Jerry's company, saying that it would slow him down. He used a shallow cave with a low ceiling he had found on one of his forays. It only went in about fifteen feet and he had to stoop all the time, but it provided shelter and solitude. He slowly added the lye and the smell was abominable. The guide had not shared that little tidbit. He stood at the cave entrance without relief. He tried to acclimate his nose but started gagging. In the end he just endured it and breathed through his mouth as shallow as possible.

The lye worked much better than expected. It was very concentrated and he had obtained huge quantities. Since they constantly generated ashes, he could experiment as long as the fat, and his nose, could hold out. After the fat had more or less dissolved, he started adding the coconut oil. Actually, he added crushed coconut. He told himself that it amounted to the same thing He stirred until his arms fell off and it still did not look like any soap he had ever seen. It did not smell foul anymore, but it did not smell like anything any woman would want to put next to her skin.

He removed the pot from the wood to let it cool down, added a little salt water and cooled it quickly by dipping it into a nearby stream pool. It hissed and spat, but he did not notice. He was depressed, he had had such high hopes and it was an utter failure. *What could I alter? More fat, less lye? Or the other way around? Different kind of fat? Would any of the others know? Maybe I should talk to Seth.*

After all the physical work and emotional burden of the day, he was exhausted. He quickly cleaned himself in the river before lying down and falling asleep. He awoke suddenly as dusk was settling in. He jumped up, and ran to the beach before he could no longer find his way.

"There he is. Goddamn him for scaring us," said Leesa.

"I am sorry I am so late, I went too far and then I got lost." He said it with assurance, but his eyes were fixed on his feet.

Jerry intervened by walking between the two of them. "It's okay, Marc. You are safe and that is what matters. We were just worried about you and had no idea of what to do. Next time you should not go alone. You are way too valuable to us to risk losing you."

"Huh? Okay, I'll let you know if I ever plan to go again." The valuable part, coming from Jerry, had shaken his old, no longer appropriate, view of himself.

"Well?" Seth said pointedly. Marc looked puzzled and did not say anything. "You were gone the entire day, what did you find? Anything useful or interesting? A MacDonald's ready to open? Tell us, Marco Polo. What gems did you bring back with you?" Marc looked around and realized that, except for Martha and Arrianna, who were asleep, all of them were focused on him and waiting.

"Uh, I...well..." He began to sweat and could not come up with a story to save his life. Everything that he thought of sounded ridiculous. *I saw a mountain lion. No, that's not right. It was a seal colony on the other side of the island. No, that makes no sense...*

"If you don't want to tell us, that's okay. We know where we rate," Leesa said and walked away. This time Jerry did not rescue him.

At last he said, "I am so sorry, I have been on my feet without any food for the entire day and I can't think straight. If I could get a piece of fruit and a good night's rest, I will tell all in the morning." To his amazement, they all accepted that and it was Leesa that brought him the food.

"By the way, did you smell something unbelievably foul around mid-morning? We were getting whiffs of it off and on and it was beyond description."

"No, Leesa, I don't think so. Or at least not that I noticed."

"Oh don't worry, you would have noticed this. It is not something any of us is likely to forget." With that, she left him to himself and curled herself up to sleep. Marc looked over at her and wished that his day's efforts had been more fruitful. He so wanted to present her with a bar of soap. It would tell her that he was thinking of her and cared for her. He fell deep asleep before that thought was completed.

~~~~~~~

REDEMPTION ISLAND

He woke up last and they were all waiting without patience, anxious to hear his story. They were children of the modern era and, like their ancestors for millennia, they required entertainment, only more of it. Without his counsel, he had been designated the entertainment for the day. Only then would the group start their work.

Marc was ready. He'd had time with which to become inventive. He related detailed stories of mushrooms large as hats, ant colonies that he had to run away from, another small waterfall with a pond on the far distant edge of his day long trip. "I saw numerous footprints of small animals. I could not identify them, but it seems that this island has more fauna than I had presumed possible." He detailed the stories, describing the tracks and speculating recklessly upon the imaginary creatures that had formed the imaginary tracks.

It took half the morning to relate his story and they were all satisfied and resumed their work. More logs were felled and the rope experiments had yielded one viable source of rope. They were ready to start building the damn raft, even though there still wasn't a crew to man it.

There was a palpable lack of emotional energy, mostly due to no one being in any hurry to go out on the raft and hope for the best. They had all experienced, one way or another, how fast bad things can occur and the thought of drifting endlessly on a raft buffeted by winds, constantly nauseated, and dying of thirst was more than they could bear. Jerry knew that, at this rate, they would never get off before the hurricane season flared into full swing.

~~~~~~~~~~

Hurricanes and tropical storms occur in the Caribbean with great frequency and ferocity. They start mid to late summer and last

REDEMPTION ISLAND

into the fall. Anyone familiar with them can vouch for the ferocity of nature when aroused. Marc, if asked, could have given a few more tidbits of depressing information. That they generate the power of a hundred atomic bombs the size that fell on Hiroshima and Nagasaki, and that a super Hurricane like Camille, that struck August of 1969 in the Mississippi gulf coast, could be many times that powerful.

Sure enough, if they were unfortunate to be out in the sea when one of the huge cyclones came by, they would all be dead, and quickly. The question that should have been on all their minds was whether they had any way of surviving a hurricane on the island. Hundreds of people die in each one. That involves people in developed civilized areas, not small, isolated, remote islands far from shelter or support services.

Mike also knew about these raging storms. He had flown airplanes in the area for years and they kept him out of the air and usually away from home. His job would be to fly as many of the airplanes out of harm's way as possible. He would hire as many pilots as he could find and they would convoy to the mainland and return as many times as necessary or when time ran out. He would fly without sleep, if necessary, to secure the planes which were his love and his livelihood. That he was breaking many of the regulations of licensed pilots bothered him not at all. That he broke many of the common sense rules of the fraternity bothered him much.

~~~~~~~~

It was not until after dinner that Marc was able to excuse himself, presumably to go to the latrine. He was beyond anxious to check the pot and see the outcome. He had come up with ideas to alter the recipe. He even started to collect fat again. He had no idea how he would manage to obtain another day to repeat his experiment, but he was sure he could think of something. Right now he needed to see the results before time changed them. Was it too thin? Too chunky, smelly, insufficiently cooked, overcooked? Too high a temperature? Too low? Without the feedback, he would not be any better off for that entire day's labor.

At that moment Jerry had colluded with Mike to meet out of sight and hearing of the others. The light was fading, but would last another thirty minutes or so. It was Jerry's favorite time of day. He would look at the setting sun, endlessly wondering how he could have ever been so casual about such a splendid event. The size of the sun grew so large, the color deepened and when clouds existed at different altitudes, they would reflect a variety of their own colors. That nerd Marc had attempted to explain the physics behind it all and he had nearly succeeded in taking the magic spectacle out of it.

He would look at the water's surface at the horizon and try not to blink—the changes were that fast and fleeting and wonderful. Each and every sunset was different. Marc said it varied with the humidity, the surface conditions of the water, the cloud dispersal, and the season. Jerry just knew that it was utterly beautiful and that tonight he would have to let it pass unobserved. They were in deep trouble and he had no idea how to fix it.

The underbrush around him rustled and Mike appeared. "Hello, I'm sorry I'm late. Leesa and Martha went on one of their 'I am miserable' jags. Why don't they realize that we are all in the same situation? The squeaky wheel principle does not work here."

REDEMPTION ISLAND

"I know. Thanks for coming. It's exactly this kind of thing that I wanted to talk to you about." He swallowed hard and committed himself. "What do you think of the morale of the group?"

"It sucks big time. There is no morale. Our work output is nil and we are barely managing to sustain ourselves. Even that is only because of the efforts of Marc, the girl and the two of us. I can't say how I appear, I certainly don't..."

"Don't worry about that, I've been watching everyone and your energy level has dropped, but in an expected fashion. The others, however, are in a deep funk."

"Is that the technical term for it?" asked Mike.

Jerry smiled, "Thanks Mike, I need the humor. But you know what I mean. They wander day in and day out hardly getting their meager assignments done. Usually the girl has to pitch in and help them."

"I have a name you know. I am not 'the girl." Both of the men jumped.

"You scared the shit out of me," said Jerry, annoyed.

"Out of both of you by the looks of it. Now what did you call this meeting for? And why did you leave me out of it? Out of the entire group, I am the most productive, energetic and the least demanding."

"That's true," muttered Mike. He looked at Jerry. Had it been lighter, they would have noticed his cheeks reddened. Nevertheless they did not need that visual confirmation to know he felt embarrassed.

"I...ah...well to be honest, I still think of you as a child and it did not occur to me to approach you, also..."

"A child?" she said angrily, "as in someone who depends on others, who cannot take care of themselves, think for themselves, or contribute to the welfare of the group? You mean like the three hopeless, gutless, spiritless cases over at the beach?"

Mike went over and held his hand out to her so she could be closer to them. She had been hiding behind a densely shrouded tree trunk and it could not have been very comfortable. He held her hand and brought her over to Jerry. "She is quite right you know. By her behavior and efforts she acts more like an adult than at least three of the group, perhaps four."

Jerry was biting his knuckle, struggling with himself. He wanted to talk to Mike to see if the two of them could hatch a plan that would bring the group back together. Now it was getting complicated. *Enough!* He told himself. *I eat complications for lunch. It's what I do. What is the matter with me? Are these doldrums of the spirit affecting me as well?* "Miss Arrianna, please excuse my behavior. I am still in the corporate world and I never interact with anyone your age…"

"Please drop the 'Miss' I am just Arrianna, or you can call me Ari, what few friends I have had usually do." It was too dark to be sure, but she thought he was surprised by her invitation to be her friend. "But, there was one other problem, wasn't there? You were about to say something before I interrupted you."

Jerry looked at Mike, who imperceptibly shrugged his shoulders. "Yes, there is. This is not easy for me to say, but I was not sure how you would take a secretive invitation to a late day rendezvous away from the others."

Mike added, "I had similar thoughts. It would be an easily misunderstood situation."

Arrianna looked back and forth from one to the other several times before she understood. "Ohhhhh! I get it." She was quiet for a ten-count, deep in thought. "Yes, I get your dilemma. You ask me to meet you and not tell the others, but it is those others who would be of help if I am worried about your intentions." The men could not see it, but she teared up. She ran to them and gave each an embrace and a kiss on the cheek. "Thanks for being so considerate of me. By not inviting me, I can be sure of your intentions. I have not always had that luxury."

The three of them walked to a place on the surf where they would not be seen. They walked up and down the beach with their feet in and out of the water as the waves rolled in. They bounced ideas about, but had not come up with any solution they liked, when they saw Marc coming out of the trees moving toward camp. He was walking fast and had not seen them. Arrianna ran up to him, which scared him silly. "I'm sorry, I didn't mean to do that, but it must be my night to scare men. Come, Jerry and Mike are over here and we are plotting to overthrow the government." Without a word, he followed her and was actually surprised to find that indeed the two men were there and they were actually plotting something.

Mike was the first to notice that Marc was carrying something. "What's that you're trying to hide?"

"What? Are you talking to me?" Marc tried vainly.

"Yes, Mr. DeNiro, you. What is it you have behind you?" This had the other two interested and they outflanked him and took it out of his hands.

"That's mine! You have no right to take it. Give it back."

Mike handed a piece to Jerry even as he and Arrianna were turning it over, feeling it and trying to figure it out. The shapes were irregular and rough, but it was not a hard substance, somewhat creamy, soft, and smelled of coconut. It was that last thing that clicked for Arrianna. "I got it! It's soap! You beautiful, wonderful man. I love you! You have made soap! Does it work?" She was right on top of him, mere inches away from his face, all thought of personal space gone. He was stuttering with the intensity of her questions. "Well does it?"

"Yes, it works fine. However..." He never finished the thought. She jumped at him and laughed and cried and hugged him. She gave him a hard kiss across the lips before she managed to get a hold of herself. She backed away only slightly. Still smiling, she held onto Marc with her arm while turning the soap over in both hands. It was clear to all three men that attempting to take the soap away from her would be tantamount to suicide.

"I am sorry. I got a little carried away. It's just that I had given up on ever being clean again, and this was such a surprise. How in the world did you manage it?" The question hit home with the other men and the three of them faced him. He had no hesitation in telling them. After all, he was still reeling from the kiss. He had never had a girl, no, a woman, ever react to him with that joy, passion and raw energy. He found that he rather liked it.

"You sneaky bastard," said Mike. Arrianna was pacing with the anticipation of getting washed up in the morning. She even considered trying to find fresh water tonight but quickly dismissed the thought.

"You know, if you don't have enough for all the women you will cause a riot," Arrianna said calmly. "And if that is the case, I want all of it, every last bar."

"Really?" Jerry and Marc said together.

"Yes, really. It is one of the two most difficult things of being here. At least for us. We feel grimy, sticky, and dirty. I can only imagine what we smell like. I have almost come to terms with it, but the others haven't, and it is bringing them down." She looked at them and the moon's reflection on their faces revealed blankness. "Come on now, a girl likes to be clean and feel that she looks and smells nice. Not like some derelict in a ditch who hasn't bathed in a month."

"That's it!" shouted Jerry. "We've been trying to come up with a way to help their morale, and this is it. We just have to think about how to best present it." He thought a few seconds, "But first, how much is there? Is there enough for everyone? Can you make more? Will it go quicker with our help?

Marc was more in control of himself now, "There is plenty made, more than enough for everyone. The amount is limited only by the available fat. As for..."His last sentence was lost in the roar of laughter from the other three.

"So that's what the fat was for! You sneaky bastard."

After the laughter had died down, he continued. "As far as your help, it will make things easier, if you can stand it. The smell is horrible beyond description."

Arrianna stood there with her jaw open as she realized what he was saying. "So that foul smell that would drift in and out, that abominable, indescribable smell was actually you making this? You endured that smell?"

Marc simply nodded. She once again went up to him and kissed him hard. Just before disentangling herself, she said to him, "Thank you Marc. Thank you very much."

Jerry changed the subject and asked Arrianna. "What is the other thing?"

"Other thing? What do you...oh, you mean the other difficult thing?" Jerry nodded. "It is the monotony of the food. Fruit, fish, fruit, fish, sometimes a bird, when we can get one. It has worn us all down, and Martha thinks that the lack of nutrients has already started its effect."

The four conspirators continued talking and broke up just before midnight with their plan ready for the earliest rays of the morning sun. Marc and Arrianna would leave at first light and collect as much of the soap as they could manage. They would then meet everyone at the waterfall pond that the hiker's had discovered.

REDEMPTION ISLAND

No one would tell the others about the soap until they were there. They wanted the surprise to be intense so as to hopefully shock them out of their lethargy. With all due speed and any luck they would reach the pond by mid-morning. However, they had not counted on human nature.

Chapter Sixteen
Intimacies

The two travelers arrived at dawn. She had woken him as the sky was barely lightening. She had pushed harder and faster than him and it should have been obvious that her intentions were not to simply pick up the soap and take it with them. However, he had never been good at reading other peoples' feelings and intentions and, although he was making real progress on the basics, this situation was more along the line of graduate level studies.

They arrived at the site in record time. He went right over to the pot and started to scrape the soap out and into the containers they had brought. He was studiously concentrating on his task and did not notice right away that Arrianna was no longer next to him. She was out of sight. "Now where in the world did she go?"

He knew she was not lost, and he wasn't worried, but was irritated that she would take this time to look around and explore. They had work to do and a timetable to keep. Jerry and Mike had been adamant about making the best time possible, so they would reach the waterfall quickly and spend as much time there as possible. He was almost done getting the soap out. Now he would have to go looking for her.

He stood up and now he could just see her. She was forty yards away, sitting in a shallow pool formed by the stream. There were suds all around her... She had gotten a bath! He sighed and went over to tell her it was time to go.

She waved at him, clearly enjoying herself and showing no intention of leaving. He placed their cargo down carefully on the path back to the beach and went over to pull her out of the water. Her hair was smooth and straight and silky. Her skin was glowing and she was clearly ecstatic. At the very same instant that she stood up, he noticed her clothes draped over the bushes to dry.

He stood rooted, completely unable to move. This was different than the time they had accidentally stumbled onto Martha bathing. She was much older, they thought her dead, and there was no way they could have known. Here he should have figured she would not take a bath with her clothes on. It had been her matter-of-fact attitude that confused him. She had shown no concern when he saw her. She had made no move to hide, turn her back, or in any way suggest he should go away or at least not look. On the contrary, from the outset she had waved for him to join her, just as one might do at a pool. No one had been this immodest around him before, not by a mile.

He did not know what to do. His mind was racing but unable to come up with a plan of action. It would not have mattered, as his brain was no longer in control of his actions. They were only three feet apart and he could not take his eyes off her. Her body, that is. And to his astonishment, she did not seem to mind. In fact, she looked like she was enjoying his admiration. She had her beautiful raven colored hair now wet and clean and hanging down to her shoulders. Her face he was familiar with and he skipped that to see the contours of her chest, hips and legs. The loose clothes she wore had hidden how remarkably developed her body was. In this particular arena, she was not some young half grown child but a fully developed woman. His reaction was as predictable as it was inevitable. He was overwhelmed with helplessness. He knew that his normal course of action was to turn around and back off, but his feet would not move and his brain could not convince his body (at least a certain part of his body) that she was not an adult. What he failed to realize was that the definitions he was using were mixed. For millennia girls became women at the onset of menses, then married, had babies and enjoyed all the rights of womanhood, as meager as they were at the time. It was only in the past hundred years that physical maturity did not coincide with social maturity.

He was scared, not knowing what to do and flustered by this seductive being in front of him. Her breasts were on the small side, but he preferred them that way. She was of athletic build with narrow hips and long slender legs. He just stood there and gaped, until she walked out of the water and came over to him. She grabbed his hand, pulled him into the water, started undressing him and began to wash him with his own soap. After he was clean, she began kissing him softly and longingly.

~~~~~~~~~~

Mike woke at dawn and was not surprised to see that the two kids were already gone. The way the girl went on about the soap, he knew she would be off at the first hint of light. He woke the rest of them and told them they had a change of plans today. They were going on a short hike and there would be a surprise at the end.

Jerry was anxious to get going and reveal the discovery. He crossed his fingers repeatedly compelling this event to snap the three people around him out of their doldrums. They need to be excited, full of energy, willing to take risks, or they would never get off this infernal island. One big push was all it would take to get them ready to go for help. For the first time in decades, he prayed.

They gathered what they would need and started for the waterfall. Jerry was in the lead, since, aside from Martha, he was the only one in the group who had been there. They expected it to take just over an hour at this pace and he hoped that everyone could keep up.

Martha was becoming animated by the prospect of returning to that wonderful place where she had relaxed. What had happened to that person? Could she summon her back or was she gone forever? Or was it a figment, a delusion of someone who was thinking she was about to die? If it had been real, why was she now so miserable and hopeless? Could she simply will herself better? To act as if she felt better and then, *Presto*, she would feel that way?

She could imagine herself there, in the cool water relaxing and cavorting with the rest of them. The spray from the waterfall tingling over her body, the fresh water cleansing her from the physical and emotional poisons of the torturous past three weeks. Would she once again find peace, comfort, and acceptance in her fate, whatever that turned out to be? Or would she be able to find hope? That seemed beyond imagining. She could not recall how that particular feeling tasted. Her pace abruptly quickened and, since she was the slowest member of the group, their pace increased proportionally.

As she walked and her muscles protested and ached, she forced her thoughts back to the waterfall, the pond and the luscious invigorating spray, plus their profound effect on her body and spirit. The picture in her mind of the four of them swimming and drifting, unaware that anything else existed. Perhaps that was what Eden had been like. Complete all by itself. The present moment all that there was. No worries, no anxieties, no depression—nothing but that moment, those people and that place.

She remembered being discovered and smiled. At the time it had not mattered that she had been seen naked. However, over time it came to bother her tremendously and she avoided those people. Had that started the spiraling downward course into her malaise? Or had it been the immeasurable weight of the colitis with its concomitant diarrhea? Both? No matter and no longer. She was now more embarrassed about being weak of mind and heart and that others had to support her. "Me, of all people. Ms. Tough Independent Adventurer. I have never been a burden to anyone and I refuse to be one now." The last sentence was emphatic and unintentionally came aloud. Seth was next to her and he was the only one to hear. She gave him a radiant smile and walked right past him.

Who had thought of going there? Whoever it was deserved a medal. She knew that a malaise had crept over them and this was probably just the thing to break it up. Already before they arrived she felt better, revived somehow; alert and observant. She noticed the riotous colors of the flowers abundant around them. Yesterday she would have dismissed them as irrelevant. Now they were a gorgeous affirmation of His presence in the world. She must not let herself get that way again. More than that, it was her duty to contribute to the group in a way that would keep their spirits up. What could she do? She resolved to come up with something by the time they arrived.

Leesa was beyond caring about anything. She was horribly depressed and apathetic. These were not new emotions to her and in some way she felt comfortable with them. She marveled at how she had lived most of her life that way. Until a doctor somewhere talked her into taking those little pills—*Zoloft*—"son of *Prozac*," was what she called them. And *Voilà*! her chronic depressions vanished. She had been on the pills for years now and had not given it much thought until she ran out. She had been furious with herself for not carrying more, but who could have possibly anticipated this?

To aggravate the situation, she felt useless. Everyone else seemed to have some skill that was useful to the group. Her acting and modeling skills were not in great demand here and even if they were, it would be so hard to perform without props, makeup and costumes. *For God's sake we do not even have a fucking bar of soap to get the oils and dirt off me.*

She knew that feeling the part, feeling pretty and clean and made-up went a long way for her to actually be pretty. She was not one of those actresses that can turn their craft on and off with the blink of an eye. She had started as a model and worked hard at acting lessons to become adequate. Well, at least good enough to get small parts as often as she wanted. It still required concentration for her to do her best. Jesus! How she hated feeling this way. She just had to get a hold of herself. They had described the waterfall and pool, and if it turned out to be half as great as Martha said, maybe that would be enough to jump-start her back into reality and life.

Seth had gone into a fugue weeks ago. When Marc announced that it was already the summer solstice, June 21st, it shook him more than he'd expected. The information he carried had a deadline and it had run out. It would no longer matter to anyone since it had already happened. The risks he had taken. The joy at obtaining it and the wonderful anticipation at having that debt of honor repaid! All gone now. Not only that, they thought him dead. He could not even go back and try again. He further realized they might not get off the island at all. Something would overcome them; illness, malnutrition, a bad storm. He remembered what it had been like when sixty mile an hour winds came upon them in the South Pacific. The devastation done by the gusts was terrible. Trees down everywhere and, for those without shelter...they never did find the bodies—washed out to sea, they supposed. If a hurricane, even a very weak one, grazed their island, there would be nowhere to hide. And the season was about to start.

Mike and Jerry's spirits were running high. For some unexplainable reason the old lady, Martha, was pushing hard and, instead of slowing them down, was actually increasing their pace. She looked better, more alive, smiled more. It was already happening! Wait until they saw the soap! They led the way and started chatting to themselves out of hope-fueled energy. "Do you think they will be there ahead of us?" asked Mike.

"They better fucking be." They had a huge head start and can travel far faster than us. If they aren't, it's because they continued fooling around."

Mike did a double take, "You mean—"

Jerry snapped back, "Of course I mean that. They might look at the surroundings and possibly explore a bit, but if they aren't there when we arrive, it won't be because they got lost or the scenery was too pretty. It will be because her scenery and his competence were too much to ignore." As an aside he added, "I don't know if you noticed, but it seems that women, unlike men, are attracted by successful, competent men and not so much by looks."

Mike nodded absently and added, still shaken, "Did you know this when we decided who would go?"

Jerry looked at him curiously, "What's the matter? Marc won't force her. If anything, she will probably have to force him, if it came to that."

Mike pondered that for a while and finally nodded his head and smiled, "Yes, I suppose you're right. I keep thinking of how young she is, but in most ways she is far more mature than he is."

"Damn straight. That girl is like no one I have ever met younger than thirty. Her emotional intelligence must be off the charts. On the other hand, Marc's EI is only now entering the measurable range. Besides, she wanted to be treated as an equal—as an adult, actually. So…that's exactly what I did. If you want to feel worried about someone, you should consider that poor, clueless bastard Marc. He will never know what hit him."

Chapter Seventeen
The Soap Festival

They did not see anyone when they arrived and Jerry had an anxious moment or two before Mike found the soap. "Look, over here. They have cut it and laid it out for us."

Jerry looked over and had to touch the stuff before his worry and anger faded. "Good, they made it and are probably looking about. Quickly, find something to lay over it so I can make a show of announcing it." Mike started pulling elephant leaves while Jerry looked to see how far back the rest of the group was. Unexpectedly, it was Seth who slowed them down. He could not really fault him because he was a good twenty or more years older than the rest of them. He heard them before he saw them. They were trampling through the underbrush and making a low-level chatter.

"Mike? Jerry? Can you hear us? Seth is going to need a break. We are pushing him too hard." It sounded like Martha's voice but with the dense jungle absorbing most of the sound energy it was hard to be sure.

"Over here, we made it. Take a look, Seth, and you can rest as long as you want."

The trio broke through cover and they all gasped at the sight. *It is still marvelous* Martha thought to herself.

Leesa had not seen anything so intensely beautiful, at least not without a house or two built up on it. She had not realized how much that detracted from the beauty. The shielded waterfall with its corresponding pond was carefully and fully framed in a cacophony of multi-hued greens. The various levels of shading and sunlight, combined with the multiplicity of shapes and the lines of the foliage, resulted in a sense of infinite detail. That it was actually there and not a picture added the three-dimensional effect that could not be duplicated even with the remarkable cinematography she lived with. The sounds of the birds and insects on top of the water sounds added a fourth dimension of reality.

Jerry broke into their trance. "Contrary to what you may think, this is not the surprise we promised you." Only Martha looked at him. The others gave no indication of having heard him. Martha touched the other two and they looked up and gave Jerry the attention he was seeking. "Mike will tell you all about it."

Mike had not been briefed and he fell silent trying to formulate the words. As Jerry passed by to stand behind him, he whispered "You would have worried too much about the announcement so I didn't tell you."

"Yes, well it seems that our inestimable professor has done it again. I think that you will agree with me that this is an accomplishment of the highest order and that proper thanks are due to him." He looked about him, "At least when he shows up."

"Get to it!" demanded Leesa, "Or I will let you go on while I cool off in that water and try to get some of this sweaty slime off me." Martha and Seth both nodded absently even as they started walking toward the water.

REDEMPTION ISLAND

Mike was flustered, but recovered quickly, "That's exactly what I'm trying to tell you. It will be so much easier to clean ourselves now, because Marc has somehow made soap." He knew that the two women would be excited, but their reaction was out of proportion to his expectations. The first thing that happened was the two screams that merged together in such an intensity and high pitch that he was struck backwards a step. Next, the two women seemingly attacked him, demanding to know where it was and to turn it over immediately.

Jerry had anticipated this and had the chunks of soap ready in his hands. The two ladies grabbed the biggest pieces and ran off to the water. He vaguely noticed that they did not take the time to find cover before starting to undress. They began peeling off clothes immediately and continued as they walked into the water.

Mike was smiling as he watched the two ladies enjoying themselves immensely with the soap, clearly luxuriating in it. He had not seen them so happy since they landed. This had indeed been a good idea, and it struck him that Marc was still such an enigma—talented and stupid at the same time.

"Is there any more left?" asked a clearly deferential Seth.

"Yes of course, there is enough for everybody and more. Besides, he can always make more," Jerry said, noting the other's demeanor.

"Thank you sir, thank you very much. If it would be all right with you then, I will go over and wash up." Seth turned with gaze averted and began walking to the shore.

Jerry caught up with him and would have grabbed his arm had it not been for Mike's interference. "Let him be a while and see if he can work it out." When he saw the uncomprehending look on Jerry's face he added, "Back in 'Nam, right after Tet, we had legions of men with that look about them. We had been fighting nonstop for days, not sure if we were getting anywhere, losing buddies at an atrocious rate. Then it was over so quick. There was little time to get acclimated to the new situation. It seemed like the mind needed to revisit the past to believe it was real. I don't know where he has gone, but I can tell you it was someplace very bad."

Jerry was dubious, "Are you a shrink part time?" It came out wrong, like a challenge or sarcasm, but it didn't matter which because either way he did not like it. "I am sorry, I did not mean it that way, I meant—"

"I know what you meant. I was not one of the walking wounded, but many of my buddies were and I worked with the shrink to try to find a way to help them. What we found out, the hard way mind you, was that it was very bad to try to force them into the present. It was best to give them a little time to work it out themselves. Most of them did."

Jerry nodded. He wasn't sure about it, but it was easier this way and they had time to burn. Besides, he felt sticky and grimy and wanted to use his fair share of that soap. He nodded to Mike, who threw him a chunk. They both stripped to their shorts before going into the water, where they finished undressing.

The seven of them luxuriated in their warm, soapy, cleansing bath. The bubbles from the soap did not last as long as commercial soaps did, but then again it was completely organic and would not hurt the environment. They were each in their own world, almost oblivious to the others. Their lack of swimsuits fretted none of them as they cavorted in and out of the water.

~~~~~~~~~

"Are you ready?" asked Arrianna.

"Uh, yes. But do you think it's a good idea?" fretted Marc.

"It's like I told you already. It will scare the shit out of them, including Mike and Jerry. Whether they know it or not, those two also need a good shock to their system to snap out of this malaise we're all in."

Marc smiled, "You certainly knew how to snap me out of mine." He unintentionally blushed and looked down.

Arrianna turned to face him. She lifted his head, looked directly into his eyes, "It snapped both of us out of it. It was your soap that did the trick, mind you. It feels good to a woman to feel clean. It is impossible to feel pretty without that. You helped me feel even prettier." Neither spoke for minutes as they recalled the events of that morning. Marc did feel better in some indescribable way, more relaxed—better able to focus on life and less preoccupied with his interactions with women. It was as if he was no longer hungry and could pay attention to other things.

"OK then, let's do it." With that they both jumped into the pond just next to the waterfall from the overhanging promontory they had discovered while waiting for the others. It was at least a fifteen-foot fall through a thin screen of leaves. To the others it would look like they had just fallen out of the sky.

To say the others were stunned, shocked, and amazed would be to understate the situation dramatically. As to how many may have actually wet themselves, well, they were all in the water and no one was talking. When the two divers surfaced, they were greeted with wordless open-mouthed expressions that started them laughing uproariously. That became contagious and the entire group began laughing deeply. Even Seth joined in after a minute. The group was well on its way to resolving its emotional and mental health issues. Although they did not know it, from that moment on they were bonded as few people ever are. Further, none of them felt like they would need to return to that place of malaise that had overcome them.

REDEMPTION ISLAND

~~~~~~~~~

They swam up to the others and showed them how to get to the promontory and, in no time, all but Seth and Jerry were jumping and carrying on like adolescents. It did not escape the notice of the castaways that it was the youngest two of the group who had provided the needed stimulus for them to "snap out of it." Particularly that it was the youngest who'd shown the most energy and emotional resources and had been so instrumental in keeping them going. What happened to that strange persona she showed earlier?

Eventually, they had enough of the cleansing ritual and finished washing their clothes. They had jumped until they could no longer climb to the ledge and one by one they dragged their tired, but spiritually renewed, bodies to the shore.

That night they camped by the shore. Not one of them wanted to return to the beach and their problems that day. As it turned out, they would not leave for several days, when their need for rejuvenation was overcome by their increased and equally intense determination to get off this island "paradise."

~~~~~~~~~

Seth returned to his normal self. Now seated next to the others, he felt the need to explain. "If you would all grant me a few of your precious minutes, I would like to tell you a story." All of them looked up, interested in anything that promised to be entertaining.

He went on to describe his life after the war. He had a wife and two children by then, a girl Ali and a boy Ari. They were all emaciated. There was devastation everywhere and there were no jobs for anyone, much less a Jew with accounting skills. He resorted to doing anything to get food for his family. Some days he and his wife went hungry, but usually it was just his wife. She insisted, saying that if he did not remain strong, he would be unable to obtain even the meager rations he managed.

It became winter quickly and their situation became desperate. There was less and less that he could gather in the fields or the barns, most people were going hungry, and homeless people like him were starving. Out of desperation, he was going to upgrade from simple theft to actually mugging for whatever he could get.

That was when the young, determined men came and made him a proposition. They were Zionists and were trying to give birth to the country that would become Israel. To this end, they needed bodies, Jewish bodies, and as many as they could get over there. They were up front with him that it would be perilous, but he jumped at it. They fed his children and his wife. Then, when they discovered his skills, they gave him work—tracking and recording people instead of money—and therefore adding meaning to his life. But most of all they restored his family's hope. The first thing they did on arriving at the camp was to receive a bar of soap that they all took turns using while getting the first bath they had in months.

"So you see, when Mike gave me that soap, I regressed to that time and place of hopelessness, despair and acquiescence. It was this young lady's unconventional entrance into the pool and her smiling face that brought me back to the present. It's not true that you can't go back. It's just that it is not wise to do so."

There were few dry eyes by the time he was finished. He was, they discovered, a natural storyteller. He had them leaning forward afraid to miss the next word. He would lower his voice to place an emphasis. He became the story and they were all transported forty-odd years back in time and felt what he had felt so long ago.

REDEMPTION ISLAND

His confession acted as a catalyst and many in the group shared of themselves, further bonding them. For many, this was by far as emotionally close as they had ever been to another person. The joy and peace that usually accompanies that filled them, and they all drifted into a restful dream filled sleep—the first, but not the last, they would have on their island home. In that way the first day of their Soap Festival ended.

~~~~~~~~~~

The following days were a continuation of the celebration. The worries and anxieties they had brought with them were temporarily on hold, placed in suspended animation. Marc and Arrianna did not repeat their intimate encounter by mutual unspoken agreement. They both felt that it had been an aberration. It was nothing that they regretted, but not something they needed to repeat just to prove that.

It was Martha and Seth who began their real physical intimacy there. They found in each other what they had missed since their widowhood started. They hung about each other constantly, the way older couples tend to. This, of course, was evident to all the others. That they would drift away to be by themselves went unnoticed only by Marc.

Marc now had much more attention than he knew how to handle. Leesa had made it clear "I am grateful, very grateful for his efforts at soap making. That if there is anything I could do in return I will be only too happy to oblige."

He was, of course, blown off his emotional feet by this and was unable and unwilling to act on it. He erroneously felt that his time with Arrianna was a closely guarded secret only the two of them shared. He needed not only physical privacy, but emotional privacy as well. The thought that the others would know what they were up to and their looks on his return caused an embarrassment within him that left him limp.

Late that day, Arrianna and Marc were trying to count the number of days the group had been stranded on their island home. They had not kept a log nor, like Robinson Crusoe, made notches on a log to keep track. Therefore there was an error of several days. They each remembered it differently and on checking with the others found that out of seven people they had four differing accounts. It ranged from five weeks, three days to six weeks even. They took the middle number and began calculating the actual date. It was then that Arrianna screamed.

"It's my birthday! I am now eighteen years old. I can't believe it's my birthday!"

The rest of them stopped whatever they were doing and turned to sing *Happy Birthday* to her. She reveled in the attention and admitted that it was the happiest birthday she's ever had..

On the second day, they discovered Seth's secret. He was now a well–respected accountant who did freelance work for international companies. He had an intimate knowledge of the many subtle differences in accounting procedures used by the various countries in the Mediterranean and he would be brought in to prepare reports for a variety of investors, customs agencies, and the like. During his last job, they started him working on one particular subdivision of a French conglomerate. He had only just started when one of the principals of the company happened to drop by to look around. That is when something very odd happened. The atmosphere at the company's corporate offices was relaxed and generally jovial. That remained so when the visit occurred, until the principal was introduced to him. Actually it was a little later when the principal absently asked what job he performed there.

REDEMPTION ISLAND

When he was told that Seth was auditing the books of the company, his face changed. The man dropped his guard only for a few seconds, then recovered and left abruptly. "But," Seth added, "in those few seconds I saw it all: the shock, disbelief, the fear and then the horror. Had it ended there I probably would have simply attributed the behavior to anti-Semitism. But the very next day, before I could even get into my office, I was summoned and assigned to a different subsidiary altogether, at an embarrassing raise in salary."

"Why on earth would they do something like that?" asked Arrianna.

"They had something to hide," volunteered Jerry.

Seth nodded, "That was my question exactly young lady. And Jerry's answer was my own as well. I went further and asked myself what it was about me in particular that had so alarmed, even terrified him."

"Was it that you are Jewish?" asked Marc in a no longer rare example of intuition.

"What else could it be? He had not known of me before that. My name is not particularly Jewish, but my appearance is very definitely so." He saw the look on the faces of Martha, Leesa and Mike. "I know, I know, I am saying that you can tell a Jew by his cover. That is not so politically correct these days, but it is true some of the time and definitively accurate in my case."

Martha spoke up, "You've told me how you make an effort to appear Jewish, that you are proud of your heritage. So it really isn't that much of a surprise that he could tell, is it?"

"No, dear Martha it is not. But you can see what was going through my mind. As you now are aware, I have felt a debt of honor to those men who rescued my family and me by taking us to Palestine, now Israel. My mind told me that here was the chance I had been waiting for my entire life. If I could only find out exactly what the secret was."

"So you went to Israel's French embassy and reported this?" ventured Jerry, not at all sure.

"No, I did not. First of all, my immediate supervisor was embarrassed beyond words. He is a good man and had hand-picked me for the job and I could tell he did not know why this was happening, but he could guess as well as I. Against orders, he let me gather my papers and belongings in private. I used the time to download the detailed records I was about to oversee onto a thumb drive. I did it on impulse, and I wasn't at all sure what I was going to do with them."

Everyone was by now sensing a mystery and eager to hear the ending. "So what did you do?"

"Yeah, can you cut to the chase?" agreed Leesa.

Seth startled as if just now aware what he had been telling them. "Oh, I suppose it doesn't matter. It is too late anyway." He paused to collect his thoughts and no one said anything. "I went home and thought about it all night. I think I was going to go straight to Israel and find someone who would give it the attention it needed, however..." this time the pause was only for effect, "...however, when I left my apartment, I noticed a car with two men who were watching me. At least that is what I thought. So I drove a convoluted route to the Louvre, just as if I had missed a turn or two on my way over. They stayed behind me all the way there."

Martha's face showed concern and her hand reached out to his. He held it, kissed it, and continued. "That was when I decided to find out more about this before I turned it in. I actually feared for my life those first few days. I flew to New York City and became a tourist for a while. When I no longer felt watched, I booked my flight to this forsaken part of the world, which is where my new assignment was."

Mike spoke up in his typically understated way, "They sure as hell sent you to the middle of nowhere. This is as far as you could get from civilization, the Middle East or anyone who knows anything about it."

"Exactly right. So I slaved over the disks and saw ledgers of purchases and sales of strange-sounding equipment. I made a list of the few items that I could not find referenced anywhere as well as the companies they bought them from and I went searching. I finally found an expert who would talk to me confidentially."

"For a fee I am sure," added Jerry matter-of-factly.

"Yes, of course, but you have to expect that if you want secrecy. Anyway, he looked at the list of materials and the companies and he told me to return in a day."

"Weren't you scared?" asked Martha?

"I wouldn't have returned," said Mike.

"Yes, but you are hearing it as a story compressed into a few minutes. I lived it, unraveling it slowly. I wasn't expecting foul play. The guy, although gruff in appearance and manner, was true to his word. He had spent the day checking his conclusions."

"Enough with the Sherlock routine already. Can we now have the chase scene? What were they up to?" Leesa complained.

"The proper question is 'what *are* they up to?' I looked at the list of clients the company had and it only fit one way. The materials as a whole had only one conceivable use. They were helping the Iraqis build a nuclear device at the nuclear reactor in Osirak."

There was a few minutes silence while they all digested it, after which Marc voiced the remaining questions. "When did you find this out and how does it tie in to us, to this time frame?"

Seth looked exhausted. The telling of his secret to them had unburdened him, but at the same time it had required a large expenditure of emotional energy. He sat next to Martha and let her rub his shoulders as he leaned forward with his hands covering his face. "OK, that is the last part. I had suspected this all along, but I needed proof before I could present this to the Israeli government. I received his confirmation two nights before our flight. I spent the next day copying records and hiding them. They are probably still where I left them the night before our trip. I was going straight to New York to meet a Rabbi I know, and together we would go to the embassy. He was expecting me and he knew the general reason for the urgency. I can't imagine what he thought when I did not arrive. As far as the time urgency, well, his best estimate was that given the type of instrumentation being requested, they were probably one or two months from completion."

"So there is still time then?" asked Jerry.

"No, there isn't. It was from the time of delivery and the scheduled delivery was two months ago last week. Israel may well have a nuclear Iraq to deal with now."

They all understood. Why he had tried to get a message out when the plane was going down. Why he had become morose when they calculated the actual date, and why he was now crying with his head on Martha's shoulder while she stroked his hair and made futile efforts to reassure him.

~~~~~~~~~~

It was on the third morning of the Soap Festival that it ended. It was becoming clear to all of them that they were in deep trouble and that they could not continue for much longer. They held a war council to discuss their options.

Jerry summarized, "So we are all in agreement that we need to make every effort to get off the island as soon as possible?" There were nods all around. "We are very short of time, so we should try to get off within days."

Marc asked, "Why so fast? Are you concerned about the hurricane season? It has already started, you know."

Mike added, "Yes, but it is still early in the season and we still have time. We don't need to rush unprepared." Most of the others nodded their agreement. It did not escape Jerry's notice that Martha was the only holdout. He waited to see if she would speak. She seemed about to but then stopped herself.

Jerry prompted, "Martha what do you think?" She was clearly surprised to be singled out like that, but after a few seconds of pantomiming "me?" She stood up and broke their equanimity.

"We don't have much time. Certainly not weeks, probably only days before—"

"Before what?" demanded Leesa and Arrianna jointly.

"Before we begin getting sick and are unable to help ourselves." She looked at their faces and saw that Mike and Jerry understood. However, the others were not getting it. She would have to be blunt. "Leesa could you stand up here with me so that everyone can see you?" While Leesa was dubiously acquiescing, Martha noted that Jerry had a very self-satisfied smirk on his face. "That little creep. He is letting me do his dirty work for him," she told herself. Leesa joined her and Martha took her hand in both of hers, "Please don't worry, you are all right, it is just most obvious on you, that's all."

She then had her turn her back on the group and remove her blouse. She pointed to the brown, irregular spots on her back, to the way that the skin had no luster and how it flaked at places. Then she pointed to the prominence of her ribs. Finally she turned her around, after having her replace her blouse, and pointed to her prominent belly.

REDEMPTION ISLAND

"She's pregnant?" a startled Marc blurted out to his immediate embarrassment.

"No Marc, she's not pregnant, at least not as I'm aware." She said this as if to a particularly dense child.

Leesa asked "What then is the matter with me? I have always shown ribs, it is part of being a model and actress—"

Martha interrupted her, "Not like this you haven't. I saw you when we first arrived. Sure you were a bit thin and, if you stretched, I could make out some of your ribs, but my dear, this is a significant change. Also, there are the other signs."

"Signs? Signs of what? What's the matter, I feel fine. In fact I haven't felt this good in days."

"Malnutrition." This was forcefully said by Jerry. He had been patiently awaiting his opening. "Leesa does not eat the fish we catch. She is a vegetarian and, although she eats a slightly inadequate amount of calories, her deficiency in vitamins and protein is huge. That is why she has the disproportionate belly. The skin changes are related to a B vitamin deficiency and we are all subject to that. Our diet is insufficient to fully support us and very soon our immune systems will not be up to the task. We will have no way to heal when illness strikes. Also, even though we may not realize it and cannot feel it, our strength and energy levels are likely much lower than when we rowed over here. Eventually we will not have the physical resources to crawl, much less paddle our way off the island."

They sat still and silent for a long time. This was fine with Jerry who wanted them to stew on what he had said for a good long while. They were emotionally ready. He had just provided the motivation necessary for them to make that final push to get off the island. He took his job very seriously indeed and now that the morale problem had been dealt with, the next step was to focus on their final objective—getting off this fucking island!

Chapter Eighteen
Escape Plans

The trip back to the beach was as full of energy and life as the one going there had been devoid of both. They sang hiking songs, silly songs, and funny songs. They told jokes and threw out riddles. They asked Marc repeatedly how he had made the soap and cringed at the ingredients required, amazed that it could turn out soft, white, and coconut-scented. Leesa, in particular, had difficulty believing there were fish parts in it. "Just the fat from the fish." Marc clarified. It did not help her accept the proposition.

Marc smirked, "If your vegetarian sensibilities are upset, you don't have to use it. I'm sure that Martha and Arrianna will take your share."

Martha interjected, "Leave me out of it."

"Me too," said Arrianna. But after a pause, "He's right though. If you don't want to use it, I will gladly take it off your hands."

There was snickering throughout the group. The way that Leesa clutched her soap, you would think it was the crown jewels.

Leesa paused a second before replying, "That's quite all right.

It's not like I am going to eat it or anything. I just can't quite see how fish are involved in the making of this oh-so-wonderful stuff."

Marc said, "Next time come with me and I'll show you. I'll even let you stir."

~~~~~~~~~~

Most of the soap was gone, but with judicious use and no further Soap Festivals, enough remained to last them a few more days. If they were still here when it ran out, they could readily make more, although running out of soap would be the least of their concerns.

Seth recovered quickly from his exhortations two days before and, in fact, felt better than at any time since arriving. He was keenly aware that with a nuclear device in the hands of the madman from Iraq, the balance of power would be forever altered. He had made every possible effort, and had fate smiled on him, he might have been able to help prevent it. Alas, it was not to be. With acceptance of the lost opportunity behind him, he decided that whatever now happened in the Middle East, it was out of his hands, nukes or no nukes. He therefore pushed it aside as he would a nagging mosquito, held Martha's hand securely in his and participated joyously in the reverie of the journey back to camp.

Leesa, on the other hand, was not so calm and mellow. She had been ignoring the pigmentation differences, as well as her slightly swollen belly. No one knew she had missed her period, which was highly unusual for her. She attributed it to stress, but now it was likely that the beginning of malnutrition was as likely a cause. Was it that obvious? Did she really have to eat meat?

She discussed this at length with Marc. His logical mind unencumbered with emotions was a perfect foil for her disordered head full of denial and magical thinking. He pointed out to her "Humans were made to be carnivores. It does not matter how disgusting it is to you. It is how your body was made. With the abundant variety of food available this century, it is easy for someone to avoid animal protein completely, but it requires some work." He made the point that the opposite choice was not nearly as difficult.

There were numerous instances where people survived on meat alone, without fruits, vegetables, or starches. They were somewhat worse for the experience, but the effects were minimal and took a very long time to surface. The specific example he used was the trip by Lewis and Clark to map out the route to the West Coast "For months all they ate was what they shot and killed. They were able to perform unbelievable feats of physical endurance on that diet."

The thought galled her, "I am a carnivore." She had pleaded with him to find some other source of protein, a plant source, but he did not know much about tropical nutrition.

She knew the basics well enough: peanuts, corn and legumes, soybeans, and, of course, milk products. All of those would do well, but none were available to her. She thought of how much she despised fish and how she would rather get sick than have to eat it. Would they notice? And what could they do about it if they did? Force open her mouth and shove food down as if she were some goose that needed to be fattened? —not very likely. "Hell. I will just hold out until we get off this island prison. The way we are going we plan to be off in just a few days anyway. How sick could I get in just a few days?"

~~~~~~~

They arrived at the beach with an energy and motivation never experienced before. All of them, every single one, were now on the same page of their hymnal. They wanted off the island desperately and had put aside their personal problems and fears to work as a championship team to accomplish their rescue. If they had come up with a motto, it might have been, "Damn the torpedoes and full speed ahead." or something much like that. They had most of what they needed in place, and with a collective effort, could have two small seaworthy rafts ready, with supplies, in the next couple of days.

And they might have actually pulled it off just as planned had fate not intervened once more.

~~~~~~~~~~

Arrianna was on a mission to find another patch of plants they used to make rope. She held a leaf from the plant so she could identify it and was making a grid search the way Mike had shown her. It was on her fifth pass that she saw him. He was slumped over, still as death and against a tree. She could not see much of him and wanted to see less. She could absolutely not deal with another dead body.

She ran as fast as she could into Marc's arms. She wanted to be held and miraculously he understood and held her without asking questions. After a few minutes, she was able to talk. "There is another one out there. I don't think I can stand it anymore," she managed to say through tears. Everyone just stared at her.

"Another what? Asked Marc and Martha together.

"Another dead body! A man—I think. I didn't get close—as soon as I saw him I ran."

They were thunderstruck. It did not compute. They were not missing anyone and no one else lived on this island. "Can you tell us where to look?" asked Jerry. There was a tinge of excitement in his voice. If there were other people around, even dead ones, there might be people looking for them.

"Over in the trees about one hundred yards away and fifty feet or so into the jungle. He's tied to a tree."

That did not make sense and it left the others at a loss for words or response. Finally, Jerry dismissed it as a creation of an overactive imagination and formed a search party. "Martha, Leesa could you stay behind and care for Ari? The rest of us will go and have a look."

Martha shifted uneasily. "How about if Seth remains behind with us? I would feel safer."

After a moment's reflection and despite his wanting the old man's wisdom along, he agreed, "OK. But I am not agreeing that there is anything to worry about. I think that Ari here is very upset. Understandably so, but she may have seen him with his arms wrapped around the tree and not tied. We will return quickly either way."

The women and Seth watched them leave. They had their somber faces on, ready to deal with whatever was waiting for them. Just before they were out of sight, Seth yelled, "Wait!" picked up something and ran to them. He gave Marc the rudimentary slingshot with a few stones. "Just in case."

Jerry nodded to himself realizing it was this kind of forethought that made the old man so invaluable. *Never mind*, he told himself, *we probably won't find anything, and certainly nothing of danger.* With that they took off on their mission to find what in the world had scared Ari so badly.

Instead of the path Arrianna took, they walked along the beach the approximate length and intended to spread out as they turned inland. Marc saw them first. "Tracks!" The others ran to him and they saw the numerous footprints over the high part of the beach.

"What can you tell us about them?" asked Jerry. The question was directed at Marc out of habit, but it was Mike who answered.

"We can count the number of different shoes, that will tell us how many there were. The size of the print and the depth will tell us the composition of the individuals, and the pattern of the prints may tell us what they did here." The rest of them looked at him dumbfounded. He explained, "My wife and I like to go on nature walks and we've taken up the hobby of recognizing animal tracks. The principles are the same for humans."

They promptly began accumulating the information Mike requested and, with minimal disruption, they identified five distinct sets of prints, although one was faint and only appeared randomly, as if being carried. They were all men of heavy build and two of them had walked in lock–step and were either much heavier than the others, or were carrying a heavy load, possibly the fifth person. They had marched directly into the woods and then marched out, partly obliterating their prints.

"I suppose it is time to go check out what Ari saw," said Mike. The reality that she may well have seen what she told them hung in the air amongst them. No one moved or said anything. Confusion, fear, and excitement all flowed through their nervous systems in the manner that blood flows through arteries, with pulsing force and anxious energy.

"Let's do it!" asserted Jerry and without looking back, plunged into the vegetation.

They found him quickly and without the need to spread out and search. He was exactly where she said he would be and in the exact condition she had described.

His hands were handcuffed around the tree and he was devastatingly motionless. They circled him as if he were a snake that would suddenly jump up and bite them with its venomous fangs. He was young, perhaps Marc's age, fairly fit with a good musculature visible and was clearly all torn up.

Caked blood was everywhere, particularly around the face. Bruising was visible as well and what could be nothing else but burn marks, too big for cigarettes, perhaps cigars—nice perfectly round patches all over his chest. His face still showed some of the effects of the agony he must have endured. Each one of the three men were nauseated by the sight and the thought of running away as fast and far as they could was not far from their minds. None of them had moved to touch him and probably would not have had he not stirred and moaned.

"Holy Shit! He's still alive," shouted Marc in a strained, high-pitched voice.

Mike, reverting to his experience from 'Nam, went right up to the man and methodically took inventory. "He has a strong pulse. It's a bit fast. His breathing is shallow, probably from broken ribs under these large bruises. He doesn't have any bullet wounds or knife wounds that I can see. We have to find a way to get him loose, clean him up, bandage him as best we can and hydrate him." No one moved. They were all stunned and when the faces of Jerry and Marc questioned him, his only response was "Nam."

Jerry and Marc found some rocks and they took turns pounding at the links. Fortunately the cuffs were old and rusty and once the initial shock wore off, their humanity surfaced and the energy they used freed him, despite their pathetically inadequate tools. "Great! Now let's find a way to carry him back to camp."

Marc spoke up urgently, "Jerry, we should not move him, he may have a broken neck or something." The other two just looked at him in disbelief. This was where his book knowledge was a hindrance, worse than ignorance.

"Let me put it to you gently Marc. He was left here to die. He will probably do that no matter what we do. If he has a neurological injury, then he is dead. Those rules that you read about are well and good but only when there is something you can do about it."

"Oh, yeah." Marc fumbled, once again berating himself for not seeing the obvious.

~~~~~~~~~~

Back at the camp, Arrianna remained disconsolate. She wept inconsolably and wanted them all close to her. Martha was beside herself with grief over the poor girl's infernal bad luck. Three bodies now. How many adults could deal with that? What could she do but hold her, rock her and reassure her? Seth sat next to them and stroked her hair. Feeling left out, Leesa started to walk away, but Arrianna stopped crying for a moment to ask her, "I just need to feel that there are still people alive, can you hold my hand?" Leesa gladly complied.

This went on for a full thirty minutes, no less. Then she was able to sit up and tell them about it between sobs. "There were handcuffs. I saw them clearly. Someone must have left him there to die!" Martha and Seth did not know what to think. It was so preposterous, yet she was alert and lucid as ever. "I wasn't all that upset about it, really. But when he moved and moaned...I sort of...freaked."

"You mean that he was alive?" asked a startled Seth. Arrianna nodded. They all stood silent and it was Leesa that broke the silence.

"I believe you. I don't know how or why or anything about what you saw, but I believe that is what is out there, and we had better prepare for them. They will have found a way to free him and bring him back."

REDEMPTION ISLAND

One look at Martha and Seth told her that they would comply, but not out of any belief that it was necessary, rather to humor Arrianna. Consequently, the look on their faces when the three men came back with the bundle on their shoulders was absolutely priceless.

The men were surprised when their patient was expected, just as if this was the jungle equivalent of an emergency room. Water, cloths, a mat of leaves and the full attention of three women were immediately available. Martha began putting small amounts of water in his parched mouth, Leesa and Arrianna began cleaning him up and applying crude bandages on the worst of the wounds. Seth joined in after a while and, without fanfare, removed the maggots and other larvae that were feeding on his dead flesh. "I really should leave them in place, but I cannot stand it."

"Leave them?" screamed the other men nearly in unison. "Whatever for?" Clearly suggesting he had lost any sense that he might once have had.

Without looking up he answered, "They only eat dead tissue. They can clean a wound better than a surgeon by eating every microscopic bit of dead meat. The wound will heal that much faster." Marc ran off and they heard him hurling, the other two looked like they wanted to join him.

Mike said, "I completely agree, regardless of the theoretical benefit, if we are going to take care of him and tend to him closely, we need to remove them."

Seth had never stopped working. He simply nodded absently while he continued with his unenviable task.

The patient responded to the water almost immediately. His lips moved, silently asking for more. Martha knew better than to give him more than a few drops at a time, and it took forever to quiet his silent lips.

REDEMPTION ISLAND

Leesa noted that despite being in the shade, he felt hot, hotter than he should be. "He must be running a fever, a high fever from the way his skin feels." The others concurred, but did not know what to do for they had no aspirin or any other medicine for that matter. Leesa used what they had plenty of, water. They irrigated his entire body with cooling water using large leaves to encourage evaporation, and the results came quickly.

"He's not as hot! Really, feel him." Leesa was excited to be part of something so immediate and useful. They all agreed his temperature was lower, but needed to continue their efforts.

Within three hours of his arrival at camp, the mystery man had been cleaned, and satiated with water. His fever was brought under control and even his pulse had slowed. All of his wounds were now insect free, cleaned, and the large ones had mudpacks on them. The intensity of the crisis was over and it was time for the inevitable questions and multiple fears.

~~~~~~~~~~~~

Jerry opened the impromptu meeting, "There is no doubt that he was left here to die a miserable death, but by whom?"

"It wasn't boy scouts. That's for sure. I would say it has to be drug related." ventured Mike.

"There weren't any signs of drug use. His arms, legs, and even his nose show no signs of long term use." Seth added. "It doesn't exactly rule it out though."

Martha piped in. "He has several tattoos over his body, arms, and legs. Some military, some…" it remained unfinished. It was Leesa that finally finished the thought.

"They were vulgar, obscene pictures of women with melons for breasts and—well you need not hear the rest." They all nodded, each having seen at least one of them. "It doesn't mean anything, though. He could just be a jerk, not necessarily a drug dealer."

Jerry summarized the feelings of most of them, "But it makes sense that is exactly what he is. A low level, stupid man who thought he could cheat the big boys and got caught. They torture him a bit and then they let him die of thirst here and they can show the bones to newcomers as a warning of sorts."

"Jesus Christ! I can't friggin' believe this shit. Just what we need now, a moral dilemma," said Seth. The reaction of the others was not what he had expected. Instead of sympathizing with him, they started chuckling. First Martha, then Leesa, followed by the others. The chuckling turned into laughter and then into tearful hilarity. Seth looked about in confusion and embarrassment. What had he missed?

He felt his face burning red, first with discomfort, then with anger. He thought *Why would they not let me in on the joke?* When he could no longer stand it, he stood up and ranted at all of them. This was exactly the wrong thing to do since it caused the laughter to renew in intensity. He wanted to storm away, but he was old and wise enough to know that he would only be hurting himself. He just had to bear it and let the laughter run its course without adding more fuel to the fire.

While waiting, he found himself snickering and eventually laughing. Not at anything in particular but just because everyone else was. The infectiousness of the laughter was great, due at least in part to the terminal seriousness of the rest of their existence.

"Do you get it now?" said Jerry. Seth's headshake was his only answer. It was Martha who broke the news.

"You are Jewish for Pete's sake. After all the hell we have been through the past few weeks you have never, ever sworn, not once. And now, the first time you do, you invoke the name of Jesus." She fidgeted a little. "I don't know. It struck me as very funny, somehow." The others were nodding their agreement. She noticed that he did not find it as amusing as they did and added, "...maybe you had to be there..." This started a new round of laughter.

That night around the campfire they decided as a group that they could not allow the man to die and they would do what they could for him. But they would go ahead with their plans to get off the island at the earliest possible moment. It was now made even more urgent by the likelihood that the ones who left him there might return to check on their victim. They discussed relocating away from this area, but decided they could not afford the time.

"Besides," Jerry said, "when they discover him missing, they will look far and wide to make sure he is not hiding. We could not hide well enough from a dedicated search by motorboat. At least... not if we are going to try to build rafts and get off this frigging island."

"It's fortunate they landed far enough away to be unaware of our presence," said Marc.

Seth said, "And that we were not here. I don't know about the rest of you, but if I had been here I would have made a fool of myself running down the beach to greet them." Marc and Mike nodded. They were quiet thinking of the inevitable conclusion of such an event: All of them dead with no one to ever know the difference.

Jerry felt the tension building and knew from experience they were at a crucial crossroads. The mood of the group was in flux. The smallest thing could make all his morale building a waste of time. He looked at the eyes of the others and saw the desperate expectation for someone to help lead them away from the despair they were beginning to feel. He stood up with a broad smile and ceremoniously raised his hand in salute, "A toast to Marc and his Soap Festival. Not only did he clean us up, he improved our outlook and saved us from meeting a group of unsavory characters." He was joined immediately by Seth and the others piped in.

Marc was the only one who remained sitting. He had no idea what he was supposed to do now. He saw them clapping and shouting his name as if he was some celebrity. He knew these people and sensed they were not trying to make fun of him, so he relaxed. When they started to shout, "Speech, speech..." He jumped up and began to play-act.

"You probably are wondering why I called this meeting..." The group roared—it was exactly what they wanted from him. He felt more free and more himself than ever before. He was able to kid around and intuitively understand what was happening. He accepted that he always had the capacity for intuition about others, their emotions, and reactions. It was as if he had suddenly been given access to a part of his brain previously denied him. He understood people's reactions. It wasn't that he lacked the ability to interpret feelings. It was that he had ignored anything not logical and tangible. It would be hard to trust these...feelings, intuitions, whatever you might call them...but at least for the moment he was fully human without any parts missing.

The merriment continued until midnight, when the nervousness eased enough for them to sleep. For the first time since their arrival, they posted a night watch.

The next morning, the energy was electric and no problem could slow them down. When an obstacle occurred, there were numerous ideas and volunteers to deal with it. So when the issue of

Leesa not being able to stomach fish came up, they dealt with it quickly and expeditiously. They did not blame her or badger her. They knew she understood the importance to the group of remaining healthy and fit and that her aversion to meat, particularly fish, was real. She acknowledged that she could stomach bird meat. So, Marc and Mike managed to make two more slingshots from donated elastic clothing and everyone searched and gathered appropriate projectiles. With a little practice they were able to obtain bird meat on a more regular basis and on a much larger scale than before. Despite herself, Leesa ate greedily. Her body craved the protein.

To Leesa's amazement, she turned out to be one of the best shots in the group and became a designated bird hunter. She had to revise many of her self-perceptions. She had helped to care for a very sick man, become an integral part of a group and contributed to their survival. And now she had experienced guilt! What an accomplishment! When they took time from raft making to help her obtain protein she could tolerate, she had felt guilty. She still marveled at that. It motivated her to proficiency with a weapon. For the first time in her life she found it intolerable to be a burden on others! That was another breakthrough. Now several others were allowing that they would prefer bird meat to fish. They had even stopped fishing and she was the main protein producer, freeing up two of the men. She carried her sling shot everywhere with her. It gave her a sense of…importance.

By the end of the third day back from the soap festival, they were as ready as they would get. The rafts were ready. The new and improved rope design had survived over ten days in salt water without degradation. Each raft had a centerboard that could be raised or lowered as appropriate. Their main concern remained the miserable supply of containers for carrying fresh water. They formed some salvaged plastic into a funnel to catch rainwater, but even so, they would be on severe water rationing as soon as they left the island.

They awoke to a hazy light rain. Falling on the water, it raised a mist that obscured everything. The sea was a vast gray-blue featureless wasteland. There was no way they could leave today.

"It won't last long, the sun will burn through it by noon," said Mike. "This doesn't happen too often and it is usually limited to a small area. In all likelihood, at three thousand feet it is sunny."

Jerry spoke firmly, "There is no way we can go into this muck, and if we don't get off within a few hours of sunrise it's best to put it off until tomorrow." There was a curious mixture of disappointment and relief in his voice.

"At least if we can't set off, it is also highly unlikely that anyone will come here," said Marc.

Arrianna spoke up in a quivering voice. She had not been the same since she'd stumbled on the last body, which was still lying motionless by the tree line. "If we are stuck here for another day, why don't we make some more soap? I know it sounds trivial, but we ran out yesterday and the thought of becoming sticky and grimy again makes me sick."

Leesa agreed wholeheartedly. "We have nothing to lose and at least we would be doing something positive, with good karma. It would give us something to look forward to."

There were indistinct nods around the group. It could well be their last day, and they'd rather use it productively to make something that gave them so much pleasure than sit about waiting for the end.

Marc jumped up. "I'd love to get another shot at it. The last batch was a bit soft. If I change the lye to fat ratio I think I can make something much easier to use and longer lasting."

REDEMPTION ISLAND

"How about a different fruit scent?" asked Martha, getting into the spirit.

"Sure. I can add mango, guava, whatever we have."

They jumped up and began their preparations. With all the help and nervous energy available this batch of soap did not take long to make. Marc expected no one would want to be near when the smell became foul, but to his surprise it was the women who had the least trouble with it and volunteered to stay throughout. "It must have something to do with the value each of us places on the end product," he said to Seth and Jerry. They both nodded and smiled.

Seth said, "You are most definitely learning about people. In a short while, with your intellect and storehouse of knowledge, you could be dangerous."

Jerry added, "Absolutely, most dangerous indeed."

Marc wasn't sure what they were talking about, but he now knew enough not to say anything. He would understand in time.

~~~~~~~~~

By the end of the day they had soap again. The men bathed quickly and relinquished the stream to the women who were taking much longer. By increasing the lye to fat ratio and not adding the coconut, the soap came out firmer and did not dissolve nearly as quickly. They only made a tenth as much, but it would probably last as long as the last batch. He had added mango this time, mostly because they had a surplus. Even the men thought it smelled great. Marc began formulating a myriad of soap possibilities. "If I ever get back to the real world, I will see if any of these ideas are viable for development" he told himself.

The mist lasted well past noon and, at day's end, contributed to the most amazing sunset they had yet seen. The Sun veritably glowed and pulsated as it descended. The colors changed by the minute and jumped out at them. Yellow, orange, red rose, magenta, plus a hundred others were displayed in a way that none would ever forget. They remained quiet and introspective even after the last few rays were gone. All but Leesa decided to walk the beach. Leesa wanted to be alone with her thoughts. She did not get the chance.

She was shaken out of her reverie by a dry, low voice, "Hello, beautiful, what's your name." To her credit she did not scream, but instinctively raised her slingshot to firing position. The man was awake and trying fruitlessly to sit up.

Chapter Nineteen
Luis

She called everyone over and refused to say anything until they were all there. She wanted no part of leadership and did not relax until the entire group was gathered around the man. To her surprise he had not been gruff, vulgar or stupid. He had stopped talking as soon as he realized she wasn't going to tell him anything. He was now looking about him, not just at the faces, but their general condition as well as the two completed rafts. He was the first to speak, "My god, you're marooned, aren't you? You must be from the plane that disappeared, when was that, two months ago, maybe a little longer?" His face was in shock at the realization.

All of them looked to Jerry for a reply. He had accepted the leadership position out of habit and pride, but now he felt the burden of it and, for the first time in his life, did not want the responsibility. Nevertheless he stepped up and responded for the group. "The most important thing is not our situation but who you are and how you ended up here. We do not know what the hell to do with you." He paused but clearly communicated that he had more to say. "As you have deduced we are stranded here and no one is looking for us. The last thing we need is some ball-and-chain loser holding us back. We certainly cannot afford the luxury of guarding you or taking you with us. Therefore, do not waste our time with stupidity. We want the truth the first time."

"The entire truth. We will not take kindly to evasions," added Seth. Jerry now relaxed, let his shoulders drop and took a deep breath, knowing he would receive help as needed. There was a time of silence as both sides faced each other. The months of deprivation, fear, and conflict with each other and with nature had hardened the group. To a person from the outside they were cold-hearted and showed it. Their faces were determined and focused. The newcomer would find no weakness or weak member to exploit.

His face was a stony mask which showed nothing but concentration. He sized up each and every one of them at a turn and ended up where he started, with Jerry. "So you are the leader of this ragtag group?"

Jerry did not answer but asked his own question, "What is your name and how do you come to be here?"

"All right, already. You hold all the cards and I will play by your rules. My name is Luis, but before we get into any long discussions, could you help prop me up so that I can talk easier?"

Jerry was uneasy but the decision was taken out of his hands when Mike and Marc stood up, grabbed the man firmly by both arms and sat him up so he could lean against a tree. Leesa took it upon herself to cover him with her weapon.

"Is she any good with that?" he asked pointing to her.

"Deadly. At least to birds," said Martha. Luis understood immediately. If she could hit birds accurately enough to kill them, then at the range she was at now, she would hit what she aimed for and cause significant, if not incapacitating, damage. They all saw his face change from guarded composure to resigned acquiescence.

"Hell, you saved my life when you didn't have to, right? I should be able to trust you. Although I will admit that it does not come easy." He paused to swallow and could not quite manage it. Arrianna gave him some water. He smiled at her disarmingly.

"Don't count on my being soft with you. You owe me big time and if you turn out to be the slime ball we think you are, they will have to hold me back from feeding you to the fish." The intensity and cold cruelty of her words, plus her hardened presence shook him visibly. To his unstated question she added, "I found you. I thought you were dead. I did not need to find another dead body. I was happy before that and I have not been since. You took my happiness away and you had damn better be worth it!"

Luis looked about him expecting to see the others smiling at the silliness of the girl's accusations. His last strand of composure vanished as he saw their nonverbal yet unquestioning support for her.

He finished the water, held the container out for more and after he drank again, he collected himself, then spoke, "At least let me tell it my way. It's going to be very hard to prove my story so at least let me have my best shot at it."

No one answered, but he saw Jerry and Martha nod. He took that for a yes and started talking. "I'm with the DEA and I infiltrated one of the drug cartels. I was only recently found out which led to my being unceremoniously deposited on your island." He saw only skeptical looks so he went on adding details.

"Three years ago, I joined the Chagas drug cartel based out of Venezuela. They focus mostly on heroin, but will occasionally bring in cocaine and hash. I climbed up to middle management, where I intended to remain for another few months before retiring by faking my death. Unfortunately, last week, a former member was unintentionally released from prison and he recognized me. They weren't totally sure that the other guy was not a plant so they tortured both of us and intended to leave me both here to die but he made a run for it and they shot him.

"He's now shark bait. I saw them cut him up with a chain saw and chum the water with him." Despite his best efforts, Luis's face showed some of the revulsion he felt as well as a pale pallor that was evident even by firelight. Everyone but Jerry, Seth and Mike had left before this moment. Now only Seth remained.

Luis's story was interesting and the way he told it used up time. He concluded with his best (and only) bit of evidence. "If one of you will look carefully on my various tattoos you will note that, in a certain order, they spell out 'Drug Enforcement Agency.'"

"Let me look at those tattoos," Seth asked.

"Sure, look at the corners in the intense detail. You will see a letter in each corner, they are randomly ordered so that, if discovered, it would be hard to put together. I can tell you the order, if you like." Seth shook his head indicating that would be unnecessary and proceeded with the examination. It vindicated Luis. "I insisted on not carrying any traditional identification whatsoever. I had them put on paper that they would pay for the removal of the tattoos once the undercover operation was over."

"I heard they can do that now. But it is very expensive, and painful."

"Right on both counts. But with the amount of cash that I have helped them recover they can easily afford it. As far as the pain goes, well…"

Seth nodded his understanding. He asked, "Will they be back?"

"Who?…Oh, you mean Chagas and his guys? Sure, they will come back, but not for a while. They are a crazy bunch but they do not handle putrefaction well, so they will wait until they are sure that I will be...Uhm...fully deteriorated. At least a week or two. You should be well off the island by then. I plan to get stronger very quickly and be well inland when they return."

"You won't be coming with us?" asked a surprised Seth.

"Not a chance. They travel these waters all the time and on the odd chance they happened to be the first to spot you, I will not go." This line of reasoning shook Seth.

"What will they do to us if they find us drifting?"

Luis became thoughtful. This lasted the better part of a minute as he obviously replayed parts of the prior three years. He concluded by nodding his head to himself, "Probably not much. They will look you over with the glasses and when they see no threat they will most likely ignore you." They looked at each other while Seth analyzed this. "Let me not kid you, some of them would love to have fun and games with you, being defenseless and all, but if they are carrying product or money, as is likely, most of them know better than to delay, even for a few minutes. You should be safe here and on the water."

"They most definitely won't help us, but they will probably leave us alone," Seth murmured mostly to himself, "at least that is something." Seth was about to thank him for his efforts when he noticed a faraway look on Luis. He waited until it passed and then pointedly looked at him.

"Well, I was thinking..." he let that hang in the air between them and when Seth said nothing he continued, "...there is a possibility that they could return sooner. This is a wonderful disposal area for them. The bodies do not float away to be found. They decompose rapidly into something unrecognizable, much less identifiable, and it is readily accessible. If they had a 'housekeeping' problem, or more likely if they wanted to show a novice what happens to traitors, they will bring them here, give them a knife and tell them to bring back a piece of the body. Usually a finger or a toe. Most of them get sick and it makes a very big impression on them. It's why we have such a hard time recruiting informants. Why I had to go undercover."

"How long will they wait?" asked a shaking Seth.

"What day is it?" asked Luis.

"We think it's, Thursday but there is no way to be absolutely sure."

"It was a Monday when they brought me here. You found me the next day—three days ago now, that makes it Friday. Without you I would have died that day." Luis stopped his monologue and looked up at Seth. "By the way, I never formally thanked any of you, especially that young girl who found me. Thanks. Thanks for saving my life."

Seth nodded and smiled for the first time since the stranger woke up. Maybe there was a purpose to this madness. It might actually turn out for the best.

Luis resumed his discourse, "In this heat a body decomposes fast. They would wait two or three more days, maybe four if they have some logistical problems."

"So you are saying they could be here as soon as the day after tomorrow?" Seth said with his voice shaking noticeably. Luis was suddenly not sure that he would recover fast enough to be 'long gone' when they arrived. The fear welling up in his gut was reaching every cell in his body and he did not trust his voice, so he just nodded.

Seth stood up solemnly and shook the sand off his clothes. "I need to tell the others." He was about to walk away when he stopped and faced Luis again. "Before I go, I'd like to ask you about something altogether different."

"Sure, whatever. I am not going anywhere and I am rather

REDEMPTION ISLAND

deeply in your debt."

Seth hesitated, thinking of the exact wording he wanted to use, "Has there been any news from the Middle East?"

Luis did not try to hide his surprise at the drastic change in topic. Was the guy a political junky? He was much too old to have any active part in the mess over there. "Uh… what part? Is there a specific area? I do not usually keep up with international events."

"Oh, nothing in particular, I was just…"

Luis interrupted, knowing that there was a lot more to this than mere interest, "I heard that Israel is having an election soon," he noticed Seth's reaction to the name of the country, but not to the rest of the message. "And that it is getting heated up because of the surprise air strike at the Osirak nuclear reactor."

Seth was shaken to his very core. They had done it! They somehow found out that Saddam was building a nuclear weapon at the reactor and destroyed the place before he could finish. Wonderful news! His only regret was that he had not been able to contribute to this and thereby erase his debt. Now it would likely never be paid off.

Luis had been prepared to say more, but it was clear that was what he wanted know. The old man's face had cracked into a faint smile for a long moment. He had not known about the attack. After all, it had only occurred, what was it, last week? Yet this old man had known of the reactor and the possibility of an attack. There was much more to him than he let on. Who in the world had even heard of Osirak before last week?

Seth stood up and walked away to find Jerry. Later he would have Luis tell him every detail he remembered about the attack. But for now, he was satisfied that Israel was safe, if only until the next threat appeared.

Luis saw Seth walk briskly away, noticed the purposeful stride, the confident set of the shoulders and shook his head wondering how the old man could keep his composure in light of the upcoming challenges, and what it would take to shake that man up.

PART THREE
Chapter Twenty
Battle Preparations

The meeting began with surprise, anxiety, and depression, but quickly degenerated into rancor and panic. It raged for what Martha would later describe as "eons" before they began working together as a unit instead of finding fault. Most of them were stuck on blaming Luis, as if that by itself would fix the problem. This line of thinking ended only when Seth stood up, quieted the group and firmly told them "The 'fault,' if there is such a thing, belongs to all of us. Had we left him to die and rot we would all be in no danger. Actually, if we put him back now, killed him and let him rot, we will still be fine."

The shock and truth of his words ended everyone's need to stay on that subject and they proceeded to the next question on their agenda, which was "What can we do about it?"

The initial consensus was that they must flee inland and quickly. This was what Luis intended to do, regardless of their decision. He'd pointed out that, with a couple of day's head start, they could be far inland and the frequent rain showers would erase their trail. They could even situate themselves to see the approach to island. The down side was that the camp would be discovered during their subsequent search and all their hard work would be destroyed.

Further discussion brought out more problems with the plan. Luis admitted that he feared they would not give up easily and would return better prepared to deal with them. Perhaps they would bring helicopters or light planes to spot them. "They even have infrared night vision goggles. They could overfly at night and pick us out. If I was by myself, once I am fit again, I could hide and move fast enough to keep ahead of them. I am not so sure if, as a group..." He left that line of thought unspoken. It was clear that the older members of the party would tire quickly and move slowly.

Marc spoke up for the first time, "With all the vegetation and tropical heat, I am confident that if we stayed under cover, the night vision equipment would not work well enough to spot us."

"Nevertheless," said Jerry, standing up to make his point, "if they make a concerted effort, it will be hard to consistently dodge them," he waited for a few seconds, clearly not finished with his comments, "particularly if they use dogs."

The use of dogs in tracking is not a novel idea. However, for a variety of reasons, few in the group of castaways had considered it. In some irrational way it was just "too damn unfair to use dogs."

Seth again spoke. "I've been discussing the situation with Martha, Leesa, and Marc and was speaking for them as well, I have to say this. I presume that you aren't just throwing stones but that you have an alternative plan, Jerry. What do you propose we do?"

It was then that Arrianna, who had been peripheral to the discussion and in a world all her own, jumped up and shouted, "That we fight and blow those bloody fuckers out of the water." She said this with such a release of pent-up rage that it stunned even her. "I'm sorry. I didn't mean to shout it. I just meant that we should use the only advantage we have while we still can." She then looked up at Jerry, "Isn't that what you meant?"

Martha nudged Marc, who eventually got the hint, went to Arrianna and tentatively put his arm around her. She leaned into him and visibly relaxed. Jerry nodded, "Yes, Ari, you are quite right. Mike and I feel that the only course of action with any chance of success is to be ready for them before they know we are here, and to use that surprise to somehow overpower them. With a little luck we could evade them long enough to take their boat and finally be off this infernal island."

That last unexpected statement shook all of them out of their victim's stupor. The idea that they could be off the island without risking their lives to the vagaries of the sea and weather served to further energize them. Even the meekest of them felt transformed, as if the frustration, anger, and hopelessness of the past months had finally reached a crossroads. One by one they stood up and expressed their intention to join the crusade. Mike and Jerry, who had clearly discussed this before, almost felt hopeful.

Chapter Twenty-One
Marc in Charge

They wasted no time getting started. The energy was there for the tapping and Jerry was fully aware that the time to act was now, not tomorrow. They set up a watch from a nearby promontory where Martha, Leesa and Seth would take turns watching the horizon. Mike showed them what to look for and in which direction to concentrate. The three of them found they were quite able to weave rope while watching. This gave them a feeling of contributing to the group effort and besides, Marc said he could use as much rope as possible. To this end they had cannibalized the raft they were building, but despite this they had all seen Marc's disappointment at the amount of rope available. Clearly he had come up with plans.

Marc was placed in charge of designing weapons. Luis was in charge of strategy and planning. The two of them became inseparable since their assignments were so interdependent. Mike, Jerry, and Arrianna were left with doing everything else such as scouting and mapping the terrain and doing the required physical labor.

REDEMPTION ISLAND

~~~~~~~~~

Marc felt exhilarated. He was in his element and at a level of intensity he'd never felt before. He now understood how having a deep personal stake in the outcome made an enormous difference in a person's productivity. He felt the flow of ideas become a flood, coming close to overpowering him.

They made an unlikely pair, the shy, almost reclusive scientist and the daring, extroverted to the max, undercover cop. Yet, they meshed well and, in some indefinable way, were attracted to each other, as if they were finally able to see in the other what they themselves lacked. The first day, they all worked ceaselessly into the early hours of the next day. Only when absolutely exhausted were any of them able to lay still and close their eyes with any realistic hope of sleep.

By then they had accomplished much. An escape route was chosen and illustrated to all. It led up to one of the peaks and had many chances for a change in direction and, of course, for setting up an ambush. All the materials available to them were gathered and inventoried. The people on watch doubled the amount of rope. Marc and Jerry collected a veritable feast of meat using nets to gather fish and were aided by Leesa using her slingshot to knock down birds. They overcooked the meat and planned to store it just in case. They erased as much evidence of their presence as possible. There would be little obvious evidence left to suggest that Luis was not alone.

Luis formulated a workable plan. It required everyone to participate and used surprise to the hilt. If any reservations remained among the 'guerrillas' they concerned their ability to accomplish their assigned tasks and letting the others down. Much as a quarterback might feel going into a Super Bowl game. The plan's genius was not simply in its strategy or tactics, or even in the maximum use of everything available to them. No, the genius was in realizing the complete potential of everyone in the group.

Marc devised a variety of weapons and traps that could readily be made or found. He even made a few prototypes to see if they could be learned quickly and effectively. At dawn they would all have a chance to practice. Those with the steepest learning curve would make the weapon their own.

"Marc, I don't understand how you are going to use the mushrooms. I know they are poisonous, but are we going to cook a feast and offer it to them and then wait for them to die?" Leesa said with not a small amount of sarcasm.

Uncharacteristically, Marc did not respond with his typical aversion. "It is part of a fallback plan. There is so little time or effort involved that it seemed like a good idea. Once I discovered that you could recognize the poisonous mushrooms, I felt that there had to be a way to use them." He stopped talking and soon it became evident that he was not going to say more.

"Well!" They all said in spontaneous chorus. Marc made no sign of saying anything and finally Arrianna, who was seated next to him holding his hand, said, "Marc, no one is going to laugh or ridicule whatever you have come up with. We all have the deepest respect for you. If it wasn't for you, we would not have survived this long." She looked around and said, "Right?" There was a chorus of nods.

It took Marc a few minutes to get his voice, "This is what I plan. We gather a cooking pot full of mushrooms and boil the mush to concentrate the poison. Leesa told me how the early American settlers used the mushrooms with milk as a way of killing flies and that the poison remains after boiling. We then mix in a little fish oil to make it sticky and we apply it liberally around the site where they left Luis." He looked up, expecting them to start laughing, or at least criticizing, but they were all silent and expectant.

"I figured we could paint the tree trunks on the path, as well as any obstacles that they might touch. We could also leave some of our stuff on the beach as if discarded by campers. This could be doused in the poison brew."

"Don't they have to ingest it?" asked Seth.

Leesa answered, "To kill them outright that would be correct, especially if you want it to work quickly. But...it will still do a good bit of damage if they simply touch their lips or, even better, their eyes. They will get burning and tingling on their tongues and lips and perhaps throats within minutes. If they get it in their eyes the intense burning and tearing will not only be disabling but occur nearly instantaneously."

Marc jumped in, "It isn't designed as a primary way of incapacitating them, but more to distract and slow them down if we have to make a run for it. Even if we only get one or two that are incapable of chasing us, they might give up or there would be only a couple left to deal with."

He sat back waiting for a reaction. Nothing happened for what, to him, seemed a very long time, but in reality was only a small fraction of a minute. Everyone smiled and congratulated Marc on his novel idea.

Arrianna came up with her contribution to this part of their plan. "Marc? What if they had to rub their eyes after they had it on their hands? We could possibly immobilize the entire group. Or at least the majority of them."

"What do you have in mind?" His curiosity was definitely piqued.

"We would have to make sure that they had some of the stuff

on their hands. I leave that to you. If, when they arrived at the tree where Luis was chained, they had to rub their eyes, and if what Leesa says is true, then they would be almost immediately immobilized, reasonably far away from the boat. We might even be able to get a gun or two from them. We could use the gun to, you know, take care of whoever is guarding the boat."

"How do you plan to make them rub their eyes?" The gleam in Marc's eyes was not yet evident.

"I thought I could climb the nearby trees and spread ashes on the leaves so that they would spill if they shook them. Or even the wind could spill them."

Marc glowed with excitement, "Or we could tie a string to the leaves and pull on them at the right moment! You are a genius! A veritable genius." He brought her close to him and kissed her on the lips. Not too hard, but not brotherly either.

~~~~~~~~~~

The Mushroom Proposal, as it came to be known, was promoted to their primary strategy. It had what they most wanted, a good chance of success, minimum effort and technology required and, best of all, minimal exposure.

They cooked mushrooms galore and the result was a naturally sticky liquid that obviated the need to add the fish oil. They painted any and every tree in the vicinity of their expected landing. They placed some of their logs on the beach and along the path with copious amounts of poison spread on the areas most likely to be sat on or touched by someone trying to step over them. They were able to make so much of the stuff that they started painting the leaves of the vegetation along the route. Despite their best efforts and ingenuity, they had a good amount left over.

REDEMPTION ISLAND

Two days after they started their preparations in earnest, they sighted the boat. It was Martha who was on watch and, despite all the efforts and expectations, she was still surprised when it became real. She dropped the rope she had just started making and, with all the speed she could muster, she ran to the beach to sound the alarm. They all went to their battle stations.

Mike, Luis and Seth were the slingshot brigade. Jerry was almost as good, but they had only been able to make three weapons using all of the elastic from the women's brassieres. They each had scoured the beach and riverbeds for the rocks with which they felt most comfortable. Seth was deadly accurate at anything less than fifty feet. The others could consistently hit a target the size of a human head at thirty feet or less. They intended to ambush their prey at distances significantly less than that and hopefully inflict enough damage to cause at least one serious casualty. The stones had been ground to create points that they then dipped into the mushroom brew. They would all aim for the same person to increase their chances of success. Considering they were in the jungle, if they took care to freeze after their first shot, they would probably not be seen or even heard.

Despite everyone's objection, it was Arrianna who climbed the tree near the site where Luis had been left. She was the only one who could readily climb trees and comfortably remain there for what could be a long time. She rigged the tiniest of vines to shake the leaves with the ashes that she had just now placed.

Jerry and Marc were left to put a fresh coat of poison brew on the most obvious places, remove evidence of their presence as they made their way to the point of the cove to be able to swim to the boat from the seaward side. They would begin their swim a few hundred meters away and the two remaining "guerrillas," Martha and Leesa, were to try to get whoever was at the boat to leave it unattended. They planned to do that the old fashioned way, lure them with their bodies.

The way they practiced was for them to stumble out of the jungle and act surprised to see the boat and men. Then they were to run in abject fear. To say that Leesa would have little clothing on was to overstate the issue. They would then run to a preset place where the slingshot brigade was waiting in ambush. Once past the site, each of the ladies would take a separate path as far away from there as possible in case the enemy made it past the ambush site unscathed and still intent on mischief.

Luis assured the ladies over and over that these guys would not be able to resist them. They had only to show fear and shock and linger long enough to make sure the men were on their way. Martha required large doses of reassurance but Leesa jumped on the plan like a kitten onto warm cream. This was right up her alley and she was desperate to contribute to the cause.

When any guards would leave the boat, Jerry and Marc would board it, take off and maneuver out of sight to the far eastern edge of the beach, where they arranged to meet. Once all of them arrived, they would be on their way as fast as the motor could take them. No one wanted to think what they would do in the rather unlikely case that the boat was too small to carry eight people. It was rather unlikely in any case. Most likely the fit men, Luis, Marc, Mike, and Jerry would draw straws and play hide and seek until reinforcements came.

Jerry's biggest concern was for Arrianna and Leesa. The first would have to scamper down from her position in the tree, avoid contact and hike over a mile to the rendezvous. He was confident she would not get lost, but he did not know how long she would have before they were found out. Leesa also had to go an unusually long distance. After separating from Martha, she would have to circle around some fairly rough terrain. The distance was not as long as Arrianna's, but he did not have as high a degree of comfort in Leesa's orienteering skills. They had marked the trail somewhat conspicuously for her, but still…

There were six of them on the boat and it was crowded. As soon as Marc and Jerry saw it, they simultaneously shook their heads. It would be a very tight fit. Doable, but they might need a shoehorn to get the last one or two people in.

They saw them land at the extreme near end of their target zone. *Great!* thought Jerry, *So much the better for us if they are closer to the ambush site.* Four of the men jumped out and ran into the jungle in the direction of Luis' tree. So far, so good.

The two men noted how every one of the six large, unkempt men had a weapon of some kind, ranging from a handgun to a submachine gun. The two remaining with the boat had a large type of automatic rifle, perhaps an M-16 and a handgun. To their dismay, they were alert and focused on every approach. Marc wanted to find a way to tell the ladies not to come but Jerry prevailed. "We have no way of getting to them. We will have to play it out. If they see us first it will be worse. Right now our only real weapon is surprise." Marc's brain acknowledged this but he was learning to pay more attention to his heart and he found it increasingly difficult to remain hidden.

Pablo, the de facto leader of the small party, was guarding the boat. He was up for a promotion of sorts and he did not want to spoil it by some unexpected freak coincidence. He had called in a lot of debts to get this chance to prove that he could lead a group of men and, by all that was holy to this most unholy man, he swore they would complete the assignment without any fuckups. It was for this reason he picked Estefan to guard the boat with him. This young idiot was the least disciplined of the five soldiers and he did not want to hear that he'd done something stupid while in the jungle. He wanted to keep a very close eye on him.

He estimated it would take the four *hombres* about fifteen minutes to complete their task. It was already five minutes since they left. So far, so good. He smiled at himself when he thought how they would react on finding the partially decomposed and completely foul body of that SOB cop that they left here a week ago. He bet himself that three would lose their lunch immediately. Sancho might hold out a while but eventually he would lose his too.

Pablo had gone out of his way to give them a large fatty meal of *huevos rancheros* just before leaving and all but Sancho had been stupid enough to eat it. The trip here had almost been enough to get them to hurl so they were primed. He looked at the bag by the driver's seat. It contained leftovers from the Chinese dinner his family ate yesterday. He planned to start munching as soon as they were out on the sea-lanes. The smell of the food should be good for another few hurls over the side of the boat. He smiled wickedly realizing how much he cracked himself up.

At the eighteen-minute mark he started to worry. He did not get a chance to make it a habit because that is exactly when the two women broke the cover of the jungle. One was young, beautiful and hardly had anything on. The other could be most tactfully described as matronly. It took him a full five-count to break his immobility.

REDEMPTION ISLAND

Arrianna heard them well before she saw them. She had been set in plenty of time even though climbing the tree had proved far more difficult now that she knew it was the real thing. "Stage fright! That's what it is, simple stage fright." she told herself. They were talking and laughing in Spanish. She did not speak the language, but it nevertheless seemed forced to her. They rummaged around looking from tree to tree, clearly unable to find what they were looking for. The tone of their speech began changing from casual, to concerned, to royally pissed off.

She did not know it, but they were actually scared shitless. They were expecting to find something beyond their worst nightmares and then it wasn't there. Was this a test? Did they not really have a body for them to find and each one of them cut a finger off as proof? They dared not hope for this, despite the relief it promised. Their worst fear was of not finding the body, having to report their failure to Pablo, who, by the way was acting, as a real shit now that he was in charge. Therefore they started to sniff the air. Nothing! No smell at all. Could they really be that far off the path?

The four men split up and started calling out to each other, apparently in an effort to avoid getting lost. She could only partially see out of her nest, but they were getting a major dose of the poison all over themselves. Holding on to trees, brushing away the plants. One time an attempt was made to climb the tree she was on to get a better view.

Her heart jumped into her throat and tried to climb in her head. She could hear little besides the insistent "thump-dub-thump-dub" of her racing organ. Fortunately the guy did not give it his best effort and he went on his way after two abortive attempts. She told herself, "I have to remember that this tree trunk has the poison on it now. Don't be stupid and wipe your face after climbing down."

Eventually one of the group found the handcuffs where Arrianna had placed them. He called the others over and an intense discussion ensued. Arrianna did not wait for it to resolve but ever-so-gently tugged at the vine in her hand. Gradually she noted the faint rain of fine ash that fell on them. They were so absorbed into their dilemma that it took them a long time to react. The screams of pain were almost immediate. The poison was doing its stuff.

She heard them scream and run blindly about and after a full sixty count without hearing any sane voice, she decided it was time to go. She slid cautiously down and after dropping to the ground, squat there very still—listening. The screams had turned to moans and, as far as she could tell, they were all rolling on the ground making things worse by rubbing their eyes in agony.

Instead of running for the meeting site as planned, she decided that she could risk getting at least one of their weapons.

~~~~~~~~

When Martha and Leesa broke cover the two men did nothing more than drop their jaws in disbelief. Martha struggled with last-minute nerves and had required Leesa's hand and steady pull to get her out in the open. Now the panic and bile were building up a relentless pressure that was quickly becoming impossible to ignore. Then in an instant the two men broke their spell. The leader was slower by a full second and tried to catch up to the other guy whose intentions were absolutely clear to both ladies.

The instant the chase was on. Leesa took off, pulling the initially reluctant Martha behind. She had not felt this alive and energized since she was a child. Her mind was so clear and working so fast, it seemed like the world had gone into slow motion. She had no trouble focusing on every detail of the plan. They had a good thirty-yard lead and besides, they knew where they were going. Still, the men had worried that they would be caught before the ambush site and had set up several trip wires along the route. Each place was carefully marked. They had practiced the run over and over until finally Jerry was satisfied that they would not get caught by their own trap, even if they were overcome by fear.

The unexpected gunshots from behind startled her but she still saw the first trap and reminded Martha, who in the heat of battle, had clearly forgotten. Once over it, the practice kicked in and they made it past the ambush in record time. They waved at the men and proceeded to go to the meeting site. Instead of splitting up, Leesa went with Martha. She was convinced that this was absolutely necessary.

~~~~~~~~

The men waiting in ambush were keyed up. The reality of what they were doing surged through them and suddenly the idea of sending a barrage of stones, poisoned or otherwise, at men with no moral compunction and armed with automatic weapons, seemed at best idiotic and at worst suicidal.

There was no time to back down now. They prepared themselves and focused on Mike's words. "If you only shoot once and you all shoot at the same time, they will not have any idea where you are. It is the second shot that will give you away."

Mike had taught them imagery techniques. He had them focus on how they felt during their endless practice sessions and to not think about the differences but to imagine that the men's heads were papayas. They needed to make the first shot count.

Suddenly they heard shots. The jungle diffused the sound so

that they could not tell where they came from. "It's too close to be from Arrianna's direction, it has to be from the beach," whispered Luis.

"I thought you said they would chase, not shoot," hissed Seth with not a small trace of anger.

"Calm down you two," said Mike. "Think about it, they screamed and started running long before the shots. They were well concealed before the shooting started. It wasn't aimed at the women. Stay down and get ready."

Hardly ten seconds later, they heard the thrashing of people coming in a hurry. All three were relieved to see the two women running unhindered and apparently unhurt. Instead of splitting up as planned, they both went the direct way to the meeting site, using Martha's path. Mike had a few seconds to wonder what had gone wrong before they heard the sounds of pursuit. They first heard someone fall, followed by a long string of curses in what Luis recognized as Spanish. There seemed to be only one person chasing and, after the fall over the trip vine, he was much more circumspect in his pursuit.

When the person broke out of cover, he hesitated as expected. They had created two evident paths that slowly diverged and he did not know which one to take. Pablo never got the chance to worry his head over it.

~~~~~~~~~~

Pablo was stunned. He could not make his mind think. It kept racing from how, to what, to whom the nearly nude woman and her older companion were. By the time the shock wore off, he saw that Estefan was already running full tilt up the beach and that, to his disappointment, but not his surprise, he had left his handgun on the sand in his effort to reach the women faster. "Stupid idiot! Come back and get your *pistola!* We'll catch them without a problem and we can all have a little fun," he yelled as he started running after him.

Estefan was a man of little brains and even less judgment. He had been fortunate in only one respect. His uncle-in-law was "upper management" in the organization and had been pressured by his family to take him in. Since the day his uncle acquiesced, Estefan's incompetence and his many instances of "stupidity beyond belief" had placed a strain on his uncle's position in the "company."

Pablo reflected on his secret talk with his boss and Estefan's uncle. When they placed Estefan in his care, he complained because of his inability to discipline someone who could later use his family to retaliate. They told him that Estefan no longer had any protection whatsoever and that if he found an opportunity to eliminate him without witnesses and with no possibility of comebacks, well…then he was to take it.

He recalled the words of his boss "His uncle is under tremendous pressure to keep Estefan, but at the same time he hears it every time something goes wrong. This idiot is eroding his power base and he needs a face saving way out. You find a way to make this easy for him and you will have a patron for life. He will owe you big time."

It was with these thoughts buzzing in his head, that when Estefan turned around and flicked him the finger, he let go a short burst from his Uzi. He hit Estefan three times in the chest, slightly to left of center. It was exactly where he'd aimed. The force of the three bullets spun the idiot around despite his already being dead. Pablo picked up Estefan's gun and placed it near the body to make it look better. He also shot a couple of rounds from the gun in case any of the others were of a mind to check. He then ran into the jungle after the two mystery women, satisfied that he'd already accomplished more than he'd expected to. He forgot to wonder what was taking his men so long.

He was just picking up speed when his foot snagged on something and he went sprawling on the jungle floor. To his credit, as a Marine he did not let go of his gun when he fell. With the Uzi in the ready position, he looked about and saw the vine that had tripped him. He swore and resumed the chase, but slower and more carefully this time. He needed to find at least one of the women to prove they were real and justify his shooting Estefan.

There was one more instance of a vine being across the path. He was puzzling over that when the path split into two. He now had to make a choice and he was about to turn around and go back to the beach for reinforcements when he was hit in the head by something hard—twice. Once on the temple and once across his mouth. Had he been focusing on it, he would have felt another projectile whiz within millimeters of his left eye.

He hit the ground partly because of the sudden pain, but mostly from his Marine training many years before. He flicked the safety off once again and waited silently for a sound, a movement, anything to betray their presence.

He'd heard no shots and it took him a few seconds to reason out that it must have been rocks. It was then he felt the one that had hit him in the temple. "Man it is sore. What did they use to throw them? A cannon?" Fortunately the one on the mouth was a grazing wound, although it did leave him with a distinctly strange taste. *Oh well, the Chinese food will take that away*, he told himself.

As he waited, he started to feel a slight tingling at both places, particularly his lips and tongue. He began using his military training to wait them out. He knew one of them would move and when he did, he would use his superior firepower to take them all out. He had enough ammo to fill the entire jungle if need be.

He heard a vague, very brief rustling from his right, and when he had one more sound to pinpoint the direction, he would jump up and spray the area. He would not stop shooting until he was down to two clips of ammo. The tingling was getting downright annoying now. He made a mental note to wash both areas out as soon as he was done.

~~~~~~~~~

Unfortunately for Pablo, Mike and Luis also had excellent training and it would be a very long time indeed before they would move one centimeter. Seth had not been involved in either the armed forces or in the police department, but his training was far superior to that of the other three men. As a young man he'd hidden from the Germans, where one sound would mean capture and a fate much worse than death. He'd learned how to keep from moving or making a sound for hours at a time.

The four men stayed that way for what seemed ages to Pablo. Could they have left while he was diving for cover? Where were his men? Despite this, he did not move until a noise came from his left. It was a most definite thumping noise. He jumped up and started shooting. The men, having heard the same sound, had also jumped up and were about to unleash a second barrage of rocks when they heard the return fire from behind them. Two shots and Pablo was history. He had barely had time to squeeze off one burst.

The three men hit the ground once more hoping to God they had not been seen by this new and unexpected threat, when they heard Arrianna's voice, "Time to go guys, I think we got all of them."

Chapter Twenty-Two
Allie Makes Her Entrance

By the time the last of them arrived at their designated spot, the boat was visible and moving toward them at full throttle. They could see both Marc and Jerry in the boat apparently unharmed. The building excitement was palpable—they just could not believe how well everything had gone and their joy at having obtained a functioning high-speed motor boat to take them to civilization was beyond measure.

They waded out as far as they could and started climbing on board from all sides. It wasn't as tight a fit as it had first seemed. After what they'd been through, it was nothing.

They compared notes quickly and Marc told them of how Estefan was shot for "God only knows what reason" and how easy it had been to swim to the boat and take it. They never saw any of the other men return. Arrianna filled them in on how each of the four had been incapacitated by the poison in their eyes and how she decided to get one of their hand guns. Just prior to her leaving, one of the guys saw her and shouted something, but he had been unable to do more than stumble toward the beach.

"If he can get to the sea water, it will wash off the poison and he will recover quickly," warned Leesa.

"Then we will stay as far away from the beach as possible as we get around the point," answered Jerry, who had by now taken over the controls.

It was hard to say which they noticed first. The guy on the beach apparently talking into something that could have been a cell phone, or the wind that picked up as soon as they motored out from the lee of the island. Still determined to make it, wind or no wind, they pushed on until they rounded the last vestige of sheltering earth and that is when they saw it.

The storm that was on the verge of swallowing them looked enormous and was not to be ignored, even by the most experienced seamen among them. It truly was an incredible, awe-inspiring sight. It spanned horizon to horizon in their direction and, for all practical purposes, formed an impenetrable wall of water, wind and waves. They had come head to head with the first hurricane of the season, Hurricane Allie.

Jerry instinctively pulled the power back and they all stared at it for what felt like a lifetime. It was the boat's increasing rocking and swaying that broke them out of their shock.

"We have to go back," shouted Jerry.

"We can't," answered a chorus.

The decision was made when an unexpected wave hit them and sent Martha overboard. She managed to keep a hold of the railing and, with the help of the others, she was back aboard. This time when Jerry turned the boat around and headed for the beach at all possible speed, no one argued.

REDEMPTION ISLAND

The castaways still worked like a well-oiled and maintained machine. Even without a plan they instinctively knew what the others would be doing and what their best contribution would be. Within minutes of reaching the shallows, four of them were in the water bracing themselves on the sand and steadying the boat enough for the rest to get off. Then, as a group, by pushing, pulling, and the sheer tenacity of frustrated victory, they managed to get the boat onto the beach using one of the higher waves.

With the jungle offering barely adequate protection, Jerry distributed the various containers of Chinese food he had discovered under the driver's seat. It was the first real food they'd had since being shipwrecked. The savageness of millions of years of ancestors poked through the civilized exteriors of all seven of the castaways. Luis, although not the most sensitive person, quickly saw the animal hunger surrounding the food that these seven strange people expressed. To his credit, despite being hungry, he passed on it saying "It doesn't agree with me," and the moment passed.

When the food was gone and each container licked clean (their pride and manners had been left behind with the plane) they all looked at Marc to get them out of this unexpected mess. All but Luis, who had anticipated that Jerry, or perhaps Mike, would take the lead.

"It's not so bad. I suppose that as soon as the storm lessens we can just run back here and be off in the boat, back to the real world and..." Leesa stopped talking as most everyone was looking at her with sad expressions. "What! What did I say that is so dumb?"

Seth was the first to speak, "Not dumb. Call it inexperience. Have you ever been around a hurricane, after it passed through?"

"No!"

"Well... There is going to be little more than match sticks left of the boat by the time the storm is over." As to underscore that statement the wind increased suddenly and lightning flashed around them.

"Oh," she replied and slumped even further into the sand, dejected and utterly hopeless.

There was a silence during which they all did their own version of cursing their gods, fate, luck, what have you. To have successfully and so easily overwhelmed an armed party of drug mobsters and to get so close to being delivered from this island hell...just to have it dashed completely was almost more than they could bear.

Even ever optimistic and cheerful, Jerry struggled, "So we're just as bad off as when we began. Worse actually, because there are armed men who know where we are and have a personal grudge against us."

Luis spoke up, "We are armed too." But it came out without any real conviction. They all knew that without the element of surprise their chances against the men and whatever reinforcements they brought in were zero, zip, zilch, nada...

The wind was picking up its pace, driving the rain nearly horizontally. Despite their semi-protected location on the lee of the boat they were all sopping wet. There were branches falling around them and the sound level was ratcheting up by the minute.

It was then that Marc stood up with Arrianna at his side. They hung onto each other for both emotional and physical support. The wind made it very difficult to maintain balance. They both had focused determined looks on their faces.

"Enough! That will just about do it for the moan and groan chorus. We have things to do, places to see, yada, yada," said Arrianna.

Marc, in a highly uncharacteristic fashion, picked up where she left off. "Goddamm straight. What is all this pissing and moaning about anyway? We accomplished things beyond our imagination and I for one am not going to stop now that we are so close. If any one of you wants to continue with these negative karma waves, fine. Just don't do it around us, go over to the surf and let it drag you out to sea, at least you'll feed the fishes."

With that utterly ruthless declaration, the two of them stormed off to the other side of the boat mostly to keep the others from seeing their hands shaking.

"How did I do?" asked Marc.

"Perfect. You were utterly perfect. They are probably still in shock." They both snickered knowing they were out of sight. Then, despite the driving rain, desperate wind and escalating surf, they took a few seconds to share a deep kiss, one of many more to come—they both hoped.

Marc's tirade, as it came to be called, spurred all of them to action and soon enough they ran after the couple. He directed them in salvaging everything possible from the boat. They also ripped out anything they could, to lighten it. They were going to try to pull the bloody thing up onto the beach and hopefully out of harm's way.

The weather was now getting truly rough. If it hadn't been for the courage exhibited by every single person, the boat would've been lost. As it turned out, the wind helped more than hindered. Inside an hour they had the boat into the woods and tied down to the trees as tight as possible. They also had an array of tools none of them had anticipated.

Apparently these men traveled prepared for anything. There was ammo, ammo and more ammo, far more than they could hope to carry, much less use. They buried most of it against the future possibility of needing it and kept as much as Luis deemed prudent. There was the outboard they lovingly, but quickly, removed and placed into a sheltered place because it was their ticket off the island. Even if the boat did not survive, with that kind of power, they could build anything that would float, rig the motor to it and limp back to civilization. A chain saw was unexpected, but not unwelcome. They placed it next to the motor.

Once satisfied that all that could be done had been done, the group gathered and, despite the now deafening roar of the wind and the random percussion of the thunder, they huddled for a moment of emotional connection before following Marc to his soap making cave.

The cave was significantly off the beaten path but it was unlikely the enemy would have found it. Nevertheless, Luis and Mike led the way with both weapons at the ready. It was perfect weather for an attack and Luis had argued for them to search out the survivors and exterminate them—that later would be too late. He had lost the vote 7-1. Being used to senseless orders, he let it go and now concentrated on not being surprised by those same men.

Arrianna described her ordeal with the bumbling gangsters. The group cackled and Arrianna joined them.

"It was hard not to laugh. I had to firmly clamp my hand over my mouth…although…"

"Although what?" asked Martha.

"I was thinking how if I had managed some kind of maniacal laughter, he would have run even faster."

Jerry mused that he must have been the one they saw on the beach with his cell phone. He asked, "What happened next?"

She looked at all of them, but especially at the three from the slingshot brigade. "I was worried about the three of you. Of all of us, you were taking the most risk." She focused her comments on

Mike. "When I saw the gun just lying there I had to get it and run to help you."

"Good thing too, he might have gotten lucky and hit one of us with his aimless fire. It sure was lucky you arrived just as he started shooting," commented Luis.

"It wasn't luck at all," said Arrianna, "I was there before you even fired your first shot."

At this they all perked up, aside from the howling of the wind and the static of the rain outside the cave, there wasn't a sound.

"I watched him get hit and was surprised how he dove for cover. He must have had some prior training. Then everything was so still, not a single one of you made a sound. It was creepy how you could do that. I figured he was waiting for one of you to betray your position, so I tossed some pebbles to the far side, and you know the rest." She sat back and visibly relaxed now that it was all out.

Marc was next. "We saw the entire scene unfold at the beach. We couldn't hear what they were saying but the guy you shot didn't need any provocation to shoot his partner. He then picked up the guy's gun and rearranged the scene as if it had been done in self-defense. He even shot a few rounds in the air. I guess for the benefit of the four in the woods." He looked at Luis.

Luis shrugged, "This kind of senseless shit happens all the time; it's hard to resign from these groups."

Marc continued, "When the two of you broke cover, the reality of it all hit us and I was scared shitless…"

"Not half as much as we were," replied Leesa "it made us run faster."

"Right, well… as soon as he reached the woods, we swam as fast as we could to get there before anyone returned. I climbed into the boat from the seaward side, lifted the anchor while Jerry started the boat. We stayed down as planned, but no one shot at us. Just before we turned out of sight, we saw someone stumble out of the jungle, his hands on his face…"

"Must have been my guy, the one who ran into the tree," remarked Arrianna.

"I guess so. Anyway, he jumped into the water as if dying of thirst. Then we made it to the meeting site and to our surprise and delight everyone was already there waiting for us."

It was Martha's turn. "I confess that when I saw the raw lust and evil in that guy's face I sort of froze. My legs would not move."

"I know," added Leesa, "that look was aimed at me."

~~~~~~~~

Suddenly they all felt exhausted. The reality of what they had accomplished meshed with the reality that it was not yet over and that a hurricane raged outside their small shelter. It was only room sized, but it was reasonably dry and safe. They looked at each other and finally, with their attention focused on Jerry, someone asked, "What do we do now, chief?"

Jerry looked up at them with tears of frustration welling in his eyes, "I haven't a clue, not a clue at all."

Chapter Twenty-Three
Battle Plans Redux

At first they had briefly entertained the notion of posting a watch. It took only a few minutes for the storm to point out with flash and fury, how ludicrous an idea that was. So, they had lay down and succumbed to the physical and emotional fatigue.

In the morning the discussion of their next move came up once more. The storm was, for the most part, past and on its way to play havoc elsewhere. Soon they would be able to leave. Everyone feared what the boat would look like. The storm had been far more severe than anything any one of them had experienced. That was true even for Mike, who had been on the islands for a while. There was little doubt in anyone's mind that what they had labored at only a few hours before was now a collection of splinters washed out to sea.

Finally, Seth broke the impasse by standing up and making for the beach. "Let's do it folks, we won't know what to do until we see what happened to the boat and equipment."

They all trooped obediently down the slight grade and the

freedom of movement soon dissipated much of their gloom. Had it not been for the presence of others on the island, others that meant them harm, they might even have broken into song.

As they approached the boat, the ones in the lead, Seth, Arrianna, and Marc slowed and they all ventured forth as a group. There was still some light rain and an occasional gust of not quite 30 knots. At twenty paces they saw the shape of the boat and it looked intact. They raced to it hoping for the impossible.

~~~~~~~~

On inspecting the boat, they saw the damage. It was major and despite their best efforts, dispiriting. A tree had fallen on one of the chairs ripping the strut out of the side of the boat. This left a grapefruit-sized gash at the waterline. Considering the violence of the storm, it was better than they could have hoped for.

Marc spoke up, "I'd forgotten that the damage to boats is almost exclusively from them hitting something hard. I guess that by tying it down so well we avoided most of the usual damage."

"We can patch it with some of the floorboards but without tar or some other waterproofing it will take water quickly," said Mike.

"How about the pump?" asked Seth.

Jerry replied, "No chance of that helping. It's just a hand pump, more for looks than function. There is no hope that it could keep up with that kind of inflow."

"Damn it all to hell! We are so close," shouted Leesa, adequately describing the feelings of everyone there.

It took a while for anyone to notice, but Marc was walking in and out of the boat checking something, his brow furrowed. He was measuring the hole and testing the edges of it. Once they saw him at it however, all but Luis started smiling. They knew that their "professor" was coming up with one of his special ideas. Luis started to approach and question Marc but the others hushed him and gave Marc plenty of elbow room and time to do his thing.

Suddenly Marc stopped, cast about him and was startled to see everyone looking at him expectantly. He started, "I have an idea…" stopped, looked again and smiled. "You already know that, don't you?"

Seth said, "You aren't the most subtle of thinkers. Let's have it, I expect it will be good."

"The hole is at the waterline, like you know, but just at the waterline. I don't have much practical experience around boats, but theory suggests that if the boat is going fast enough, the hull will rise and lift that hole right out of the water. What I was trying to figure out was how fast is fast enough?"

"And?" asked Martha.

"I just don't know. There is no way I can think of to calculate it. I suppose that we will have to simply go and find out."

"That won't be necessary," said Jerry moving to the boat and looking it over. "I should have thought of it myself. I have been in similar boats and I have water-skied behind them more times than I can remember, certainly enough to have paid attention to how high the boat rides so as to judge it's speed. I can tell you that the hole will be completely in the air after twenty knots, give or take a couple. That motor can easily reach forty. Marc has once again saved our bacon."

The shock and fear held them back a few moments, but finally hope and joy overtook all of them and they all smiled at the resourcefulness of their "mad scientist."

They began the heavy work of getting the boat close to the water and placing the motor back on it. By lunchtime, the storm had faded into memory and reality began creeping into their consciousness. There were still four armed men out there and with the noise no longer masked and distorted by the swirling wind, they would be easy targets. Even more menacing was the scary thought that now those four could count on reinforcements arriving. If they didn't get off the island soon, they'd be in deeper trouble.

Progress in patching and re-loading the boat was painfully slow. It became evident that it would take more time than they originally thought. Instead of losing focus and despairing, furious urgency surged through nearly all of them and they formulated a plan. They would simply have to buy more time.

~~~~~~~~

The plan was simple in concept but difficult in execution. If they "eliminated" the remaining men on the island and hid them, not only would they be better armed, but the new group would not know what, who, or where they were. It would take time to coordinate a search. Luis opined that it would undoubtedly be interpreted as a raid by a rival gang. By the time they had their act together, they would not have any way of knowing whether anyone remained on the island.

The only question left was "Who would go after them?" They had no shortage of volunteers: Mike, Luis, Arrianna, and Seth all wanted to go. With only two weapons at hand, however, it was senseless to send more than two or three people. It was surprising, even to Arrianna, that she volunteered for such a mission, but after her dispatch of Pablo, she had felt powerful for one of the few times in her life. She had some control of what happened around her. She wanted to feel that again.

Seth was rejected due to his age and reasonable concerns that he would slow the others down. Luis had to go, but the other two were equally adamant about going. Arrianna had the advantage of being young, fit, and had recently proved her ability to use the weapon effectively. Luis settled it with a question. He asked, "Would you have any problem shooting them in the back without any warning or provocation whatsoever?"

Mike answered without the slightest hesitation, "No problem. As far as I'm concerned they've had all the warning they need."

Arrianna hesitated, clearly unsure how to respond. The guy in the jungle yesterday had been different. He was firing and trying to kill them. She just did not know how she would do in an ambush situation. Reluctantly, she nodded her acquiesce despite her deep desire to carry the weapon and be in on the assault. She would go with them, but mostly to help them carry stuff.

The three of them left immediately and without fanfare. Arrianna carried the extra ammo, some food and a whole lot of resentment. They headed to the guy she'd killed to see if he'd been found, and if not, what else he might have on his person. The previous day they'd been in a hurry and all they had managed to get was his Uzi and a couple of clips. This time they would search him thoroughly.

Jerry and Seth continued refitting of the boat, trying to be as quiet as possible. Martha and Leesa set up an observation post at the only practical approach to their camp. They took turns manning it while the other gathered food. Without any formal discussion, Marc was left alone to let his remarkable mind ruminate. They hoped for another of his ever-so-practical ideas. Talk was short and curt. Each of their hearts and minds were with the raiding party.

~~~~~~~~

The raiding party reached Pablo without incident. They

approached slowly, methodically, looking for a trap. When they found none they searched the former leader. In some indefinable way the hurricane had made his body much more accessible, as if it had been cleansed and no longer retained any of the stigma of death. Arrianna found a palm-sized 25 cal. automatic strapped in an ankle holster. Behind his neck they found a savage looking knife that only Luis appreciated. They also found his wallet and thereby discovered his name, a rough estimate of his wealth and, if it had not been for Mike, they would have seen his family.

Mike knew that it was vital not to see this lump of soon to be decaying flesh as an actual human with a wife and family. This was especially true in Arrianna's case. He casually closed the wallet, put it in his front pocket and signaled for Luis to lead on.

They heard them well before they saw them. Stumbling, cursing, and whining all the way down the hill. When they saw them collapse on the sand, they knew they had precious little time. If a boat or plane approached and landed before they could enact their plan, then they would be lost.

Arrianna moved into position, screwed up her courage and set herself up for her performance. Luis and Mike carried the waterlogged body of Pablo to the edge of the woods, and then threw him out onto the sand.

At the same time Arrianna fired the .25 cal twice yelling at the four morons lying supine with their weapons scattered where they had carelessly dropped them. "You filthy pieces of Hispanic shit. You couldn't give your grandmother an enema much less catch me." She then went into a fit of hysterical laughter of the type that used to infuriate her mother.

While Arrianna waited for the four to get themselves up and moving, Mike and Luis fell back into the blinds they had hastily created. In retrospect, Luis noted that they could have quietly walked up to them and shot them point blank before they could have reacted. "Who knew?" he asked himself.

Once up and roused, the drug runners' speed was impressive. So much so that the first one got by the ambush. Mike and Luis started firing as soon as the last one passed their position. Two dropped immediately, dead or seriously wounded. The third one started firing blindly, unable to tell where the firing was coming from. Both men let loose on him and he was dead before his knees flexed on his way down.

The last of the men had wisely kept going when he heard the shooting and was only now turning around to face the threat. Arrianna saw him clearly from her perch. She only had to move slightly and she would have a clear shot at him.

Unfortunately when she moved, some of the ammo she had been carrying in her pockets shifted and fell, causing enough noise for the man to suddenly twist around. She still had plenty of time to shoot but inexplicably hesitated, unable to shoot until he started firing. He smiled knowingly and squeezed the trigger.

Mike and Luis were on their way but did not reach her in time. The man tried to fire, but the gun jammed. He would not get the opportunity to file a complaint with the manufacturer for Arrianna, now realizing her near fatal error and how fortunate she was at getting a second chance, did not hesitate a second time. She fired over and over until she emptied her clip, well after it was clearly unnecessary to continue. Had she had another clip she still would have been shooting when her two friends reached her.

She was shedding tears of rage and all that Luis could get her to say was, "You were right after all."

Chapter Twenty-Four
Wicked Witch of the West

The boat was as seaworthy as they could make it. There was enough food gathered for a day or two and the group left at the boat was teeming with nervous energy. They'd heard the gunfire ten minutes before and they could not resolve the exchange. The first shots had not been from the automatic weapons carried by Mike and Luis, but from a handgun, or so Seth said. Then the next and final shots were from the same handgun. They could not come up with an explanation that did not include one of their friends hurt or dead.

They discussed what to do next and if their friends did not return promptly they planned on running for the hills. They were readying to go when the plane showed. Marc heard it first, but Martha was the one who spotted the plane. It flew low and in such a direct line for the island that no one doubted for a second who was in it. Significantly, it only served to fortify their resolve. They were now absolutely determined to make it off the island regardless of the obstacles.

REDEMPTION ISLAND

They watched mesmerized as it lumbered over the island and circled many times, first to the left and then to the right. Apparently they were looking for something or someone. The longer the plane circled, the higher their hopes reached. Marc nervously checked the boat once more to convince himself it was not visible from the air. It had been Marc's idea to camouflage it and he'd done an excellent job. Logically they knew it could not be seen, nevertheless the five castaways felt terribly exposed.

The plane circled for what felt like forever before it disappeared to the far side of the island. It returned ten minutes later and circled again. Finally it started dropping altitude in preparation for a water landing in the general area where the boat had arrived.

"What do you think we should do, Marc?" asked Martha.

"We should go and hide, but I hate to leave until Arrianna returns. We can't leave a message in case they find it first." What remained unspoken was that their friends might not ever return again. "Why don't we give it ten more minutes and use that time to get ready. We will still have a good lead even if they know exactly where we are." The others nodded in agreement and continued preparations.

It was a full eight minutes later when they heard it coming. They'd forgotten to post a sentry and they all looked at each other, the dread evident on their faces. They had no weapons and were essentially defenseless. Their trepidation did not last long, for Arrianna broke through with a huge smile on her face and ran to Marc. Mike and Luis came half a minute later.

They began a war council to catch up with each other, but once informed of the plane, they began formulating a response. Mike had not seen the plane, but he'd heard it and with the rough description from Marc, he deduced that it was a plane similar to his own–at least in seating capacity.

"They could get four, maybe five guys in there, if they skimped on the gas and did not carry anything heavy."

Luis said, "You know they will be heavily armed, at least twenty or thirty pounds to the person." He pursed his lips, looked like he was going to say something, but thought better of it.

Seth said, "I don't think these people would worry too much about recommended weight limits. After the war, when we were fighting off the Arab attacks, we would load a plane until there was no room left. We let the pilot worry about it."

Luis nodded and smiled. Mike closed his eyes and calculated. "Then it depends on how crazy the pilot is. In this humidity he'd be insane to carry more than 1100, 1200 pounds somewhere around there. Even then he would need an awfully long runway."

"So figure five soldiers max. Possibly four if they wanted to carry a lot," said Marc. "That doesn't sound too bad. They will be very careful and slow when they can't find their buddies." He paused to look at the other three. "You're sure they won't find them—right?"

Mike spoke up, "Like we told you, we were late because we took special pains to hide them. They are in the jungle and well into the underbrush. We took some uh, additional precautions. They won't find them." The rest of them looked at him for three full seconds and decided they probably were better off not knowing what he meant.

They all went silent for several wave cycles. They could hear the birds and the sea but nothing human. No one wanted to ask the next question. It took some time but eventually they discussed their options and quickly decided. All ideas of trying to repeat their search and destroy mission were gone. The enemy was now on alert, doubly so because they could not find anyone. They were fresh, not demoralized and beaten down by a hurricane and probably far better armed than they were. They would also now have real leadership. There would be little hope of luring them into a trap so easily.

They discussed taking the plane from them, but they could not figure a way of boarding it and overpowering the pilot without alerting the others. If they left no guards, it would be out in the bay where the pilot could see all the approaches. Even if someone swam to it, as soon as he stepped on the pontoon, the pilot would know.

Only Luis was surprised when it was Marc who came up with a workable solution. He'd been working on a way to fix the boat well enough to get them to the main island. He had several ideas but he'd learned from the raft episode to test them first. What he needed most was time and they would have to get it for him. Once he had the fix tested and dependable, then and only then could they motor out.

As an afterthought to his plan Marc added, "Oh yeah, by the way, we will have to disable their plane so they can't follow us. On this island with the sound carrying over the water, they will hear the motor right off. They may not be able to tell from exactly which direction, but in a plane it won't take them long to find us—we'd be flightless ducks out there."

Arrianna volunteered to lead them on a not-so-merry goose chase. "I will know where I'm going. I won't be weighed down by equipment or fear an ambush. I will be way out ahead of them leaving them just enough signs for them to follow. Then when they are far inland, I will sneak back here and we can be off. How much time do you need?"

Marc looked uneasy, "I don't know. It depends on how many things I have to try to get it to work. Too bad we don't have radios or phones." At this the raiding party managed huge grins.

"You mean like these?" said Luis.

Marc's jaw nearly touched the sand, his mind clearly working double time to comprehend the impossible. "You've had phones all along? And you haven't called for help?"

"Not phones, but radios, walkie-talkies. We found one on the leader, the guy we ambushed yesterday. One of the others had this one. We almost didn't bring them, their range is very short and undoubtedly the new bastards have identical ones and are listening in."

Marc had his faraway look considering this new datum. "OK, OK, but we can still use it. We will come up with a code and signal Arrianna when she is to come back. That leaves only one thing."

"To disable the airplane," said Mike matter of fact.

"Right."

Seth spoke up, "Mike and I will take care of it. Luis will stay here to provide security. I need Mike because he will know how best to disable the plane."

No one could think of an argument and after a few moments they dispersed in their assigned directions.

~~~~~~~~~~

Manuel was more puzzled than angry or frustrated, but those would come later. They'd circled the island several times and at different altitudes and with everyone looking out, they'd seen nothing. No boat, no wreckage, no people. No signs of people—nothing! He'd tried the walkie-talkie without success. It only had three frequencies and he'd tried them all. He could not very well report this to his boss. Not yet anyway. If he could find a body or two with some clear and convincing evidence of how they'd died then he'd be off the hook. Even if they couldn't determine cause of death, they could arrange for a pickup and have a post mortem done—they had ways. Once they all were off the plane and waded ashore safely, he'd sent scouts to search the beach. They found nothing, nothing at all. The storm had done a lot of damage and any traces of footprints or habitation were long gone, yet...

"*Jefe!*"

"*Si, diga.*"

"We found something." A wallet and one of the weapons were in his hands.

"Where were they?" asked Manuel, clearly excited with the new possibilities.

"Over by the tree where they told us the DEA shit was chained, although... he isn't here anymore."

Manuel thought it over. Someone had taken Luis's body. Further, one of his guys had dropped his gun and wallet. It only added up one way—ambush. He put them on alert, set out a perimeter guard and reported his findings on his cell phone. His call lasted only three minutes. In that time he had his instructions—search and kill anyone that remained on the island. They agreed it was likely they had left before the storm, but he had to make sure.

"And try to find out as much information as possible!" his boss had emphasized, "I need to know who did this." It was unlikely but conceivable that some of their men had been chased inland and been hurt enough that they were unable to come down and meet them.

"We will go along the coast for a while and scout the edge of the jungle, and then we will go inland." They started in the direction where the boat and castaways lay, but had not taken ten steps when the female voice broke the silence. Manuel could not disguise his shock that it came from his radio.

"*Hola muchachos.* I hope you guys are more durable than those spineless pantywaists from yesterday. They just couldn't handle little old me."

REDEMPTION ISLAND

Manuel clicked the mike and restrained his impulse to scream. Instead he kept his voice low and firm. "Who the fuck are you and what are you talking about?"

"Well, someone with brains, what a change. You'd better watch that language though. I don't think your mother would approve. For your information, I live here on this island and your buddies intruded on my privacy, so I killed them—every last one of them. Would you like their cojones? I haven't eaten all of them and I have some left."

"*Que*?!" yelled Manuel, unable to control himself.

"I don't get such a delicacy very often so I took my opportunity when I had it. I will take yours also if you're not careful."

"Get off this frequency, bitch! Stop playing games!" Manuel shouted. He replaced the radio and told the men to continue with the plan. Obviously someone with a similar radio on a nearby island was playing with them. He did not have time for games.

"Oh I get it, you don't believe me. I need a little credibility. Why don't you have one of your tough *hombres* look behind that large tree you just passed. Have them go twenty paces or so and look on the far side of the fallen tree, under the pile of palm fronds. I will be here when you are done."

Manuel wasn't sure what to do. She knew what they were doing and where they were? How could that be? She also knew about the other group. It could be a trap. Still he had to check it out. Quickly he set up a tactical plan, just like he used to do in 'Nam when he was an NCO. To his surprise, it turned out that there was no trap and just where she said, they found one of their men—with his balls cut off.

~~~~~~~~

REDEMPTION ISLAND

"Shit! It still leaks like a sieve. I can't find anything that works, except maybe..." His voice trailed off.

"What?" asked Jerry. Martha and Leesa were both there and they had heard the same thing. Marc was holding something back. "I can't say it, it's just too..." he never finished the sentence.

"Too what! Come on damn it. We have an eighteen-year-old girl leading a platoon of heavily-armed, morally deficient men on a merry chase and taunting them. Our oldest member is sneaking around trying to disable a plane with the pilot still in it. Whatever it is, we need it now! No! We needed it yesterday. So cough it up, we are completely, totally out of time. It has to be now!"

Marc looked up and saw the anger in Jerry's face, but he also saw the caring.. He simply knew that Jerry was not angry with him as much as he was worried about the others and feeling the urgency to get off the island before something bad happened, something real bad. Still, how could he tell him what he'd thought up? It would work for sure, but could they really do it?

They saw his hesitation and Leesa tried a different tack. "It's okay Marc, we aren't angry with you. We just need to get off this damn island. And we have no time left. None at all. Arrianna is, at this minute, running away from five furious men intent on doing her no good. We know you are able to think in unusual ways and if it doesn't work, we won't hold it against you. We can't even come up with a single idea."

Marc looked at them with tears streaming in his eyes and a hollow haunted look that silenced the three of them. It had been the vision of Arrianna in terrible danger that spurred him on. "It's not that. I thought I could come up with a plant product that would expand with water and remain strong, but one idea keeps coming up that I can't get out of my mind. It will work all right, but..."

Martha spoke, "But what Marc? You can tell us, we're all friends."

REDEMPTION ISLAND

He took a huge breath, followed that up with another and said, "Promise that you won't think less of me?"

The three of them looked at each other puzzled, not comprehending what in the world Marc was referring to. "We promise," said Leesa with the other two nodding their assent.

Marc began telling them. He looked down at his hands throughout the explanation. "I had the idea when I looked at the chainsaw. We could cut the leg off one of the dead men high up—at the hip joint. The leg is shaped as a funnel at that point and it would wedge nicely in the spot. Then we could cut the dangling part off." He looked up to see their faces.

Martha had a look of horror on her face. Leesa appeared to be holding bile back—these were the reactions he'd expected and feared. It was Jerry who saved them—his face was a mask of concentration. There was absolutely no emotion for at least five seconds, at the end of which he looked at Marc and said formally, "Good work. I am deeply impressed with your out-of-the-box thinking. Don't feel bad because it is distasteful. Once we are back in the real world you can get therapy for years if you need it, and I will pay for it. Now I better tell Luis what he needs to do." He stood up and started to walk away, leaving the three of them slack-jawed, but better. Just before he was out of hearing range. Martha called to him and said, "Better have him bring two just in case."

~~~~~~~~~~~~

Arrianna was not scared. She was actually enjoying herself. The teasing and acting came naturally to her. She would have to look into this as a career choice if she got back. "Stop that!" she told herself, "When you get back!"

She was on an outcropping that allowed her to see the beach.

REDEMPTION ISLAND

She could see the men reporting back to the leader and wished she could see his expression. On her way up, she had gone by the easiest body to reach and performed her amputation. That job she hadn't liked much, but it was necessary to get their attention. These boys pretending to be men are so attached to their manhood. Luis had helped her with it, but they both agreed it would be best not to tell the others.

Finally the leader was calling her back.

"What is it you want?" said Manuel, his voice cracking with undisguised fury.

"So you found him, did you? Is my credibility any higher now?"

"Yes! You fucking bitch, we believe you now. What kind of game are you playing?"

"Tsk, tsk, watch that name calling. You might make me angry."

Manuel had to physically release the frustration he felt and he went up to a tree and punched it. He felt no pain. "Why are you doing this? What's your game?"

"No game...uh, by the way what is your name? You can call me Ari if you want."

"Manuel."

"No game, Manuel. I just want you off my fucking island, and now. I don't like people and I don't want visitors. Tell your boss that if he dumps his bodies on my island again, then he must bring me supplies. I will give you a list. Don't come back otherwise, or you will end up like your friends. Remember, I don't get much chance to eat meat, or brains." She smiled as she said this. Playing mind games was second nature to her and for the first time in her life, she entertained the thought that something positive could have come from her miserable childhood.

Manuel was speechless. On top of that, his men were looking at him and at the jungle, not scared but definitely alarmed. What was he supposed to do now? He could not leave and report this... this woman to the boss. The idea was ludicrous. Yet she did seem able to surprise armed men. It was his mucho-macho culture that finally rescued him.

"She is taking credit for something others did. The body had bullet holes you said. They were ambushed by the Colombians and she took their radios but nothing else." The others nodded their assent. It was a far better thing to believe than the alternative. "If we only knew where she was we could silence her for good. Perhaps even find out what happened." As an afterthought he added, "and maybe we could find some time to have fun." They all laughed.

It was at that precise moment, when his men had leers on their faces, that she stood up on the rock outcropping and said, "Manuel, I am up here, just look up." They did, were stunned to see the voice materialize into reality. Before they could react, she was gone and they went after her. The chase was on.

~~~~~~~~

Seth and Mike saw the group of five disciplined and impressively armed men take off at a dead run. It was their cue. They counted to twenty as slow as their hearts would allow and stealthily approached the beach.

At this point in time, their main purpose was to scout the area, check-out the plane and come up with a plan for disabling it or, at the very least, chasing it off. The timing of "Operation: deny flight" would be tricky and had to be coordinated with Marc's boat fix, Arrianna's diversion, and, as far as Seth knew, Jehovah's sense of humor. He followed the men's tracks into the woods and stopped.

He would now remain stone quiet listening for the first signs and sounds of anyone's approach.

Mike waited until the old man reached the woods before leaving the shelter of the trees and proceeding with his assignment. The amphibian was floating far out in the cove bobbing up and down with the gentle waves. There was no sign of anchor and it needed to be far away to avoid being beached. The wind, as light as it was, had caused the pilot to face into it and, at this moment, the plane was turned so that its tail faced them—good. The pilot would be unable to see them unless he stepped out of the plane.

He measured the distance in his head, looked at the motion of the plane, and tried to remember where the fuel tanks were on this model. Like his own, this one was army surplus and built for war. It would take a lot to disable it. Particularly true from this distance and armed with only light automatic weapons.

"I suppose one of us could swim to it without being noticed," he said to himself, surprised when it came out loud. "Then what? Shoot holes in one of the props? In the rudder? Swim with a machine gun strapped to your back, try not to drown and hope the gun works?

He paced up and down the beach analyzing the best approaches to the plane. Once done, he signaled to Seth with his whistle call and they both scurried back to camp to await instructions.

Seth saw his face and decided against asking what he thought. His face told him that he did not want to know.

~~~~~~~~~~

Arrianna was so exhilarated by the role she was playing that she was now speeding through the jungle without visibly expending any effort. She'd seen them break toward her and reach the tree line. There was no way to check if they were still after her, but that was not her concern anymore. If that act did not work then nothing would.

She had a good ten minute head start, but she was losing it quickly by the care she took to leave tracks. These had to be obvious enough to follow, but not so overwhelming as to be suspicious. She went out of her way to step on plants, land on soft ground, avoid rocky terrain. After twenty minutes, she stopped and found a perch in a tree that overlooked the rock outcropping she'd been on. She wanted to see how many made it there and possibly entice them some more. She needed to get them as far from the beach as she could.

She'd only been in the tree three minutes when the first one arrived. He looked around, checked the area, and then signaled the others to approach. "A scout! Damn! These guys are good," she muttered to herself.

All five eventually showed themselves in their careful scrutiny of the surroundings. They saw the outcropping and looked down at the beach. They could easily see the plane from there. The scout noticed her trail immediately, but instead of following it, they hesitated and their leader gave them instructions. She was alarmed when two of them were about to head back down to the beach.

"I wouldn't do that, Manuel."

Manuel tried to hide the jump he felt at the sound of her voice. "I don't give a rat's ass what you would or wouldn't do."

"Again with the language, oh well. Your dead friends said the very same thing—exactly. Do you guys go to the same school for training? Like the army sends its people to a war college you guys go to Drug College?"

"Shut the fuck up!"

"Yup, exactly what the guy I had for dinner last night said. You know what I call you guys?"

Manuel felt stuck, if he did not respond he would look outmaneuvered by a woman. But she was taunting him to his limits. "I call you dead, bitch!"

"Truly amazing! Word for word what he said. Did you guys practice it before you came? What to say if you are talking to a crazy, dangerous mountain woman." Arrianna paused, "And believe me, Manuel; I am very dangerous. I will be your worst nightmare while you remain on my island. You will never hear me approach. Never see me when I snatch one of your men. You guys are my 'Meals-on-wheels." Arrianna cackled her worst laughter that she could manage. She used to do a mean Wicked-Witch-of-the-West imitation and it had served her well.

Manuel's deep self-confidence was cracked by the exchange and the maniacal laughter at the end. This was one very mixed up woman. Was she a real threat? Could he afford to ignore it? Should he really send two of his men back to the beach as he intended? Would they be safe? In the end, his mucho-macho ego ruled the day. There was absolutely no way he could go back and report this taunting by a woman without a satisfactory resolution. *She'd better be half as good as she says she is because once we catch her she will sorely regret putting me through this.* With that unspoken thought the five of them resumed their chase.

She was relieved that they were all after her. Another twenty minutes or so and they would be so disoriented that getting back to the beach would take at least as long as getting up here. Two hours is what she'd promised; she was now well on her way to fulfilling that promise.

Unfortunately, her early and easy success had the consequence of decreasing her vigilance. Immediately on resuming her flight, she stepped on a hidden root and went down sprawling. Her right hand landed first and took the brunt of the fall. She heard a snap followed by a searing pain. She rolled around holding her wrist, biting her tongue to keep from screaming. After what seemed like hours, but was probably only minutes, she regained a modicum of composure and realized that she had to go.

However, she couldn't get up. Her wrist hurt so much. She had to motivate herself to get moving, now! She dug deep into her horror closet and brought out the ugliest of her repressed memories: the time that her mother's boyfriend tried to rape her and nearly succeeded. She remembered the hurt of her mother's indifference. She had been eleven at the time and aged a lifetime that day. She remembered the pain, understood what these men would do would make that pale by comparison and found the strength to get on her feet. She swayed a couple of times and then felt much better. She took a few cautious steps and found that the wrist did not care unless she jostled it. She took off not making any effort to advertise her direction.

Once moving, endorphins took over and the pain of the broken wrist eased markedly. She was able to move at nearly normal walking speed, slowing down only for large obstructions. She did not know how long she'd been down or how close the men were so she made every effort to increase the distance between them. The "fun and games" were over and the cold hard slap of reality had been as sharp as it had been unexpected.

~~~~~~~~

Jerry walked away as calmly as he could manage. He had to project control, approval, and leadership. Once out of sight, he fell to his hands and knees and vomited everything that he'd eaten that day and more. It took three minutes for the spasms to pass and the revulsion to end.

REDEMPTION ISLAND

His training as CEO had prepared him well for this. He was a pro at hiding his feelings, particularly of sweaty, nauseating fear. He then got up, dusted himself off, and finished the trip.

He arrived at the blind simultaneously with Seth and Mike. One look at Mike's face told him all there was to know about disabling the plane—not very likely. They saw his face and paled. They knew something wasn't right.

Seth spoke first, "Is Arrianna all right?"

Jerry answered, "As far as I know, but she can't hold out all day, we have to get going."

Mike was about to ask something when two mike clicks came over the radio. They all stood rooted to the ground. Not a single one took a breath hoping against hope that one more click would not come. Despite their silent supplications, the third delayed click came and went. It was Arrianna's distress signal.

The four men thought it through quickly. She still was at large or she would have broken radio silence, but was in some sort of trouble, injured perhaps. What were they to do? They had no clue as to where she was. Jerry came to a decision and clicked once paused for two seconds and clicked twice—the signal for her to return; the signal that the boat was ready. She responded with her one click of confirmation and they all breathed a big sigh of relief.

After their hearts slowed to a manageable level, Luis said hopefully, "So you came to tell me that you've fixed the boat?"

"Not exactly. I signaled the return code to confirm that she could still get back on her own. Besides, Marc has come up with a rather unorthodox solution. " Jerry then took a big breath, braced himself and told them what the four of them had to do—now more urgently than ever.

REDEMPTION ISLAND

Arrianna was fading, and despite her sluggish thinking, she knew it. The energy it took to keep going with her wrist in such torment drained her to exhaustion. Had she not had the emotional toughness from living with her parents, she would not have been able to continue to push herself forward. She revised her initial assessment that she could return unaided and was about to break radio silence to ask for help, when she heard Manuel talking to the plane. He'd said far more than necessary and gave away the ranch, outhouse and all. The instant she realized he was not following her anymore, she collapsed exactly where she was and began sobbing desperately, yet quietly, still holding her wrist to her body as someone might hold a dead baby. She had accomplished her duty and had not been caught.

They could not point to her as the reason for failure—this gave her more relief than anything else could have. With the relief came hope. It took time, but after the wrist had been still for several minutes, the throbbing eased, her exhaustion diminished proportionately and her thoughts switched to whether they would leave without her. Her better half told her that it would not even occur to them, yet the abandoned, betrayed child within brought up the many times other adults had done exactly that. She stood slowly and began a deliberate walk. She discovered that by planning her steps carefully, she could keep the wrist from moving and the pain would only reach intolerable levels every few minutes or so. She realized she would make it back alone and would not need to call for help after all.

REDEMPTION ISLAND

Everyone wanted to be the one to disable the plane. The alternative was too bloody awful to consider. Jerry winced at what he had to do. As leader, he knew that he could not ask of others what he would not do. They arrived at the boat and informed the others of the sudden urgency. They just had to have that boat sea worthy and in the water. The seven of them had jumped into action and begun digging a trench from the boat to the water. It did not take long and now it was time.

"OK, here's the plan. Mike, Marc you two are our best shots. You will go and take pot shots at the plane. Remember it is highly unlikely that you will do any significant damage to the plane at that range, so you are to scare it off, nothing more. Take one shot at a time. Aim for the pilot's cabin. Keep low and hidden. We don't want him to see you. That way he won't know when it's safe to return. Ladies," he addressed Martha and Leesa, "I want you out in the jungle as far as you dare go, remain hidden and quiet and listen for Arrianna. She may need help. The rest of us will fix the hole in the boat and start pushing it into the water.

They all took it in and accepted his leadership. He placed himself in the middle of the worst of it. Luis and Seth winced but said nothing, the rest of them simply tried not to show their enormous relief.

Chapter Twenty-Five
Arrianna Reaches Her Family

Arrianna was now stumbling through the jungle, unable to be either quiet or gentle. The pain shot through her arm and down her back with every step her right foot took. She was curious why it did not hurt when she used her other foot, but her brain could not focus enough to analyze it. Fortunately for her, she was making so much noise that the two ladies heard her well in advance. When they saw her condition, Leesa gasped and froze but Martha ran to her immediately. She reached her just in time to keep her from collapsing. Martha sent Leesa for help while she looked Arrianna over carefully.

The wrist she was still cradling was swollen, discolored and distorted. She felt her stomach flinch in revolt but sternly ignored it. Arrianna had risked her life and was forced to rescue herself to give them the time they needed to escape. She hadn't even asked for help. Martha remained quiet, but was unable to stop tears from flowing. She knew some of what Arrianna had endured before this and it broke her heart to see that her life continued to remain brutally and painfully unfair.

Arrianna's eyes opened and after three seconds of disorientation, a smile grew on her lips, "Martha, how good of you to come. Everything is all right then?"

Martha had to wipe her tears and swallow a sob before replying, "Yes, my dear child. We are just fine, thanks to you. The boat is fixed and we are ready to leave. All we needed was you."

Arrianna's smile intensified, despite the evident pain she endured. "See, I told you so, I told you they would not leave me behind." And with that she either passed out or fell asleep.

By the time Seth and Luis arrived, Martha was weeping openly. Nevertheless, they picked Ari up and, between the four of them, carried her as gently as they could manage. Martha noted that besides looking pale, her skin was clammy and her pulse pounded as if her heart would come out of her chest. It also seemed to be far too rapid.

Once at camp they placed her in the boat and treated her for shock. Her legs were elevated, layers of clothes placed on her, and bits of fresh water were dribbled into her mouth. Seth looked carefully at the wrist. He had a yeoman's knowledge of injuries and was able to diagnose it, "Colles' fracture of the wrist, but severely displaced and macerated by all her movement. We will have to splint it." They made a rough splint from what they had and left Martha to care for her. The choice was made easier by Martha's obstinate refusal to leave her side. She understood her and knew how often her parents had ignored her needs or completely abandoned her. She would not be another person to abandon her and, when the girl came around, she would see a familiar face. While stroking the young girl's hair and whispering soothing words to her, she resolutely fixed her gaze on her patient and thereby avoided seeing the front of the boat. They had plugged it in, as per their plan, and covered it with a shirt.

The rest of them, now galvanized by the urgency, pushed and pulled the boat into deeper water. They tried to get it out as far as possible, for once the engine started they were committed—it would be heard for miles. They reached chest high water, but were unwilling to advance further until the two sharpshooters arrived. They came at a dead run only two minutes later.

It had taken half a dozen shots each to convince the pilot to leave. He took off and, as far as the two of them could see, he did not turn around. They heard the shots and so had everyone else. They knew all too well how little time they had. Resisting the urge to check on Arrianna, much less discuss what happened, Marc joined the others in pushing the boat into deeper water past the breakers. Once the water was chin high and the propeller had adequate clearance, Jerry and Leesa climbed aboard. The other four remained in the water to avoid weighing the boat further.

Jerry carefully checked the fuel, primed the carburetor, checked the prop and fired the engine up. It took two tries before the engine hummed to life. He steered slowly to deeper water and then idled long enough to allow the four men to climb aboard. Leesa screamed and Jerry throttled up.

"On the beach, they're coming!" Indeed, five men were just breaking out of the tree line, surprise and disbelief evident on their faces. It took them a few precious seconds to recover and begin firing.

On board, it was clear to everyone who saw the men begin shooting that they had not left in time. They would be cut down even as they were about to effect their escape. One bullet managed to bounce off the side after skipping off the surface of the water, but didn't have enough force penetrate. Jerry pushed the boat hard, ignoring any waves, or any concerns he might have about flipping.

REDEMPTION ISLAND

He knew if he did not put distance between them and the shooters, they would be dead anyway.

Several factors were in their favor, two markedly so. First, Jerry did some amateur speed racing as a young man and, although rusty, he had no reticence of going full throttle and dealing with the consequences—no timidity here. Second, the man who purchased the boat had money to burn and needed powerful toys to feel manly. Within seconds the boat was pushing forty knots and still accelerating. It was only when one wave nearly sent them cart wheeling that Jerry cut the power a bit.

Arrianna, now conscious again, tried her best to not scream with the pain that the boat's thumping caused. She knew they were on the verge of escaping and Martha, seeing her dilemma, helped her by holding her face tight against her shoulder so she could scream without being heard. After the longest ten seconds of their lives, particularly Arrianna's, one by one they began to realize they might make it. Jerry throttled down and glanced passed from one to another and those who could rise. In one instant of pure and complete exhilaration, they all yelled out their unsurpassable joy of success. Even Arrianna joined in the celebration by forcing a smile before passing out again.

Chapter Twenty-Six
Civilization

The high performance plane spotted the departure of the amphibian without waiting for the landing party. That had generated a quick response. The pilot was ordered to follow the plane while the cutter dispatched its scout helicopter to the island and changed its direction to head there directly. At full speed it was still forty minutes away.

The very last thing that the crew of the helicopter expected to find was a damaged motorboat speeding away from the island filled with a decidedly odd group of refugees. When at first sight they started to take evasive action, the pilots were sure of their quarry, but as they approached closer, they saw that the people on the boat, instead of being men firing guns, were a mix of men and women, old and young.

Initially the people in the boat seemed to be afraid, but when they turned their side to them so the Coast Guard markings were visible, they jumped up, started waving their arms and turned the boat in their direction. The pilot and copilot were perplexed but could not ignore them. They radioed the cutter and signaled to the motorboat the direction that they needed to take. Then they resumed their assignment.

It took a little work but eventually the boat made off in the assigned direction. The helicopter proceeded to the island with increased caution. The pilots remarked to each other how the people never stopped waving even as they sped off.

~~~~~~~~~~

They wanted to go at full throttle, but the shaking tortured Arrianna. She was now sitting propped up against the wall of the boat, looking more like a little girl than ever. She was nevertheless enjoying the attention from Martha and Marc. When Leesa, sitting at the front of the boat, spotted the cutter steaming at full speed directly at them, they understood why the helicopter was insistent on them taking this course. They resumed their manic waving and jumping right up to the moment that the cutter's outboard stopped alongside and took them aboard.

For the castaways, the shock of being back in civilization was nearly too much. Martha, Arrianna, Seth, and Marc cried fervently and joyously. Jerry and Mike could not stop talking and touching everyone in sight. Leesa was the one who took it most in stride, perhaps because several of the crew recognized her and paid her the kind of attention she was used to. Luis had only been gone a few days and necessitated no adjustment. He made his way quickly to the bridge where he found Ricardo, his control officer and the ship's captain. He had not known that Ricardo had been undercover and smiled ruefully at himself. Once everyone's credentials were established, he proceeded to bring them up to speed.

The cutter did not have a doctor on board, but did have a very experienced corpsman who'd served in 'Nam. He checked them all over carefully before replacing the makeshift splint on Arrianna's wrist. He was attentive, concerned and appropriately diagnosed the potential for *osteomyelitis* in her wrist. He ordered a landside helicopter to take her to the nearest trauma center. Apparently the subsequent trauma to her wrist after the initial fall had ground the jagged ends of the bones and created a breeding ground for bacteria.

Within hours, the world's press heard the news of their miraculous survival, their successful battle against drug runners and the rescue of the seven castaways. It was not only a huge human interest story, but had intrigue built right in. Headlines blared about "Modern day Crusoe's" and "*Gilligan's Island* re-discovered." For better or not, the seven became celebrities. Everyone wanted a part of them. As a group, they had "presence," and the media loved them. It was their closeness and utter comfort with one another that the public loved and the demand for their appearance increased.

Despite their significant accomplishments, many problems remained to be worked out. Death certificates had been issued and had to be repealed. Family and friends began arriving in droves, disbelief still evident in their faces. Some had already started distribution of the estates–rather too quickly, and everyone knew it.

It took a week for the group to be willing to leave each other for more than a few hours at a time. This necessitated their stay in a hotel next door to the hospital where Arrianna was being treated.

During these first two days, a couple of significant events occurred: The first was not in any way humorous but it did not stop the group from reminiscing on and off for days. Apparently, no one informed the Coast Guard about their nasty, but necessary, choice of material for plugging the hole in the boat, and one of the crewmen discovered the nasty surprise and jumped overboard just to get away from it.

The second event of note involved Seth. He'd shared with them his failure to communicate his information on Iraq's nuclear reactor at Osirak yet how Israel had managed to knock it out anyway. They felt his pain at being unable to repay the debt of honor. Then the first morning after their rescue, he strolled to breakfast as if he owned the world. It took several minutes of badgering for him to tell all.

"I was getting ready to sleep when someone knocked at my door. I did not know these men but they said it was vital I talk to them. They had Israeli passports, so I let them in." Seth looked at each one of the others and enjoyed every minute of their anticipation. "As it turns out, when my New York contact heard of my disappearance, he was sure that I had been killed. He believed that the plane had been blown up to get to me. He contacted a friend at the embassy and, within hours, their agents visited the hotel room I'd stayed at and searched it thoroughly. I had done as best I knew how to be careful, but apparently, and fortunately, I was not careful enough. They found scraps of my notes in the garbage. I had left enough information that they were able to retrace my steps and obtain the confirmation they'd been looking for. It was because of my efforts and due to my disappearance, that their Prime Minister authorized the attack on the reactor. That same Prime Minister issued a letter of commendation erasing the debt I owed." His smile lit up his face. "Can you imagine such a thing? They said that they are in my debt." he said, beaming.

REDEMPTION ISLAND

Arrianna's father arrived a day late with another one of his alcoholic bimbo's in tow. Despite everything that he and Arrianna had been through, he continued to find abusive women. Arrianna discovered, to her own bemusement, she had little she wanted to say to him. Instead it was Martha and Seth whom she clung to. During her stay on the island, she'd made a decision. She told her father "I will no longer live, or have anything to do, with you. At least, not until you reach for help and stopped being an enabler. I'm now 18 and I just proved beyond doubt that I do not need you. I'm choosing not to put up with you anymore." It had not gone unnoticed that the woman he was currently with looked relieved at this ultimatum, or that her father had been unable to rise to the occasion.

After he left, Martha squeezed her hand, "You did very well. Someday, perhaps, he will come to his senses. In the meantime, you deserve far better and we will make sure that you get it."

~~~~~~~~~~

A few days later they were at the Miami airport, from which they were headed in their particular directions. They were hit hard by the pain of separation.

Marc stood up on one of the molded, purposefully uncomfortable chairs and called for attention. All he said was, "I have an idea." This by itself silenced all of them. They all knew about his ideas and how he had been essential to their survival. Indeed, the press had labeled him, "the Professor." He smiled, still amazed at the serenity he felt around them.

"What is it Marc?" asked Leesa.

"Ninety days from now, we will meet for a week and catch up

REDEMPTION ISLAND

with each other." He saw in their faces the instant joy at the statement. His intuition was right! They were having as hard a time leaving as he was! This intangible, non-linear intuition/feeling shit worked! He promised himself to explore this new world fully.

"Sixty days!" shouted Seth, "I am an old man, and I may not be around for ninety days." The rest of them laughed while nodding in approval. Seth might be older than all of them and twice as old as most, but fragile he was not.

"Leesa and I will take care of it." This came from Jerry. "We will be in touch with each one of you as to the location and time."

~~~~~~~~~~

The first boarding call for Arrianna's flight came and went. Arrianna was locked in an embrace with Marc. Tears streamed unheeded down her face and remarkably Marc too had moist eyes on the verge of overflowing. They had discussed their relationship and, by mutual agreement, decided not to pursue it further. The connection and intimacy had been out of desperation and necessity. They could not recapture the feeling they had on the island under such stressful conditions.

Her life was forever altered by him. She'd discovered the love of learning and the unimaginable amount of knowledge available to her. She could not handle school quite yet, but she knew that at some point she would be ready, and even anxious, to return. Right now, however, she needed to finish her education about LIFE, people and most of all, love

She broke off, waved with her left hand, and wiped the tears with her forearm the way a five-year-old might. She turned quickly and followed Seth and Martha onto the plane.

REDEMPTION ISLAND

~~~~~~~~~

Mike's flight to the Midwest was the next to leave. He was extremely nervous and found himself clinging to people. His wife was there, of course, but so was Jerry. He had initially not liked him much and felt he was a pompous fool. But that was before he'd gotten to know him. They worked well together, shifting authority smoothly and easily as the situation demanded. He now felt comfortable around Jerry and feared his destination more than he acknowledged. With a handshake and a hug, he bid Jerry "goodbye." He waved at Marc and Leesa and boarded the plane headed for North Dakota.

~~~~~~~~~

The remaining three sat at the airport for a long time seeing the ghostly images of their friends fade. Finally Jerry stood up, made a show of brushing himself off and said, "I suppose we better get the car." The other two stood in silent agreement, still unable to speak. Jerry started rattling on about their plans and, within minutes, had their attention diverted from their pain and onto the challenges that faced them.

Epilogue

For each of the castaways, the sixty days felt like a hundred. The continued interest of the world's media accounted for most of this. For all of them, the experience had abruptly changed their lives–although more for some than others. They could not wait for their reunion.

Jerry devised a plan by which they would meet without the scrutiny of the press, and, although elaborate, it worked rather well. He had them meet in the far reaches of North Dakota, where Mike was spending much of his time now.

~~~~~

Mike's fame had plastered his face on the globe's stage, and his fifteen minutes had brought him to the attention of several people who should have recognized him, but only one did. Her first impulse was to deny it—it just couldn't be. Not after all this time and all that pain. It took her only a short time to realize she could not ignore it. She had been his fiancée when he'd been blown up and lost his identity. He'd been listed MIA by the Air Force and she had waited for years until accepting that he was not coming home. She was now married to someone else and, although not unhappy, not terribly happy either.

She'd finally given in and called Mike's brother and told him what she suspected. He had discounted it at first and, being a farmer, paid little attention to TV or news outside the local area. Two days later, however, in a show of uncharacteristic sloth, he stopped working after only ten hours, cleaned up, told his wife, Allison, to join him at the TV, and watched a group interview of the castaways by none other than Barbara Walters.

The show started with typical silliness by repeating what the public had started calling the castaways: Ginger (Leesa), Maryann (Arrianna), the Professor (Marc), Mr. Howell (Jerry), the Skipper (Mike), and Mrs. Howell (Martha). Left out was how Seth remained un-cast and that, in desperately poor taste that only the media can manage, Dan was cast as the lovable but incompetent Gilligan.

An entire hour of programming was devoted to them. They were hot news and everyone knew it. Arrianna explained how she was going to take a year off from school to recover. Jerry, Leesa and Marc described their respective plans and finally Mike told his story of having lost his identity while in 'Nam.

It was many minutes into Mike's narrative before Allison noticed that her stoic husband of twenty-one years had tears running down his face. Her husband and Mike were twins and his being listed as MIA had been a source of unending pain for him. Now, after seventeen years, he was back and not dead or decaying in some faraway jungle. She wiped away one of her own tears, stood up, kissed her husband on his head and went to the phone to figure out how to call ABC news and get in touch with Mike, who they both knew as "Howard."

She was surprised at how easy it was to reach him. Apparently they had set up a special line in anticipation of this possibility. On the second call, she was talking to him.

"Hello," said Mike tentatively.

"Hi Howard. It's Allison, your sister-in-law."

She'd heard sobbing then and while she waited for him to compose himself. She reflected that within the scope of an hour she'd heard crying from two of the most stoic men she'd ever known.

~~~~~~~~~~

During those same 60 days that felt like a hundred, Leesa was having the time of her life. She could not recall ever feeling so fulfilled or busy. Although she could not fully accept it, she was even happy. It had been Jerry's idea for them to team up with Marc and form a new company. This became a viable option once Jerry learned that his second-in-command had taken the opportunity to sell his first company for millions.

It would have been much harder on the three of them had the prior company not been registered in Texas. For reasons that are obvious, Texas inheritance law requires anyone from another state to go through an extra probate regardless of where the person dies. This undoubtedly is a boon for Texas lawyers and the Texas economy in general. It has the unfortunate effect of slowing the process to a crawl. In this case however, the second in command had bribed a few low people in high places to speed-up the process, expecting that, since Jerry was dead, it would never be discovered. When he heard of his survival, he had nearly choked on the squab he was eating and almost saved everyone a lot of trouble. They settled quickly and quietly. Jerry received the lion's share of the millions and his former associate stayed out of jail.

So LMJ associates was born. Jerry, of course, was the money and management man, his business sense now tempered by his lessons in humanity and humility. Marc was the idea and product man. He still required regular praise and reassurance that he was capable, but that need was waning. Leesa was the face the world saw–their marketing chief. She was learning how to use her fame, but not become enamored with it.

LMJ's first product, called "Castaway Soap" was already a best seller and Marc promised much more. Up to now, soap was simply something to wash with. Marc intended to make it a decorator item, a beauty item, a gift item.

A few weeks after the rescue, Leesa had a brief fling with him and, although they continued to enjoy each other's company, they stopped the affair by mutual consent. In a remarkable example of two persons growing up simultaneously, both realized how they were using each other, Marc to bolster his inadequate sense of maleness and Leesa to overcome her sense of being unable to think logically. Their relationship now was that of close confidants and as incompatible as they were, they became best friends. Leesa was his guide to the world of women and dating and from that time on he made few egregious dating etiquette errors, certainly none outside the norm. Leesa on the other hand, with Marc's encouragement and tutoring, enrolled in a local university and started taking courses in biology and archeology, subjects that had always intrigued but intimidated her.

Jerry was back where he wanted to be, in charge of things he was comfortable with. He sold his boat, bought a satellite phone, and kept the battery charged at all times. Furthermore, he kept a fully-charged spare battery readily available—he was not going to be stranded ever again.

~~~~~~~

It took Seth only two days after the rescue to ask Martha to marry him. It took her as many seconds to say "yes." To Seth's mild, but delighted, surprise, no one in his family voiced any concern that Martha was a gentile. Through the entire process she was welcomed as a long lost and well–loved relative. The ceremony took place in Tel Aviv, and was attended mostly by family. It was nevertheless rowdy and lasted well into the early morning hours. As planned, and despite her cast, Arrianna performed well as maid of honor. Marc flew in to be best man. His reaction to being asked is plenty of grist for another story. When the reunion was over, they planned a world tour during which they would stop and visit each of their six children as well as every friend who would take them in.

Arrianna vividly remembered the best day of her short, but all too eventful life. It was the day when Seth and Martha came into her room at the hospital and asked her to be in the wedding. Her father had left the day before and she felt lost and alone in the world. She had no idea how to proceed with her newly-declared independence. The wedding request was a brief, but welcome, respite from deciding what to do with the rest of her life. Then the magic occurred—she often replayed it in the theater of her mind.

"We have another request," said Martha.

"Another request! I am already to be your maid of honor in Israel and you want more!?" she'd kidded with them. "What do you want now?"

Martha tried to talk but choked up so Seth spoke, "It seemed to us that you might have a vacancy in your parent slot and we wondered if you'd do us the honor of adopting us as your informal parents."

Arrianna remained silent for only fifteen seconds, but it felt longer than the ten seconds on the boat waiting for a bullet to hit the gas tank; longer than her entire life. She must have heard wrong– she could not get her hopes up to be dashed again, but then she remembered how Martha had waited for her on the island and how she had not left her side, even riding in the helicopter with her. When she finally allowed herself to accept the love and caring the older couple were offering, she cried and managed to nod her head yes. Most definitely yes.

From that moment on she'd been in a fairy land. The three of them had gone traveling, visiting, and exploring parts of the world she'd never heard of. She met people far different than she could have imagined. Just like Martha was accepted into Seth's family, so was she as the long lost, and now found, cousin. She was filling up with the love from Seth and Martha that seemed to be in endless supply both for each other and for her. She had never felt happier and any decisions about her future would wait.